# Ellie

by

## Seymour Hamilton

Library and Archives Canada Catalogue

Hamilton, Seymour

**Ellie**

Published by Seymour Hamilton "Colophon"

ISBN: 9798756205022



Cover art and page illustrations by Shirley MacKenzie, whose portfolio can be viewed at www.shirleymackenzie.com

Formatting the cover and the layout by Mary Montague.

Visit the author at www.SeymourHamilton.com *or* on Facebook at www.facebook.com/seymour.hamilton

# CONTENTS

# Also by Seymour Hamilton

*Angel's Share (Colophon/Old Salt Press, 2021)*
*Angel's Share* begins two generations before the beginning of
The Astreya Trilogy

*The Astreya Trilogy (Fireship Cortero Press, 2011)*
*Book I The Voyage South*
*Book II The Men of the Sea*
*Book III The Wanderer's Curse*
The story runs seamlessly through the three books

*River of Stones (Colophon/Old Salt Press, 2020)*
*River of Stones* begins twenty years after The Astreya Trilogy

*Ellie (Colophon/Old Salt Press, 2010)*
*Ellie* begins almost three years after *River of Stones*

*The Laughing Princess (Açedrex 2014)*
Twelve stories involving dragons of great power and authority
Illustrated by Shirley Mackenzie

*The Hippies Who Meant It (Colophon 2015)*
Two Americans and a Canadian homestead in Nova Scotia at
the time of the Vietnam War

Author's Website: SeymourHamilton.com

# Acknowledgements

## The Old Salt Press

My grateful thanks for their patience, encouragement and valuable contributions go to Shirley Mackenzie, for drawing the portraits of my characters; Mary Montague for formatting the cover and the layout, Antoine Vanner for information about cannons, Alaric Bond for many necessary corrections, Rick Spilman for useful suggestions, Jessica Knauss for catching many slips and errors. Special thanks to Ben for doing all the shopping while I hid away from the Covid virus, and always and especially Katherine.

# Prologue: In which Ellie
# speaks to Astreya

"Permission to speak frankly, Uncle?"

Astreya looked up from the chart table at his slim, black-haired, green-eyed niece and smiled.

"Don't you always, Ellie?"

"I brought you enough shipstones to triple the size of our fleet, equip a dozen navigation officers, and give out 'get me home' rings to all the crew. So why are you sitting on the whole lot like a broody hen?"

Astreya frowned.

"Eliana, that is not an appropriate question. I am your commanding officer."

Ellie stiffened her spine and stood at attention.

"Very well, Grand Commander Astreya, why are you hoarding stones that could vastly improve the number, efficiency, and overall functioning of the ships under your command?"

Astreya took a deep, calming breath and spoke softly.

"All in good time, Ellie."

"When? It's been nearly two years. We could be training officers and crew for when Drew gets the next schooner off the ways and ready for service."

"When the ship is completed ..."

"She'll need two mates and an experienced commander, which we've got. Except that you haven't given them the clasps they need to do their jobs."

"As you well know, it is because ..."

"Because of a ridiculous tradition of keeping the lore of the stones in the family. We haven't even started training Cam and Damon and Marley in celestial navigation, let alone how to navigate with the stones."

"Any changes in our customs will be discussed by the council of wielders."

"Bilge, Uncle."

"Eliana!"

"With all due respect, Grand Commander. What happens at every Council of Wielders is that you decide and the council agrees. You know that. So do I. And so does everyone, though they won't say it for fear of your green-eyed stare."

"Eliana, that is quite enough. You will consider yourself reprimanded for …"

"You gave me permission to speak frankly."

"And now I command that you not to speak further."

"You want me to pretend that we can all sail off into a future in which nothing changes, no emergencies occur, no …"

"Eliana, you may leave."

"At your command, Grand Commander. I'm off to teach basic seamanship to Fred. He already knows celestial navigation."

"Ellie…"

Grand Commander Astreya glowered at the cabin door that Ellie had closed with a precision that said more than if she had slammed it. More than an hour later, he was still pacing a well-worn path in the deck of the schooner *Cygnus'* stern cabin.

# Chapter 1: In which Seafoam comes under fire

Half Moon Bay was smooth under a clear, autumn sky, even though out to sea, a brisk wind was raising whitecaps. A gaff-rigged fishing boat rounded the line of breakers beyond the southeast point and headed into the bay's calmer water.

A flash of light glinted off polished brass as a lookout at the northern end of the bay brought his telescope to bear on the little boat. He saw the sail shiver as it turned into the wind, apparently about to tack north into the bay. The lookout lost interest and was about to return to pacing the circular earthwork around the gun emplacement when he saw the boat's mainsail change shape. The gaff rose until it became one with the mast, the sail took the shape of a bird's wing, and a huge jib blossomed into a smooth curve above the foredeck. The boat sped out of the circle of his telescope's view. The lookout frowned, blinked, and a heartbeat later ran to tell his officer.

~^~

Rigged for speed, the longboat *Seafoam* sailed out of the bay to a faster rhythm. No longer plowing doggedly through the waves under a slack, almost square mainsail, she skimmed the surface under smooth, curving canvass, heeling to port with the wind abeam. Her crew of three pulled up the hoods on their sharkskin jackets against the spray that wetted the foot of the jib, hissed onto the foredeck, ran along the port scuppers and left a foaming white wake astern.

Ellie tucked her ankles under the foot-strap, leaned out over the weather side, put her head back to scan the sails, glanced astern at Fred's hand on the tiller, and eased the main sheet.

"Take your hands off the tiller, Fred."

His sandy eyebrows rose in disbelief.

"But..." Fred began, then did as she told him, his pale blue eyes wide, his teeth clenched.

The tiller pointed down the boat's centre line, quivering. Fred grabbed at it.

"Fingertips, Fred!"

Gingerly, he relaxed his death-grip. His mouth opened in wonderment.

"Feeling the speed now?" Ellie asked, her green eyes bright with enthusiasm.

Fred nodded, entranced by the power that was thrusting the boat onward, racing along the windward side of the waves, her wake merging with the white-capped crests. He unshipped the tiller extension so that he could sit on the weather side of the cockpit beside Ellie. They leaned back above the water, their combined weight maintaining the angle of heel at which *Seafoam* sailed best. Ellie nodded approval when Alan, the third member of the crew, glanced back at her from his position on the foredeck where he was keeping the big jib full and drawing evenly. He grinned as spray plastered a few strands of his curly red hair onto his forehead. They raced southward, attentive to the harmony of sounds generated by wind rushing along the tense sails, strumming a sustained note from the stays, and resonating in the boat's wooden hull.

Ellie glanced over her shoulder toward the rocky point around which they had clawed their way to windward under so much less sail. Rocks combed the white-capped breakers on their way to smash into a sand beach below a tree-clad shore. Already she was anticipating the moment when they would harden in the sails and head westward towards home, leaving the easternmost point of land behind them. With any luck, she would complete Fred's lesson in helmsmanship in time for supper.

A hole bigger than a man's fist appeared in the mainsail. A high, keening wail cut through the sounds of wind and water. A moment later, they heard a sound like a distant clap of thunder. Fred flinched. *Seafoam* yawed.

"Canon!" yelled Fred.

"Keep going! Maintain course!" Ellie shrilled.

A second hole appeared in the mainsail; another wailing scream, another distant thud.

The boat's chorus of sounds sagged a halftone. The masthead arced overhead, waves slapped over the cockpit coaming.

"Starboard stay's parted!" Alan's shout barely reached astern.as you go, Fred,"

"Steady as you go," said Ellie. "We'll ease her when we're around the point. On my count head west. Five … four … three …"

A third scream. Something punched a white splash onto the wave on which *Seafoam* was poised in her headlong rush southwards.

"Keep her sailing, Fred," Ellie yelled. "We're a sitting duck if we luff."

The mainsheet screeched through its blocks. The mainsail clattered and flapped, streaming to lee of the mast.

"Why did you…?" Fred began.

Ellie was no longer beside him. He slid into the cockpit to glance astern. *Seafoam* yawed. A black-haired head broke surface, one arm pointed westward. Fred held the tiller between his knees, seized the sheet and hauled hand over hand. Ahead on the foredeck, Alan eased the jib. *Seafoam* lost momentum and wallowed amid the whitecaps.

Buoyed up by the air captured in her black sailing jacket, Ellie waved with both hands and shouted.

"…sail! … pick up … round the point …"

Alan's head appeared over the cabin top.

"Fred! Stay on the starboard tack! We'll bring Ellie aboard when we're on the other side of the point!"

Fred nodded, still frantically sheeting in the mainsail. Alan deftly played the jib to catch air, *Seafoam* climbed a wave and scudded south-east.

Ellie kicked, took two quick strokes, and body-surfed towards the shore, letting a breaking wave pitch her onto the sand beach. She did not hear the scream and thud of a fourth shot that plunged into the water behind her because she was struggling to gain her footing in soft sand. She staggered up the beach and onto the grey bedrock spine of the point in time to see *Seafoam* brace her sails and head towards her. Another shell screamed. She threw herself face down. Stone chips pattered onto her jacket like heavy, stinging rain.

She leaped to her feet, waving *Seafoam* away. A shell shrieked over her head. A plume of white spray leaped out of a wave between her and the boat, which yawed, righted and headed south. Ellie pointed west towards home, although she knew that Fred and Alan were much too busy to see her. When she lowered her arm, she saw blood on the back of her right hand from the rattle of rock shards that had showered her moments earlier. Realizing she was as much a target as her boat, she ran along the wave-splashed point toward the forested mainland. A dozen quick strides and the weathered rock under her sailing boots was patched with lichen. Then she was forcing her way among waist-high bushes, their branches catching at her jacket. She slowed, seeking an easier way; then as another shell smacked into the rocky point where she had stood to wave, she threw herself prone and lay panting under wind-stunted trees, listening for the next scream and thump from the distant gun. Another shot shook the bushes close by. She wriggled to where the trees were not so wind-bent. Branches snagged the hood of her sailing jacket and twigs caught in her long black hair. She edged forward on knees and elbows until she was beyond the tangled branches and intertwined roots.

Ellie crawled onto a soft, yielding carpet of needles fallen from the pines above her. Suddenly limp with exhaustion, she lay panting on the forest floor, resting her cheek on the resin-scented needles. Her heartbeat slowed. The rushing, crashing sea sounds dimmed to a distant susurration at the edge of hearing. Her eyes closed.

After what seemed only a few moments, she stared at reddish-brown trunks of big, wide-spaced pines. She crawled to the closest and leaned against its rough bark. Tipping her head, she looked past dead twigs to where intermingled branches blocked even a glimpse of the sky. She raised a hand to brush her hair out of her eyes and felt pine needles stuck to her cheek. When she started to pick them off, she saw the scabbed-over trickle of blood on the back of her right hand. She started to get to her feet, staggered, and clutched at the tree's gnarled bark with both arms. Her light-headedness faded, but when she tried to think, she could only marvel at the sheer size of the tree. She leaned against it, fascinated that her outstretched arms spanned less than a quarter of its girth.

She shook her head and deliberately focused on where she was and what she should do next. The process was disturbingly slow and difficult. Her train of thought kept being broken by unexpected bursts of trembling. Calming herself by breathing deeply, she strove to consult the mental chart that unfailingly told her where she was. With an effort, she recalled her way home from Half Moon Bay, expecting to remember an exact record of significant physical features like notations. Instead, she saw indistinct images of the cliffs that ran along the southern side of the big peninsula past the little town of Charton, on to Matris, her birthplace and home port. Then gradually, and with increasing clarity, direction and waypoints came back to her. She nodded. All she had to do was make her way southward until she reached the cliffs, and then look westward, where she would soon see the ship that Astreya would be sending to look for her after Fred and Alan sailed *Seafoam* home and told the family what had happened. In her mind, she sailed with them to Matris, keenly aware that if they suddenly took the wind on the port side with no stay, *Seafoam* could be dismasted. She frowned, frustrated that all this thinking took far too long.

*But what about the Two Feet!*

*They'll have to tack through the channel ...*

*But if they do, they'll capsize...*

*Fred doesn't know...*

Ellie pushed panic down, ordering her thoughts.

*But Alan's handy; he'll think of a way through, and then they're in sight of the dockyard ...*

*And Mairi will have Cygnet ready in no time at all...*

*I'll be back home and dry before nightfall.*

Calmed, she walked westward in the forest before making her way to the coast, only a short distance to her left. She was composed, tranquil, in charge of herself and the situation. There was neither need nor point in even trying to use her stone while deep in the forest. When she reached the cliff edge, she would be able to message her rescuers exactly where to find her.

Ellie opened the flap on her left sleeve and consulted her navigator's clasp. Bracing herself on a tree, she looked for the north-pointing spear of light at the centre of the stone, then picked her direction away from where she had landed. She strode confidently along a way through the greenish gloom, on which she could walk many strides before she would have to detour around even one of the huge trees.

# Chapter 2: In which Seafoam returns

"She's not there," Alan shouted.

"What?" Fred shouted back.

"I can't feel her stone."

Fred swore profusely into the wind, wishing for a wielder's stone like Ellie's. Though he had invented the waterproof coating that protected the gems for all six of the fleet's wielders, he had not even been allowed a ringstone with which to begin the first stage of training. Now they were dependent on Alan's ring with a stone of far less power than Ellie's navigator's clasp, which allowed her to both navigate and communicate with other wielders. All Alan's stone could do was home on a shipstone and sense a wielder's stone, provided the bearer was close.

"If we go back without Ellie, Trogen is going to kill me," said Fred.

"Not if we can get back tonight."

"Without losing the mast, or capsizing, or smacking into a rock, or…"

"We can do it."

"It might be simpler if I drowned myself right now."

"Don't. I can't sail *Seafoam* alone."

"You're assuming I can."

"Ellie does."

Alan's words were convincing. Ellie was the sixteen-year-old prodigy who had befriended him despite the palpable disapproval of her family. Fred supposed that her decision to teach him to sail was because they had survived an explosion that should have killed both of them. But he also knew that her family viewed him with suspicion because he had manufactured the explosives for that very blast.

As Ellie had taught him, Fred kept the extended mainsail and big jib full, and the boat poised on the waves. Helming, sail-tending and staying on course were at first all he could manage. He barely noticed the rush of spray on either side and the foaming wake astern.

As time went on, he began to think ahead to the headlands called the Two Feet and the passage between them through which they would have to sail to reach the big salt-water lake that was harbour to the fleet. Once in the shelter of the surrounding hills and cliffs, they could dowse *Seafoam's* press of canvass, and even if they failed, they would be in sight of their destination, close enough for a rescue by one of the dockyard's rowing boats. That would be ignominious, but safe.

The difficult part would be getting through the gap. For the present, Fred and Alan were under-manned, over-sailed, and condemned to remain on the starboard tack. Fred could not leave the tiller and the main sheet, and Alan could not retrieve the big jib single-handed. Even with a full crew, tacking while flying the big jib was a delicate operation that usually was avoided by lowering the ballooning canvass and breaking out the smaller, working jib. With a crew of two, striking sail was beyond them.

As long as the wind held out of the northwest, they could arrive outside the Two Feet in one long reach. However, the passage between the cliffs pointed almost northeast. Wind funneled between the cliffs, sometimes accelerating, sometimes diminishing, always unpredictable. Running the narrow passage required enough speed to ensure steerage way between rocks on either side. They had to tack, but when they came about and took the wind on the port side where the stays swung slack, the mast would almost certainly fail. The boat would be knocked down, sails flat in the water.

Fred set his teeth and concentrated on sailing. For a while, it was enough to cheat movement out of the complex interactions between the sails, the wind and the water. Then the irony of the situation snuck out of the analytical side of his mind in a realization that he was sailing towards eventual disaster using skills of which everyone save Ellie had thought him incapable. He knew that they saw him as a dry, mechanical thinking machine; a practitioner of technologies long lost well over a century before, when the world Before changed to the After in which everyone now lived.

The sun was westering towards the dim hills in the far distance, and he still did not know how they could tack with a broken port stay. Even if they made it to Matris, where *Cygnet* was prepared to head south the next day, it would still take her crew time to raise sail, and that meant Ellie would have to spend the night in the forest. Unpleasant, perhaps, but he was certain she could cope. His mouth set in a sardonic grin, Fred squinted into increasingly level light. If Ellie thought him competent to sail *Seafoam*, that was reason enough for him to try.

"Fred!"

He became aware that Alan was shouting at him.

"What?"

"… the port stay."

"I know. It's only holding by threads."

"I've an idea. I'm moving to the port side. I've belayed the jib sheets."

Fred felt the subtle consequences of Alan shifting his weight, and made adjustments to compensate. Part of his brain confirmed what he had done, and even registered mild surprise at how well he had done it. Then the boat swayed and the big jib swung back and forth. Fred's fist tightened on the tiller, and the boat yawed.

"Keep her sailing, Fred!"

Fred bit his lower lip, remembered what Ellie had said, and counterintuitively relaxed his hand until only his fingers held the tiller. As he did so, his hand and the tiller moved in accord. The jib's edges no long fluttered, the masthead steadied.

With *Seafoam's* equilibrium restored, Fred was able to take a succession of quick glances at what had happened. The cannon shot had cut the port stay almost in half. Above, rope-ends fluttered uselessly downwind, below they streamed into the wake. Only a few strands still ran all the way from the masthead down to where they were secured to the hull at deck height.

Fred watched as Alan cut away the trailing rope-ends. The deadeyes on the gunwale were now empty. Alan then moved to the mast, where the halyards were belayed on their pins. Taking the coil for the peak halyard, he went back to the blocks and passed the bitter end through the deadeye holes. This required both hands, which meant he had to kneel on the deck and brace himself between the low cabin top and the rail, where every second wave sluiced water onto his knees and spray into his face.

He then returned to his position at the foot of the mast, belayed the end and then loosed the peak halyard from its belaying pin. Immediately, the halyard no longer ran up the mast, but instead went from masthead to the deadeye above the gunwale and then back to the base of the mast. Alan then repeated the process for the throat halyard and the downhaul that turned the gaff into a topmast and re-shaped the lug-sail into a vertical wing. When he was through with all three, the sail had slipped down the mast by less than a handspan, and its shape was barely compromised.

While Alan had been jury-rigging the port stays, *Seafoam* had passed the cliffs at the mouth of Charton harbour, which meant that they were almost two-thirds of the way home to Matris. For a brief instant, Alan and Fred grinned at each other, then both of them concentrated on what lay ahead. There was no opportunity for them to plan or practice what would happen when they put the substitute stays to the test.

As the Two Feet hove into view, Alan glanced astern and nodded. Fred winched the mainsheet tighter to bring *Seafoam* closer to the wind and steered towards the shoreline. As they entered the lee of the cliffs, there was not so much wind and thus less stress on the mast. However, both knew they were gambling that there would be no puffs or patches in the wind to jerk or strain the improvised port stays.

The closer they came to the shoreline, the more they encountered waves reflected from the cliffs. *Seafoam's* rhythmic lean and sway, pitch and yaw became irregular. Cross-waves and chop caught at the foot of Alan's jib, drenching him with spray, some of which reached Fred in the cockpit. They were now so close to the cliffs that wind and waves were roiled and fluky. They divided their attention between sail-tending and looking anxiously for the gap in the cliff wall. When the narrow passage came into view, they had to judge their turn precisely. Too early, and they would end up downwind of the gap: too late, and they would have the wind astern, and the mainsail would rob air from the jib, causing it to collapse. If this happened, the big foresail might catch a wave, fill with water, yank the bow down, and the boat would founder.

The decision to turn had both of them glancing at the cliffs, at the set of the sails, and at each other. Then like a door opening, they looked through the passage between the Two Feet into the sea lake beyond. They had no time for worry or doubt.

"One, two, three…" Fred counted, forcing himself not to make the turn too early.

There could be no second attempt at going between the oddly shaped peaks in the cliff that towered high above the masthead.

The gap came fully open.

"NOW!" they yelled at the same moment.

They coaxed *Seafoam* into the wind's eye, hauling and then easing the sheets to minimize the force when wind came onto the port side of the mast. The sails fluttered, filled, and steadied. The mast swayed and bent to leeward as the jury-rigged halyards took the strain, slacker than the stays they replaced, but holding.

Fred and Alan trimmed their sails in the erratic wind within the narrow passage between the headlands. Teeth clenched, they sailed in the confused air of the gap, the waves splattering on rocks less than a stone's throw away. Ahead, beyond the narrow way lay the smooth water of the sea-lake and the harbour of Matris.

Not much more than a dozen stressful seconds later, the gap was astern, the sails slack, and *Seafoam* slid through calm water towards her home port.

# Chapter 3: In which Ellie is lost

The woods were eerily quiet. Not the faintest whisper of wind came through the canopy far above her. Her feet made no sound on the soft carpet of needles that had fallen from generations of trees whose trunks stood around her, many steps apart.

Ellie chose a tree in the distance, took a bearing with her stone and started walking. When she reached the tree she had aimed for, she walked carefully around it, glanced at her stone again, and continued. After many repetitions over what she guessed had been more than half an hour, she had an unexpected moment of unease. She glanced upward, but the pines' canopy still blocked the sky. Reassured, she walked onward. At the last of a dozen guide trees that were the way-points on her mental chart, she noticed that the forest was darkening. Reasoning that clouds could have blown in above the trees, she decided that it would be a good time to head due south to the cliffs.

Ellie consulted her stone again. Something was wrong. She was heading east. She tapped the stone, knowing as she did so that this was pointless. She gave her head a little shake, winced, and did it again. Her knees gave way under her, and she sat down with a thump. Wondering how far she had gone astray, she stared at the clasp on her arm, summoned the bright line at the heart of her stone that pointed north, stood up, and began walking as fast as she could. The spaces between the trees became shorter. A sense of urgency constricted her throat. Her mental chart dimmed in her mind, replaced by a single, compelling obsession.

*I have to get to the cliffs and message Mairi!*

She almost ran to the next way-point tree, where she consulted her stone again. It appeared that she was about to head northeast. She turned until the southern end of the bright spear of light in the stone lined up on a tree, and hurried on as fast as she could in the gathering gloom. Halfway to her destination, she staggered and almost fell. Thinking she might not be heading for the tree she had chosen a few moments earlier, she consulted her stone. It told her she was heading east. Tension rose up the back of her neck, transforming into desperation. She stopped, breathed in and out slowly three times, and deliberately went back to the first lesson she had learned about using the stones.

"Think North," she said out loud, echoing what Astreya had taught her.

She stared at her stone, expecting the bright line to swing northward, as it had done every time she had used it to navigate, ever since her first day in the Forbidden Room, years before. The line swung idly, stopped, and swung back the other way. Wide-eyed, she tried again. The bright line faded. She was looking at a meaningless green stone in a silver clasp.

Ellie, the youngest fully competent navigator, acknowledged by Astreya himself as the strongest wielder in the family, the cool-headed and incisive thinker who had faced danger on land and at sea, Ellie was lost.

She stood, irresolute.

*So many trees in my way. A giant fence of trees, but not so close that I can't go between this trunk and that one. Like a doorway. Quick, before it closes, run through. Do it again. I still don't know where I am! Run anyway. Now I do. I'm back where I started running. Where I slept because it was dark. I must rest again. Sleep away the dark. Then try again. Run faster, further.*

Ellie crawled into the hole she had dug a day ago and fell asleep under the branches and dreamed of running between trees. When the light woke her, up she got again, and ran and ran and ran.

An indeterminate time towards the end of the second day, Ellie tripped, fell full length, prone on hard ground, her heart pounding, her breath rasping in her throat. She lay still, her face a finger's width from the ground, staring at a patch of trodden earth. She did not notice that she had lost the hood of her sailing jacket. She raised her head and looked through tall, sun-crisped grass along a barely noticeable path. Light slanted through oval-leafed fruit trees that overhung where she lay.

"Orchard," Ellie muttered. She closed her eyes, and mental pictures crowded her mind.

*All I have to do is push through the tall grass, open the gate, and I'll be only steps from the back door into the kitchen. Mother will have supper ready. I'll wash up, comb my hair, sit on the window side of the big table between Lena and baby Maia. Seren's opposite, trying not to show that she's holding hands with Marley, who's frowning to hide a smile. Becky's serving corn chowder, and I can see Father watching all of us with that special soft look we all love.*

Then she remembered.

"He's dead ..." said Ellie to the gap in the grasses.

The image of her father's gentle, shy smile faded like windblown smoke, taking her whole family with it, leaving her alone at the edge of the strange forest where she had hidden from the screaming, crashing fall of cannon shot. She lifted her cheek from the earth, got painfully to her feet and stood, waiting for the path to steady into something more substantial than a wandering line into the grey, shadowy distance. Her eyes growing less and less reliable in the gloom, she put one foot in front of the other. When the trees on either side wavered, she shut her eyes and let the grasses swishing against her black-clad legs keep her on the path.

She smelled the goat a moment before it bleated. Her eyes opened wide. In quarter-light, just before everything fades to black, she glimpsed the little animal's slotted eyes, saw its floppy ears shake, and realized that it was as surprised as she. It retreated with little toe-tapping steps, then turned and ran off, bleating, its wagging tail summoning her like a beckoning white hand. Resisting an infantile desire to weep, Ellie followed. After a few steps, the baby-like bleating faded and she lost sight of the flickering tail. Ellie stood, swaying with exhaustion. A heavy-chested goose appeared in the path, neck outstretched, wings flapping, honking an alarm.

"Boo!" said Ellie, without thinking, and the goose was silent.

A tunnel of yellow light opened ahead of her. She squinted against its sudden brightness. A grotesque shape eclipsed most of the light, then as it came closer, resolved into the silhouette of a woman. A husky voice came from the looming figure.

"Blessed be."

The woman's words were soft, almost reverent.

Bewildered, Ellie echoed the words and collapsed.

# Chapter 4: In which Fred is unpopular

Fred took hold of the weedy rungs of the ladder at the end of the wharf and climbed, leaving *Seafoam* in the capable hands of the boatbuilders who had escorted them to the shipyard. An angry face looked down at him. As Fred's head appeared over the edge of the wharf, Trogen's hands fastened onto his armpits and heaved him upward, feet dangling.

"You wretched, pointy-headed, useless lubber, you've taken Ellie from us, and now I am going to throw you in the sea and keep my foot on your head until the bubbles stop coming up."

Angry blue eyes stared at him, only a finger's length away. Over Trogen's left shoulder Fred saw Ellie's tall elder sister Seren, her blonde, curly hair bright above her anxious face. Her chosen man, Marley, stood beside her, scowling. A step behind them stood Cam and Damon. A frown replaced Cam's usual grin; tension narrowed Damon's eyes.

"Put him down, Trogen, immediately," said Grand Master Astreya.

At Astreya's command, Trogen slowly lowered Fred until he stood, surrounded by grim, condemning faces. Astreya's green eyes stared at Fred, without blinking.

Alan climbed onto the wharf, talking eagerly.

"It's not Fred's fault. We were being shot at. One shell parted the port stay. *Seafoam* yawed, pitching Ellie into the water. She swam to shore, made it onto the beach safely, but when the shooting didn't stop, she ran into the cover of the forest. We had to stand off until we were out of range."

"Why didn't you …" several voices started, but Astreya held up a hand for Alan to continue.

"We wanted to pick her up on the other side of the point we'd been rounding when the shooting started, but Ellie waved us away, and pointed further along the coast. With the port stay gone, we couldn't tack, so we headed home."

"Did you feel her presence on your ringstone?" Astreya asked.

Alan shook his head.

"At first I was seriously busy with the big jib. We couldn't maneuver. We couldn't strike sail. We had to continue to fly the big jib, sail home as fast as we could, so's to get *Cygnet* to go pick her up. When I could concentrate, I couldn't feel anything. She had disappeared into dense forest behind the cliff-edge."

"We'll go look," said Mairi, Trogen's twin sister. "Seren, Marley, come with me. You too, Alan. I'll need another … thank you, Cam. Did you want to come as well, father?"

Astreya shook his head.

"I can't add anything to what can be done with *Cygnet's* stone and two wielders."

He waved them to their ship and all five headed for boats to ferry them to *Cygnet*, Mairi's little schooner. Fred sidled shoreward, trying to get away from the crowd on the wharf. He startled when Astreya spoke his name.

"Fred, walk with me. We have to tell Becky what has happened before she learns second hand."

Fred opened his mouth to beg off, then closed it again and followed Astreya up the road to the Home. The Grand Commander's quiet request had the compelling power of a direct order.

"Tell me how *Seafoam* came under attack, Fred."

"Alan can tell you more than I can about how the boat, and …"

"Alan knows little of guns. You do."

Having spent nearly three years watching masters and mates reporting to the Grand Master, Fred delayed his answer until he had collected his thoughts.

"First there was the sound. It was a whistle-whine, not the whirr-buzz of a small-bore rifle. Less than a minute later, another whine, and I saw a splash where a shell went into a wave. I must have shoved the tiller as I looked around because *Seafoam* slid into a trough, and the big jib started to collapse. The boat rolled towards the wind, but not like when you tack. The mast whipped, Alan yelled, and I saw that the port stays had parted. I let go the main. I don't know what

Alan did to keep the jib from catching a wave. It all happened so fast … so very fast. I never saw Ellie go over the side until she was behind us and we were wallowing in the trough of another wave, making leeway towards the shore."

Astreya nodded.

"You reacted. Many would have frozen."

"Ellie yelled and waved at us to go around and pick her up on the other side of the point. We got the boat going again while she was swimming to the beach. Then as we rounded the point, I saw shards of rock fly up. They were aiming at Ellie. I think she didn't know at first, but then she caught on, and ran for the bushes. I lost sight of her. Then another two shots came at us: one hit the point, the other went into the water astern as we headed west. Then we just sailed as best we could. On the way back, Alan did clever things with the halyards, or we wouldn't have made it through the Two Feet and into the bay."

Fred made his report as seamanlike as he could, but he could not tamp down his guilt at having left Ellie behind. As they walked past the gap in the Home's defences, Astreya's stride slowed. Fred matched his pace, noticing that the tall, black-haired man beside him was walking with the care of someone doing his best not to limp. As they continued on their way towards the big old houses up the road, Fred glanced at Astreya, whose green eyes looked back at him, holding his gaze.

"Fred, considering the circumstances and your relatively brief experience with nautical matters, I don't see how you could have acted differently."

Fred blinked. Astreya's approval did not lessen the shame of returning without Ellie, but it encouraged him to say what he had intended to keep to himself.

"I won't know until I see it, but the gun must be old. Not just Before, but even older — a relic. Now, how did they find or make ammunition? If found, it's got to be unstable — really dangerous. If made, then who has discovered — re-discovered, really — how to do it? I'd like to know…"

Astreya's raised finger stopped Fred's musings.

"I need you to tell Becky what happened."

Fred nodded and fell silent. He had no idea how anyone might tell a mother that he had lost her daughter, especially when she was still grieving the death of her husband. Fred was out of his depth. Things were what he worked with. Analyzing things to find out how they worked gave him satisfaction. People presented levels of irrational complexity that he chose to avoid.

As they approached the three-storey house where Becky had birthed and cared for her four daughters, Fred became increasingly apprehensive. He had been accepted in the big house because Ellie insisted, and even Astreya could not deny her wishes, but there was no sense in which he had ever felt at home. Fred had spent more than two years observing the mutual affection, respect, and trust among the extended family, but always as an outsider. His own bleak childhood in an uncaring orphanage had not prepared him for living among people closely linked by blood and shared experience. And now he was about to tell a mother that one of her daughters might be dead. Nothing in his life prepared him for the task. The nautical terms and seamanlike language he had recently learned would not be adequate. It was too late to refuse or even to run away.

He hesitated at the door, then opened and held it for Astreya. They found Becky sitting at the big kitchen table. She looked up at them; strands of strawberry blonde hair clinging to her cheeks.

"Ellie's missing," said Astreya. "Temporarily. Seren and her crew are looking for her in *Cygnet*."

Becky nodded. She wiped her cheek with the back of a hand.

"How did it happen?"

"Fred's going to tell you."

Fred stood still. Astreya touched his arm, and they both sat down opposite Becky, whose face was slack, expressionless.

"I'm sure she's alive," Fred blurted out the first words that came to him.

"So am I," said Astreya.

"Yes, yes, I know," said Becky. "But she's so … so far away. Tell me what happened."

"Ellie wanted to teach me how to helm the longboat. She'd explained to me how it works, sailing that is, but doing things is different from knowing them, and I wasn't sure I could. She was so sure that I believed I could learn, and … and … she made me believe it too. It worked. I mean, she made it work for me."

As he stammered into an awkward silence, Fred could feel Astreya beside him, listening, assessing, judging.

Becky nodded, her eyes on his.

"Go on," she said.

Fred looked into Becky's eyes. For Fred, it was as if he had suddenly discovered that he could walk on water. As long as she kept listening, words flowed out of him. Her eyes were steady on his, and she nodded almost imperceptibly from time to time as he told her how the gunshot had parted the port stay, how Ellie had swum ashore, how confidently she had waved them home, and how the trip back to Matris had proved how well she had taught him. Eventually, he stared at the tabletop between them, his hands feeling the grain of boards she scrubbed every day. The sensation recalled how Ellie had taught him to feel the longboat's tiller. When Fred felt Becky's fingers touch the back of his hand, he looked up into her eyes and saw they were bright and clear.

"She's going to be all right, Fred," said Becky. "If it weren't so, I'd know."

# Chapter 5: In which Ellie finds Maisie

Ellie lay on a low couch in a silent, darkened room. When she opened her eyes, she saw a scarlet cushion so bright that it glowed in the light of the dimmed lamp on a table near her elbow. When she moved her hands questioningly, she felt the woolly softness of a blue blanket pulled snugly up to her chin. The slit-eyed face of a large tortoise-shell cat examined her with a supercilious gaze. The animal stood on the rounded back of the couch, stretched elaborately, raised its tail and sprang to the floor. Ellie sat up, the blankets fell away, and she realized that she was wearing a white cotton nightgown she had never seen before. Her right hand flew across her body to cover the stone in its silvery clasp on her left arm, as in her mind she reached for its power. Her fingers closed around the metal armband, but there was no answering response.

A soft voice spoke out of the shadows.

"You're awake. Good. Well, my love, you're all kinds of a surprise. Tell me, girl, why did our Goddess send you to my door?"

"I'm lost."

The words were out of Ellie's mouth before she could stop herself. She peered fearfully into the room's darkened corners.

"Indeed and for sure you were, as are we all from time to time."

"But where am I?"

"A little west and south of Salterton, a couple of hours walk from Half Moon Bay."

Ellie's shock diminished at the assurance in the woman's voice, but her heart still pounded in her throat. She set her back against the arm of the couch and drew the blankets up to her neck. A lean, brown hand appeared in the light, turned up the lamp, and Ellie looked into black eyes in a dark face framed by exuberantly curly, astonishingly bright red hair that gleamed in the lamplight. Fine lines above full cheeks recorded both laughter and pain. When Ellie stared, wide-eyed, the face receded downwards, and Ellie heard a clicking, tinkling sound as the woman settled herself cross-legged on the floor beside the low couch, her hands folded in her lap, her face in shadow.

"No," said Ellie, desperately striving for control. "I am a navigator. I always know where I am and which way to go. I am never lost." She choked back tears, and whispered. "But I was. I am."

"Well then, the Goddess must have helped you find your way here."

Ellie considered the woman's words, searching for a suitable answer that would respect beliefs she did not share.

"Perhaps."

Her voice sounded tight and shrill.

"Tell me what happened."

Ellie hesitated, unwilling to unburden herself to a stranger. Red hair gleamed as the woman's chin came up. Her black eyes were kind, but there was determination in the set of her chin. Before she could stop herself, words spilled out of Ellie's mouth without control or forethought.

"I must have gone crazy. Out of my head. For sure I walked in circles, fell down, got up, ran, fell again. It was as if I was two people. One of me knew I should stay still, but when I tried to think, I couldn't. So the other me got up again and again, and ran and ran and ran in the rain until I couldn't see for dark. I fell into a hollow where the rain hadn't reached. But the mosquitos had. I was bitten all night. And then … and then … I saw I was back where I'd been before … where I'd started from. Then both parts of me were so … so defeated that I… that I…"

She heard her voice break.

"You slept in the forest, then."

Ellie nodded, grateful for the interruption. When she thought her voice was close to normal, she replied.

"I did. I walked for a whole day, taking rests, but keeping on walking — sometimes running — until there in front of me was the same spruce tangle. I was back where I'd started. Again! That's when I went crazy scared. I heard someone sobbing. It must have been me. I dug the hole in the spruce needles a bit deeper, and slept. Then I got up to what must be today and walked. No clue where I was going. Nothing behind me except the fear of going back to where …"

Ellie checked herself from babbling into tears.

"And so the Goddess did your thinking for you."

"I don't know about that. I just kept going."

"Nothing to eat or drink, then?"

"I drank at several streams. Or maybe it was the same stream. I couldn't think. I just walked. Except that second day, I didn't go circling round and round. I must have held a steady course, because I came out of really big trees late in the afternoon, saw the sky, kept the sun on my left. I knew I ought to go south-east towards the coast, but that would have meant going back into that awful forest, so I headed north because… because…"

Again she bit off her spate of words.

"Because the Goddess was leading you to Maisie's door."

"Who's Maisie?"

"Why, that's me, girl. And what would your name be?"

Words tumbled out of her mouth.

"Ellie. Eliana, daughter of Becky and Dabih. Ellie for short."

"Then, Ellie, you must eat something."

"I don't feel hungry."

"You are, love. But it's that you've gone so far past hungry you've forgotten you need to eat. So now you must nibble sparingly and drink in sips until your body remembers what it needs. I have some soup warming on the back of the stove, close to where Curmudgeon is toasting herself."

"Curmudgeon?"

"She's the one who was looking after you while you slept."

"The black and gold cat who was staring at me as if…"

"That's the one. She has a knowing way about her, and she's a fine judge of character, too. Took one sniff at you when I brought you in the door, led me to the couch here, showed where I should put you down, then settled in to watch over you. Didn't leave you all night. Even when I dozed off, she was there, awake. Now she's decided you'll live, she's probably off to find herself a mouse for breakfast. So I'll fetch you the soup."

Maisie rose to her feet in a single, supple movement that was much younger-seeming than the lines of her face. Again, Ellie heard soft jingling and clinking. Maisie's necklace of bright stones swung across her dark green blouse and Ellie realized that the clinking was from her necklace and the jingling from many bangles on her wrists.

Talking to Maisie had purged the mind-numbing panic, but Ellie still was gripped by the fear that she had lost control of the stone that Astreya had clipped to her arm when she was barely thirteen, the youngest ever to have become a wielder. The green stone with the spear of light at its heart was more than a means of controlling the shipstones that guided Matris' fleet of three schooners. It was a part of her life that individuated her by far more than her slim, lean body, green eyes, and long black hair. The stone held the secret power that she shared with the other wielders, making her one of them, despite her youth. Excepting only Astreya, she was their superior in power and skill. If the stone no longer responded to her will, it was not just that she could not know where she was or where she was heading. It was much worse: she no longer knew who she was.

For a while, she lay with her eyes shut, balanced between wanting and dreading to know the extent of her loss. From nearly three years ago came the memory of the adventure in which she had been kidnapped. Then, she had deliberately flared her stone to broadcast her position to her sister and cousins aboard the schooner *Cygnet*. But here ashore, there had been nothing controlled or deliberate about how the stone had failed her, leaving her lost and terror-stricken, running mindlessly through the forest, bereft.

Clutching the blankets around her with her right hand, Ellie set her teeth, raised her left forearm so that she could look into her stone in its clasp, and opened her eyes. A soft green glow lit the edge of the blanket. Slowly, she let go of the breath she had been holding. Her stone was not entirely dead, even though it had stubbornly failed to guide her through the forest. It glowed, but there was no guiding spear of light at its centre. Perhaps, if she could only be patient, it might eventually respond to her will.

Maisie's jewelry clinked and rattled as she came back from the stove at the kitchen end of the room and slid a tray onto Ellie's lap.

"Now here we are. Warm soup and crumbly bread with the crusts cut off. Mind you only sip and nibble while I let in some more light."

Maisie's bangles jingled as she raised her arms to open the curtains to Ellie's left. Warm daylight revealed a room she had no recollection of entering. Crowded and yet not untidy, the space spoke of a solitary and independent life. Bunches of herbs hung drying from the dark rafters, their fragrance an elusive background to smells of cooking.

Maisie was watching her from the opposite side of a big table. Behind her was a stove, and next to it, a sink below a window. Outside its leaded panes, four sunflowers stared upward. When Maisie pushed the window open, the brindled cat leaped onto the edge of the sink, stepped around the pump handle, poised on the window-ledge and disappeared, leaving two of the black and gold blooms swinging. Maisie took down the largest of several iron pots that hung from the rafter above her head, filled it at the pump by the sink, placed it on the stove and then turned to look at Ellie, who was obediently sipping the milk she had been given. Light from the window behind her turned Maisie into a silhouette crowned by hair that glowed as if afire. Her face invisible, she bent over the scrubbed-white table, half-filled with green-glass bottles, stoneware jars holding knives, forks and spoons, and wicker baskets of vegetables.

"Soon as the water's warmed, we can wash your hair. I sponged you off and put some salve on your mosquito bites when I got you out of those strange clothes to make you ready for bed, and again when you were up in the night — you probably don't remember that, do you?"

Ellie shook her head, her eyes wide.

"Did I say anything?" she asked.

"Nothing joined-up and orderly. I did hear a few words that sounded like they were meant to go together. Sea foam? Serenity? 'Streya?

"They're names. The first one's *Seafoam*, a made-over longboat. The second's not serenity, it's Seren, my big sister — my older sister. She doesn't like it when people call her big, because she's tall, and blonde, and beautiful, and doesn't know it. The third name is Astreya. He's Grand Master. And also my great uncle, sort of. Our family is complicated."

"I heard you say the name Fred, for sure."

"He's … he's my friend. He was aboard *Seafoam*."

"Uh-huh."

"Not that sort of friend. I'm teaching him to sail. At least I was, until the shooting started."

Speaking of the cannon-shot flooded Ellie's mind with the urgency she had forgotten in the terror of being lost.

"I have to go. They'll be worried about me, and they need to know about the gun, right away."

Ellie put the tray on the table, swung her legs onto the floor and stood up. Her vision blurred, her head swam, her knees buckled, and she sat back down like a marionette whose strings had been cut. She sat blinking away the purple cloud that dimmed her vision.

"Woah there, girl. Best you stay where y'are."

Despite her anxiety, Ellie had to agree.

# Chapter 6: In which news reaches Matris

Fred walked away from the big house to escape the unnatural silence. Everyone was quietly waiting for news of Ellie. Even the two little children played too softly to be heard. He followed the road until he reached the ancient earthwork defences around the Home, then he climbed their steep, grassy slope and stared westward towards the outline of the Two Feet. As he watched, wind drew dark clouds out of the west across the face of the setting sun. The surface of the sea lake grew steadily darker until he could no longer distinguish the water from the cliffs and from the sky above. When he could barely see the ground at his feet, Fred knew that *Cygnus* would not attempt the passage from the sea into the lake that night. He descended the earthworks by feel, walked the road back to the house from memory, then stole up the big stairs to his room, where he lay wrestling with his conscience about his part in the ill-fated afternoon of sail training that Ellie had arranged for him.

Remorse was an emotion he had left behind him when more than a decade earlier, he had escaped an orphanage that controlled the children in its care with whippings and guilt. When at last he was deliciously in charge of himself, Fred parlayed his skill with mechanical objects into becoming a maker of precision instruments, with a sideline in chemical experimentation. His enterprise flourished. Forward-thinking people sought his telescopes, watches, sextants, and clocks, because most of what remained from Before had been lost, broken or worn out in the century that had passed since After began.

Everything that Fred did was mechanical, predictable, clean, and untroubled by human emotions until the day when two black-haired men came into his workshop. The tall man with green eyes was Astreya, the other his squat, heavy-set, half-cousin, Walt. They brought with them a gemstone the size of a thumb, with which a wielder could control a crystal shipstone the size of a fist in order to navigate when compasses failed. They wanted Fred to proof the stone against losing its power if it fell into saltwater. He took the job and was successful at the price of exploding the test stone while subjecting it to all the tests he could imagine. He waterproofed the remaining six, pocketed his fee, and remained intensely curious about the stones' potential.

A year or so later, Walt returned, looking for help in resurrecting several long-barrel guns and their ammunition from the rust-encrusted box he had discovered. Fred enjoyed refurbishing the weapons as further proof of his metalworking skills. Pleased with the results, Walt introduced him to Mirak, for whom Fred brewed up two cases of explosives at the cost of a few burned fingers and the temporary loss of both eyebrows. It was interesting work, and Mirak was appreciative. Fred succumbed to the old sailor's promises and threats, and found himself swept up in a storm of violent revenge he had not initiated, could not control, and for which he felt no responsibility. An act of piracy, a war between predominantly Black villagers and all-White townspeople, plus a hurricane later, he still saw himself as innocently involved on the wrong side of a conflict that ended on a beach in the tiny northern Village where Astreya had been born. Fred observed with amazement as Ellie, a black-haired thirteen-year-old girl, nudged and inveigled wicked old Mirak into making the decisions that led to them escaping death when the explosives Fred had manufactured were detonated.

When Astreya arrived in time to tidy up after their adventure, Ellie took Fred into her family home at Matris. He expected to occupy a room until he could board a ship and return to his business at Cottontown. However, months stretched to more than a year during which none of the three schooners' commanders cared to revisit the port where they had been embroiled in a race war. Waiting was easy for Fred after he discovered Astreya's library of books from Before. Two decades of collecting had filled a room lined with bookcases. There were well-used books on the sea and ships that fell flat at the page where Astreya had studied them, and there were books whose spines creaked open for the first time in more than a century. Fred found solutions to practical problems in metallurgy, metalworking, pyrotechnics, explosives, and the behaviour of gases under pressure. He spent hours taking notes, copying formulas, analyzing processes, and speculating on what more he could do when he had a workshop again.

The library would have been enough to hold him in Astreya's big house, but it was only a part of why he was content to wait. For the first time in his life, he had someone with whom he could talk about his expanding knowledge. Ellie's intellectual enthusiasm matched Fred's fascination with how things worked. The members of Ellie's extended family were puzzled by their relationship, which was based on learning together much more than either of them could have achieved alone.

Watching Astreya's family opened a new dimension in Fred's thinking. He was fascinated by the contrast between their easy affection at home, and their formal relationships at sea as officers in Matris' fleet of three schooners. As his studies in Astreya's library increased his technical knowledge, living within a family expanded his understanding of people.

Until the brush with death that he had shared with Ellie two years before, Fred had never really connected the inanimate world of machines and chemistries with their consequences if they were used to kill and maim. Over the months at Matris, he became increasingly aware of the moral ambiguities of what he had done for Mirak, but it was not until Astreya had him tell Becky how close Ellie had come to being killed that Fred saw himself as responsible for what had happened to her.

He had gone walking to calm unexpected emotions and to untangle, analyze, and comprehend his confusion. A dark hour later, when Fred returned to the big house, he lay on his bed and stared at the ceiling, trying to make sense of what had happened to him since Ellie had become involved in his life. It was she who had talked Astreya and his wife the ever-reasonable Lindey into accepting him into their home and family. This was no small matter, since the general opinion among all the sailors was that Fred was a dangerous incompetent who should not be put in charge of a rowboat, let alone aspire to wear a navigator's clasp. Ellie thought differently. She set about teaching him to sail.

Their relationship was nothing like her sister Seren's choice to handfast with her first mate, Marley. Nobody, least of all Fred, saw anything sexual or even affectionate in the way sixteen-year old Ellie made Fred of nearly thirty her student and protégé.

The years between their ages melted away as they learned from each other. Ellie taught Fred the Bag of Rocks game, at which they were soon evenly matched. Fred explained how to fabricate, machine, shape, and mill metal into sextants, clocks, pistols and rifles. She reciprocated by teaching him how to sail other than by instinct and intuition, as did all of her family. They drew diagrams about the intricacies of celestial navigation and calculated the vectors involved when a sailing ship steals forward momentum from the pressure of wind on its sails. She had been showing him how to put theory into practice aboard *Seafoam* when she had fallen into the sea and then disappeared into the forest.

Fred was still amazed that he had successfully brought the crippled longboat back to port without Ellie. But he could not take pride in his unexpected feat of seamanship because he had failed to protect the youngest and most adept wielder of the stones of power, who amazingly was his friend. Worse, he was why she had been at risk. Though not sensitive to other people's emotions, Fred felt the family's revulsion from him now that Ellie, who they all loved, was missing, possibly dead. They had acquiesced to his presence in their lives in deference to Ellie's wishes. Now only Astreya's calming influence held them from allowing Trogen to carry out his threat.

~^~

Two days after the start of *Cygnet's* hastily organized search mission, the little schooner returned at sunset in the rain. The sun gleamed briefly as the ship slid across the darkening water of the sea-lake toward the shipyard, where a crowd waited on the wharf. Fred lurked in the shadow of the big boat barn, eager for news, hoping not to be noticed. Astreya arrived last, walking at the deliberate pace that concealed his limp.

The faces aboard the schooner told of failure even before they landed. Fred edged close enough to hear Mairi's terse report about twenty-four hours of cruising as close to land as they dared, looking and listening for any sign of Ellie. Fred was about to take a circuitous route back to his room when he saw Astreya draw Seren and Mairi aside.

"Could she have been trying to send you a location, a message?" Astreya asked.

They shook their heads.

"We tried to make contact, together," said Mairi. "The way we did when she was kidnapped by Mirak…"

"Nothing," said Seren. "Although… I felt a … a presence … I think."

"I may have felt the same," said Astreya. "Putting it the other way around, none of us felt an absence … a nullity … a loss."

"I felt nothing at all," said Mairi sadly.

"I wanted to land …" Seren began, and then checked herself.

"I know, Seren, but where? We'd gone close to every headland, and into every cove. I really had to …" Mairi's voice failed her.

"She's alive," murmured Seren. "She must be."

Fred shuffled back into the shadows behind the boat barn, his eavesdropping unnoticed. He returned to the house long after supper was over and snuck into his room without being seen.

The next day, Fred arrived late for breakfast. Nobody was sitting at the big table or working in the kitchen. He made his way to the stove, poured the dregs from the coffee pot into his mug, then went to his place. A half loaf of bread stood cut side down on the breadboard, and beside it was a saucer containing a pat of butter. A spoon stuck out of a pot of strawberry preserve, inviting him to help himself.

He had been chewing and sipping for the time it took to drink half his coffee when he heard footsteps. Big boots took short thumping steps that mingled with a slightly uneven tread, and soft, almost inaudible footfalls. An unseen draft swayed the connecting door open.

"I seen 'em. They was there along with a bloody great pile o' rifles an' pistols an' big metal boxes for the bullets."

The man with the big boots spoke indistinctly, slurring his words, talking as if his lips were numb. Fred slid out of the line of sight. Two silent strides took him into the vee between door and wall, his ear close to the hinges. Chairs creaked, clothes rustled, feet slid on the floor.

"Where did you see all this, Enoch?" There was urgency in Astreya's question.

"Yer 'member the big old library? Well, back a few years ago, when they was goin' t'fix the roof an' doors, someone fell through a trap door into the cellar below, what turned out t' be a bloody great storehouse fer machines an' military stuff. Y' know, swords, an' knives, an' guns, an' stuff like that."

"An armoury."

Fred recognized the precise voice of Damon, the tall, moustached second mate of Trogen's ship, *Elusive.*

"What did the Learneds have to say about that?" Astreya asked.

"Nuffin'. Not a peep. 'Course a few of 'em wanted to study the guns an' things, but Gov'ner only let Sandy play wi' the machines, 'cause he's got the touch for it, not like them green-gowns all filled up wi' ideas an' arguments and stuff. Gov'ner's got them Castle folks under his thumb. He told 'em to forget about their theorizin', 'cause him an' Sandy wanted the guns fer his army."

"The Governor?" Astreya asked.

"Jus' Gov'ner. That's what he likes. Even from us what knew him when he wore a green scholar's gown an' ran around cutting people up for fun."

"Carl controls the Castle?" Astreya's voice was incredulous.

"And the town," said Damon. "As I said, Astreya, the irony is palpable."

"'E's made it so that curfew's at dusk, an' you'd better be off the streets afore the sun's down, 'cause there's soldiers goin' about in pairs, all tooled up wi' swords an' pistols."

"It would also appear from what Enoch told me earlier that Carl claims authority extending eastward to Salterton on Half Moon Bay," said Damon.

"E's got most everyone diggin' holes lookin' fer more stuff from Before. It's the only work left since the Castle emptied out."

"Is the Castle no longer a place of learning?" Astreya asked.

"There's some o' them green gowns still there, but when he took over, the Gov'ner sent the most o' them back off to their towns and villages."

"It's unclear how far his influence extends," said Damon. "Perhaps not as far as Markham, but it's likely he's having an effect on Teenmouth."

"Goin' east, 'e' got more'n half o' the local farmers workin' on the roads so's he can move his bloody great gun around. Word is, the road south's next."

"Charton," said Damon. "And then …"

"Matris. Predictably," Astreya agreed.

The back door to the kitchen creaked and the high voices of little girls mingled with Becky's patient tones as Lena and Maia came into the house. Fred had heard enough to make him intensely curious, and also determined not to be detected. He pressed his fingertips on the door behind which he had been hiding and shoved gently. When it was almost closed, he tiptoed past the gap and on to the main hall, where he softly entered the library. Astreya continued to ask brief questions that elicited long, rambling answers from the big-booted man, interspersed with precise statements from Damon. Their conversation reached Fred as sound rather than speech as he scanned the shelves, removed a handful of books and then ran up the great staircase, taking the steps two at a time.

Fred spent the rest of the day in his room reading books about guns and ammunition. He started by thinking about technical issues, but soon he was speculating about what he might do next. Should he remain, hoping for Ellie's return? Or leave, hoping to discover more about the gun with wheels and whatever else had been preserved from the past? Perhaps consult with the man named Sandy who had been allowed into the armoury? Search for Ellie himself when everyone else had failed? Whatever he decided, he would be on his own, with his motives deeply suspect – not least by himself.

# Chapter 7: In which Ellie and Maisie talk

Whenever she thought about her days at the cottage, Ellie's best memory was of Maisie washing her hair. It began with heating a cauldron of warm water delicately fragrant with lavender. Then came the blissful moments as Maisie's firm fingers massaged lather all over her head. Warm water trickled down the back of her neck, washing out the salt from swimming ashore, along with the dust and dirt from the forest, and as it did so, cleansing away much of the lost days' lingering horror. A creamy lotion smelling of rosemary let the comb painlessly separate tangles, smoothing her black hair all the way down to her waist. Then Ellie sat in the sun drying her hair, feeling contented.. Around them in Maisie's garden there were the sounds of late summer: the rustle of drying grasses, the hum of bees fumbling the petals of flowers, the call of birds. The feeling of well-being brought with it a return to normal eating at suppertime. Maisie smiled as Ellie cut a fresh slice of bread to mop up the gravy of the evening's vegetable hot pot.

The next day, Ellie woke to the rumble of Curmudgeon's big-cat purr. She put out a hand and stroked soft fur, then sat up without even a hint of the previous day's dizziness. She looked around the room, this time noticing much more than the homely kitchen area that had been all she could deal with the day before. The room was full but not cluttered. Tall stone walls and timbered beams held up a peaked roof. Baskets of onions, garlic, and apples hung from hooks in the age-blackened rafters. An iron frame beside the stove held billets of wood. A broad-bladed hatchet lay on a basket of kindling. Pottery bowls glazed in bright swirling colours sat along the windowsills. Black iron brackets supported a chest-high shelf of books that ran most of the way across the back wall. A dozen or more well-preserved books marched upright, flanked by leather-bound tomes with faded spines. Clusters of well-worn volumes leaned precariously against each other sprouting paper and fabric bookmarks from their pages.

In the corner furthest from Ellie, a three-legged table held a collection of coloured stones, dried flowers, curiously shaped pieces of wood, all interspersed with stubby little candles set in green glass bowls and brown bottles that Ellie guessed must have been made long ago. Above them was a woven drapery, its soft colours suggesting a landscape of tree-clad hills receding into the blue distance. Ellie stood, smoothed her borrowed nightgown, took three barefoot steps and examined the intricate knotting and weaving. Almost beside her, the door to Maisie's bedroom opened.

"Blessed be, Ellie. You're up and doing very early."

"Um … blessed be, Maisie," said Ellie, her voice unsure.

"No to worry, Ellie. I know my words are not your custom, but I also know that what they mean is a part of your way as well."

As Ellie puzzled about what to say in reply, she heard Maisie laugh. It was a descending, musical ripple that chased away any possibility of offence given or taken.

"I should get into my own clothes," said Ellie.

"Not much left of them," said Maisie. "All ripped and torn they were, even before I peeled them off you."

"If you can give me a needle and thread, I'm sure I can fix them."

"Doubt it. That sharkskin is some kind of tough. But we'll wash and dry them, and then you can try. In the meanwhile, best I lend you something you can wear," said Maisie. "Tighten up the drawstrings in the waist and blouse, and they'll fit after a fashion."

A little while later, wearing the clothes Maisie lent her, Ellie felt strangely different from the sailor she knew she was, and more like a person who lived ashore. Her face and hands were no longer swollen and itchy, the bruises and strains that she had not noticed when they happened were healing, but though she was moving with her accustomed ease, she was still disturbed by the state of her navigation stone. It still glowed a pale green, but the colour lacked its usual intensity, and the spear of white light at its centre stubbornly refused to appear, no matter how hard she concentrated.

Now that she was safe, rested, and well-fed, Ellie started to analyze what had happened to the stone. Like all the other wielder's stones, it had been waterproofed by Fred, but nobody had ever tested this with anything more than a quick dip into the sea. She had spent several minutes in the waves, enough for water to seep up her sleeves and down her neck. At the time she had not noticed, because her sailing jacket kept her warm until it dried from the heat of her body. She did not know if her stone had been weakened by prolonged dampness, but it seemed a reasonable explanation. But why had it not recovered now it and she were warm and dry? Was it permanently damaged? Or was it that she was no longer able to wield it?

She deliberately ignored the twinge of panic, and since there was nothing she could do, decided to concentrate on the present. In this, she was greatly helped by Maisie, who had the ability to take pleasure in the ordinary. She would pause during her day to be momentarily entranced by a flower, a bird or one of her animals. Ellie recognized a similarity to her own delight in the interplay of wind and water at sea. They were comfortable together, refraining from asking questions, even though Ellie wanted to know how and why Maisie was content to live alone; and Maisie was puzzled by Ellie's maturity beyond her years.

Late in the day, Ellie became distant and withdrawn as she wondered how to make her way home without guidance from her stone. Maisie saw her distress and took practical steps to cheer her. Handing Ellie a paring knife, she indicated a bowl of green beans fresh from her garden.

"Top and tail them, please. You do like mushrooms, I hope? They're one of the advantages of having a cellar."

Ellie sat at the table opposite Maisie. As her hands performed a familiar task, she began to talk.

"We pick mushrooms in the autumn," she said slowly. "There's a stand of oaks nearby where they grow. But the season is short, and we're often at sea and miss it. This year, we had a longer stay at home than usual. That's why I was aboard *Seafoam*, giving Fred a lesson in helming a longboat. But then I fell off."

"How could that have happened?"

"Guns. A shot clipped the port stays, *Seafoam* yawed, I fell in."

"Didn't they stop to pick you up?"

"They couldn't. We were being shot at."

"Why were you there in the first place?"

"Sailing to Half Moon Bay is … it's like taking a walk for exercise. If the wind and tide are right it's a day's trip to go out between the Two Feet on the ebb, sail to the Bay, and then come home in time for the flood. Seren and I used to do it just for fun. But all of us do the run every now and then to stretch new sails, try out a new longboat, train cadets in boat-handling…"

Ellie paused, thinking of how Fred's seamanship had risen to the emergency, and hoping he had been able to return safely. For a moment, Maisie and Ellie sat chopping mushrooms and trimming beans in silence. Then, noticing Maisie's questioning look, Ellie started to explain how *Seafoam* had to stay on the starboard tack or lose the mast. When Maisie looked puzzled by the nautical details, Ellie told her how she had swum to the point at the southern end of Half Moon Bay, where further shots at her and the boat had forced her to push her way into the underbrush and then on into the forest.

"It seemed like a sensible course of action at the time," she ended, unconsciously echoing one of Astreya's favourite sayings. "I was expecting to walk to a cove where *Cygnet* could pick me up, but…"

"Your mother and father must be worrying about you."

"Father died almost three years ago. He was murdered. Mother … Mother hasn't really recovered from his death. She goes on with all the things she always did, keeping house, looking after my little sisters, being there when we're in harbour, keeping us all fed during the winter months now there's ten of us. But she's … she's empty at heart without Father."

"I'm sorry," said Maisie, with an understanding that went beyond the conventional words. "Ten of you? I thought you said you had three sisters."

"That's right. Seren, Me, Maia, and baby Lena. Seren's got five years' more sea-time than me. Mother's hanging on to Maia and Lena like there's nothing else left in her life. Seren has her Marley, so he's now part of the family. Fred, too, but he only gets on well with me. Then there's Mairi and Trogen. They're twins. Daughter and son of Lindey and Astreya. The four of them spend the winter haul-out with us."

"What's a winter haul-out?"

"During the two-three months when the weather's at its worst, we haul the ships out of the water, scrape, apply fresh pitch and tar, refresh and replace cordage and sails … it's like spring cleaning a house, except we do it in the winter."

"It must be a big house for ten people," said Maisie.

"Yes, it is a really big house. Built Before. Three stories. High ceilings. Huge kitchen. And a dome over the front hall that's roof-high. Astreya's painting birds, and animals, and ships, and people, all around it. Every year he adds to it. Lindey mixes his paints. That's how they met," she stopped, frowning that she had let herself run on.

"Astreya. He's your grandfather?"

"Not really. Father is … was … his cousin. Both their fathers are gone. Astreya calls me his niece, so I call him uncle, but that's not quite right. It's complicated. He's … he's legendary. Just about everyone's in awe of him. 'Cept me. I horrify people by *cheeking* him regularly. He lets me get away with it … even seems to like it. He has this gleam in his green eyes that's like a knife-blade with sun flickering on it. Never raises his voice. But what he says, goes. Of course, he and Lindey are close, so close there's not much room for Mairi and Trogen."

"And why does he let you … what did you say, 'get away with it'?"

"'Cause I'm super good with my stone. Even better than Trogen. Seren and Mairi working together can equal Trogen, but I can detect, dead reckon, and message, further and faster and stronger than anyone ... except Astreya.  At least, I could … right up to when the shooting started. After that, I couldn't even find north …"

She fell silent, her mind spiralling back to the horror of her two lost days.

Maisie swept chopped mushrooms into an iron pot on the stove, where they sizzled in butter. She raised one black eyebrow enquiringly while stirring the mushrooms. As a rich smell filled the little cottage, Ellie reminisced.

"Astreya sent the four of us who have clasps to the Sunny Isles so that we wouldn't get caught in Mirak's revenge. But Mirak fooled him. I got kidnapped, used my stone to call *Cygnet* for help, which was a mistake because *Elusive* heard and headed to Cottontown where Mirak's men murdered Father. Mirak guessed that the mother lode of stones must be the Village where Astreya was born, so he forced me to navigate him there."

Maisie stopped stirring. Head on one side, she let Ellie's account wash over her.

"So Trogen in *Elusive*, and Mairi in *Cygnet* followed my stone to rescue me, and we all sailed right into a huge hurricane, which we survived, but only barely. Then when we got to the Village, it turned out that Walt … who was sort of like my great-uncle … had a gun, and Mirak had explosives, and one thing led to another, and Mirak and his crew were all blown up. Anyway, I found more stones in the Village stream, which was good, because everyone thought there were only the ones handed down in the family from Before."

"What do you know about Before?" Maisie asked as she added a sprig of thyme to the mushrooms.

"There was the falling apart of the cities, and then the plague that spread everywhere. Unconscionable numbers of people perished, but some escaped in amazing ways. Nearly a dozen great ships stayed at sea for almost a century so that they would not be infected."

Maisie put a lid on the mushrooms and stared at Ellie.

"You're descended from the Men of the Sea, aren't you?"

Ellie heard misgiving in Maisie's voice. Suddenly aware that she had been compulsively telling her private family history to a stranger, she spoke slowly and defensively.

"A descendent, yes, but now only two great ships remain, and it's all different. Astreya changed things. Now we trade up and down the coast from Matris to the Sunny Isles and back. That's all."

Maisie poured cream into the mushrooms and slid the pot to the back of the stove.

"Trade? That's all?" she repeated Ellie's words evenly.

Ellie nodded vigorously.

"We deal fairly, but we don't get involved. But it wasn't always like that. There were some of the Men of the Sea who were pirates. You see, at first, they had one nursery ship where two generations of children grew up, but somehow there weren't any more babies, so they had to..."

"Kidnap men and boys?" supplied Maisie, looking up from chopping green onions.

Ellie nodded again, wishing she had never started talking.

"That was years ago. Fifty or more."

"Not as long as that. Your ships come to Half Moon Bay often."

"I've told you why we do that, and we've never landed or tried to engage with anyone. Until they shot at us from the northeast point of Half Moon Bay. I have no idea why."

Her eyes focused on the table in front of her.

"I think I do," said Maisie.

Ellie's green eyes widened.

"It's the men from the Castle. They started arriving about six years or so ago. First a healer, and my goodness what a disappointment he was. I wouldn't trust him to birth a sheep. But more followed. They bought land, and they paid well for it. People were happy to sell whatever the newcomers needed, especially when the newcomers were willing to pay more than anyone expected. So they settled in, a few of them married local women, which by the way made them the richest wives around. And so the jealousy began, and prices for everything rose, because with all that extra coin around everyone expected more."

"What does this have to do with ..." Ellie began.

"When the soldiers started to arrive last year with money in their pockets to spend on food, drink, and lodging, they were welcomed.

Farmers and foresters left their usual work and earned good wages improving the road from Salterton to the Castle."

Ellie's concentration wavered.

"The gun arrived about a month ago," said Maisie.

Ellie's green eyes looked up, bright with interest.

"Fred and I were shot at three years ago, when we were at the Village. That gun was a lot smaller, and it exploded, but not before it killed four very bad men and one big friendly fellow who saved us."

"You and your friend Fred do have adventures," said Maisie blandly.

"Why bring a gun here?" Ellie demanded.

"To defend us from the Men of the Sea," said Maisie. "The ones who sail into Half Moon Bay."

"Like me? That's ridiculous. Half Moon Bay is a turning point, not a destination. Ever since — oh years ago, when I was little — when we tried to get them to trade with us, and they told us — it was father, actually — to go away. It struck us as really strange, because everywhere else we go people are willing to trade. But lubbers ARE strange, so we left the silly people alone.… Oh, I'm sorry, Maisie, I didn't mean you."

'I think that silly people like me would want to trade, especially now we all have more coin in our pockets than before, all thanks to that self-important Governor at the Castle. But it wasn't old Salterton people who said no to the men on your big ship, it was the mayor, who'd come from the Castle only a couple of years before. And the priest, and the healer, and the head man of the soldiers who had been building the road."

"… who told you what terrible people the Men of the Sea are," said Ellie.

Maisie nodded.

"And how we needed the soldiers from Castle to defend us."

"And the gun," said Ellie. "Where did they get that from?"

"Apparently, they found a cellar full of … oh, I don't know … machines, tools, weapons, stuff from Before. Along with other stuff that goes bang. Which some of it did, killing a few of them, which they blamed on the Men of the Sea."

"Why us?" Ellie began, then shook her head at what she realized was a foolish question, and answered it herself. "They needed a boogie-man, a scary evil collection of monsters."

Maisie nodded and went on sadly.

"Ans so they brought a gun on wheels from the Castle. And all the good people of Salterton felt much better because the Castle was protecting them from the black-haired raiders from the sea."

Ellie's green eyes narrowed. She lowered her head so that her long black hair concealed her face. Then using both thumbs she lifted the heavy tresses and released them so that they cascaded over her shoulders. Her voice hardened into a challenge.

"My father had black hair. So does Grand Master Astreya, and his father the first Astreya, and his father Oron, son of Zubin, who started the century of what we call the Wandering."

To Ellie's surprise, Maisie laughed, but it was almost a bark, very different from the peal of joy Ellie had heard the day before.

"The Goddess guided you to the right door, Ellie-girl. It's certain that I'm not the one to judge you by the colour of your hair or those green eyes of yours. We are each and all of us children of the Goddess."

"That's pretty much how we think about people, too. It's the way Astreya encourages us to deal ashore and afloat," said Ellie. "It's only good sense. But… how do I say this … you're not like most of the lubbers … sorry … the land people. They're all convinced that they're the only people who matter, and that they're better than everyone else. Which is odd, because they fear anyone who's different from them. It makes dealing with them difficult. They're suspicious, even hostile. They'll deal, but always as if they didn't trust us. Not at all like the way you've taken me in, looked after me…"

"Tell me, Ellie, have you been thinking all along that I'm a heavily suntanned woman who was born with red hair?"

Ellie frowned, and Maisie laughed again, this time with real amusement.

"I'm Black, Ellie, and that's not what you'd call well-regarded or welcome around here. "

Ellie looked puzzled.

"Marley's Black. Wonderful black that sort of soaks up light and then glows from within. He's from the Sunny Isles, and he's family. He and my sister Seren are going to have a baby. More than one, if I know her. Which I do."

Maisie tilted her head and raised one eyebrow.

"Mushrooms," she said as she took pots off the stove, served them onto two plates and sat opposite Ellie. "Enjoy. Then tell me more about your family."

It was late and after much more talk that they blew out the candles and went to bed.

The next morning, as Ellie was sitting on the couch in her nightshirt, lost in the thought that her family must think her dead, there was a knock at the door.

"I'll be there in a moment!" Maisie called.

She spoke as she moved swiftly around the table, scooped up Ellie's legs, pushed her onto the couch and threw the blue blanket over her. A wave of anxiety swept over Ellie as it had when lost in the woods, and she froze. Then she heard the door creak open, and curiosity drove off panic.

"Isobel," said Maisie. "Blessed be."

"Don't say that!" whispered a female voice. "Someone might hear. There are so many suspicious people. You really mustn't draw attention to yourself."

"The Goddess will…"

"Maisie!  There is only one god, and he's not a she."

"Isobel, I'm cleaning house," Maisie began. Under the blanket, Ellie heard heels tapping towards the couch on which she lay.

"Please… oh well, come on in. What can I do for you, Isobel?"

"It's what I'm trying to do for you. But you keep on making it more difficult by running on about being blessed and talking about a … female spirit. You're in danger, Maisie."

Ellie heard the woman's voice start wheedling and conspiratorial, then become critical, finally breathlessly dramatic. The couch creaked as she sat on its arm only a handspan from Ellie's face, her shadow dimming what little light filtered through the blue blanket.

"Danger, Isobel? Of what?"

"Listen to me, Maisie. The preacher, the mayor, and, well, everyone is in danger from the pirates. You know, the black-haired kidnappers who steal children. They're close. The soldiers used their big gun to scare off one of their strange ships. But it's possible that they could have landed people to capture more victims."

Ellie bit her lip.

"It was brave of you to walk all the way here, Isobel."

Maisie's words were flat with sarcasm, but the woman took them at face value.

"I had to. Because that's not all. Someone has made up a story about what you do and how you do it. All about spells and dead babies and potions made from churchyard bones, and stuff like that. And so of course they told the parson, and he's talked to the sheriff, and they've both talked with the mayor."

"Gossip, Isobel. Every little while they go through the same ructions, and then things settle down."

"Not this year. The mayor's up for re-election and he's been saying that with the raiders along the coast, nobody should be isolated and alone."

"Like me," said Maisie. "Living alone. Always a reason for pointing a finger."

Isobel's voice rose.

"They've seen the invaders Maisie! That's why the soldiers have come from the Castle to protect us. They shot their big gun at them and chased them off."

"Soldiers to protect us from men in ships?"

Isobel did not respond to Maisie's derision.

"They're billeted in many homes. I've got two of them." Isobel's voice went from eager to complaining. "And a more demanding, prying, leering pair of young freeloaders you never want to meet."

"Are they pressing themselves upon you, Isobel?"

"Not when my man Bill's around, they don't. But when he's not there, they stare at me and whisper to each other like I didn't know they're talking about what they'd like to do."

"You want me to give you something to put in their tea that will slow them down. That's why you're here, isn't it?"

Isobel gave a little shriek of dismay.

"Potions? The minister says any woman who would give a man a potion is…"

"A witch? A woman who's sold her soul? Made a wicked bargain with dark powers? Set loose arcane forces that will devour me and all those whose lives I touch? "

As irritation sharpened Maisie's tone, a heavy weight landed on Ellie's stomach. The couch creaked as her gasp blended with a "Prrrp!" from Curmudgeon.

"Maybe Curmudgeon here is my familiar spirit? Perhaps Dora my goat is actually the hornèd one?"

Ellie heard Isobel's shoes clattered towards the door.

"Don't say such things! I wish I'd never heard what you just said. I don't want your wicked potions! I only came to warn you."

"Warn me, Isobel? Or collect evidence for the witch-finders?"

"Take my advice and leave, Maisie, or you'll be very sorry, very soon."

Ellie peeked over the arm of the couch in time to see Maisie at the door. Her farewell was soft.

"Blessed be, Isobel, for coming to warn me. I'll remember you for that kind thought."

"I never… I wasn't here."

Ellie heard Isobel's footsteps recede out of earshot.

"You can come out now, Ellie."

Ellie emerged, her hair tousled.

"She made me cross," said Maisie. "She was here not three weeks ago to buy potions for her husband's digestion, by which she meant his performance in her bed."

"Maisie, could she …?"

"She's all of a tizzy. Wants to be right with the important men from the Castle, but can't quite forget that she and I were friends, sort of."

She glanced at the kitchen table, and then at Ellie. They blinked at each other, both wondering whether Isobel had noticed that the table was set for two. Maisie's bangles jingled as she raised both her arms in an elaborate shrug, as if unwilling to do what she had already decided. Then her jaw set and her eyes narrowed. She plucked a dark blue wool cap from a peg beside the door and tossed it at Ellie.

"Ellie, you must leave. Here, take this and stuff your hair under it. Pull it well down over your brow. If you don't take it off, you'll pass, at a distance, anyway."

She strode to her room. Curmudgeon leaped out of her way with an indignant "Prrrp," and then strolled across the floor, her brown-and-gold tail held high. Maisie returned moments later with a soft green shirt, and brown skirt-like riding trousers. Ellie found herself doing as she had been told, almost as if ordered by Grand Master Astreya. While she pulled on the clothes, Maisie darted around the cottage stuffing a shoulder satchel with clothes, bread, apples, preserves, a bottle of water, a box of fire-starters, Ellie's clasp knife, and a little pottery jar, its cork sealed by red wax. Her whirlwind tasks completed, Maisie stood by the cottage door and beckoned, her dark eyes compelling.

Ellie hesitated, searching for words. Maisie did not let her speak. She hung a green cloak over Ellie's shoulders, handed her the satchel, kissed her firmly on the forehead, and stepped back.

"Now, girl, you must go, and go quickly. When you get to the orchard, take the path on your right. It goes uphill steeply at first, then it levels out and heads westward for … oh I don't know how far.… Anyway, it eventually meets the north-south road from the Castle to Charton. Keep going. Don't come back, whatever you do. It's not safe here."

Ellie did as she was told.

# Chapter 8: In which Astreya re-assigns ships

After another restless night, Fred decided that he had been skulking long enough. He went down to the kitchen, found it filled with people, took his place, tried not to glance at the empty space where Ellie usually sat, and tucked into his breakfast. The only person who acknowledged his presence was little Maia, who gave him a gap-toothed, egg-yolked smile. Cam pushed the coffee pot in his direction. Becky looked at him, blinked, and returned her attention to the two little girls.

Astreya's black-haired head was turned towards Lindey, whose blonde hair curtained her face. The two of them were deep in a low-voiced discussion, their words inaudible above the sounds of cooking and eating. Across the table from where Fred sat, Mairi and Trogen were arguing, their food neglected. Trogen complained, Mairi responded evenly. Trogen rapped the table with one finger, both looked up at the same moment, their eyes focussed briefly on Fred, then they glanced away. Fred chewed toast and guardedly looked around. Seren's blue eyes were staring blankly at the place where Ellie should have been. Marley's gaze was on Seren's face, and one of his big hands covered hers protectively.

One by one they all followed Seren's stare. Even the little girls' spoons were stilled. The silence became oppressive, foreboding. Fred felt their eyes drift over him, pause, then look away.

Astreya stood and spoke into the silence.

"At the conclusion of the afternoon watch, mates and all those with clasps or rings will assemble in *Cygnus'* Forbidden Room to witness inductions, promotions and the re-assignment of roles and responsibilities. Cam, kindly ensure that Damon is present. Seren, please bring Marley and Alan."

Lindey rose from her chair and accompanied Astreya out of the kitchen. After a brief silence, everyone except Fred began talking at once.

Fred opened his mouth to ask what was going on, but nobody noticed. When he stood, he realized that provided he avoided everyone's eyes, he was invisible. Unwanted and excluded, he walked away from the table, muttered thanks to Becky, but did not stop to find out if she had heard.

Once outside the kitchen, Fred trudged up the stairs to his third-floor room, where he remained until the house was silent. He packed his spare clothes into a backpack, then stole downstairs to the door of the big kitchen, where he paused to listen. Outside in the yard, he could hear Becky talking to the two little girls. He quietly entered the larder where he added bread, cheese, apples and a water bottle to his pack. Pausing to ensure that the children were behind the house, he stole out the front door and down the wide steps that led to the tree-lined road. Soon the mansion was out of sight behind him. Half an hour later, he was on the cliff-top trail to Charton.

~^~

Later that day, rowing boats converged on the great ship *Cygnus* as she lay at her mooring buoy. When the masters, navigators, and cadets were all assembled, Astreya led them below to the Forbidden Room. Alan was in his best shore-going ship's uniform, shifting his weight from one leg to the other. Above their uniform breeks, Cam and Damon wore shore-going shirts and waistcoats; Damon's blue, Cam's red. Neither was comfortable to be in the Forbidden Room: Cam's usual grin was lopsided, and Damon preened his moustache nervously. Mairi's hair fell loose to her shoulders, Lindey wore the homespun skirt and blouse favoured by the farmer's wives, Seren's bright blonde curls were a halo around her head, and a green dress clung to her tall, athletic body. Marley stood proudly at her shoulder, his dreadlocks tied at the back collar of his shirt. They stood close-packed in the cramped, dark space, watching as Astreya pulled the cloth from the pit-like table navigation table. Green light flared from the shipstone at its centre, gleaming on five silver clasps, each with its own green stone, but it was Astreya's face, lit from below that held their attention.

"Throughout more than a century, men and women navigated the Great Ships with a diminishing number of shipstones and clasps.

Thanks to my niece Eliana, we have stones to spare and a source of more as and when they are needed. It is past time we made better use of them."

Subtle movements showed that all were thinking of black-haired, green-eyed Ellie. As they focussed on Astreya's angular face, half expecting a eulogy, he paused to let the ripple of small movements and sounds die away. His tone was that of a teacher reciting history.

"The habit of years has been to hold the lore of the stones within the bloodline of my grandfather Oron, and his father, Zubin, the Grand Master who initiated the Wandering. It seemed to them that the chain of command demanded the security, secrecy, and loyalty of a family, so to that end, all the masters were connected by blood or adoption. Only if a man or woman shared the family looks would he, or very rarely she, be even considered as more than a second mate or boat commander."

Astreya's voice hardened.

"There is absolutely no reason for this restriction. Nobody can tell by bloodline or appearance whether a man or a woman is capable of wielding the stones."

Lindey and Mairi nodded, their blonde hair swinging. Damon and Cam glanced at each other and then at Seren, whose curly fair hair gleamed in the shipstone's green light.

"Now that we have more stones of power, we need more men and women who can use them and more ships for them to command and navigate. We need to train more wielders in the same way as we train young men and women in the practical arts of seamanship. Cam, Damon, Marley, Alan, step forward and claim the clasps you deserve."

One by one, they each held their breath, picked up a clasp, clipped it to their left arms and exhaled when their stones glowed bright green. When they all left the room, one clasp remained unassigned. No one mentioned that Fred was not aboard.

# Chapter 9: In which Maisie's cottage burns

Maisie's hand on Ellie's shoulder pushed her gently but firmly through the door, which closed behind her with the double thud of a wooden bar falling into place. Ellie paused under the eves to look and listen. Suddenly relieved of doubt, she was entirely focused on carrying out Maisie's instructions. Nonetheless, half-formed questions prowled the back of her mind.

Apart from distant clucking from hens in their fenced run, there was nothing to hear except the brittle sound of crickets in the summer-dried grasses. When she looked up, she saw a sky dotted with small, fluffy clouds. Neither Dora the goat nor Gobbles the goose had sounded an alarm, so she reasoned that nothing was untoward. Ellie shouldered her satchel and despite the sun, drew the green cloak around her. Her slim, hurrying shape blended into the tall grass of the meadow as she followed the path towards the orchard. Less than a hundred dusty strides from the cottage, the path intersected with a fainter trail leading westward. Behind her, she heard Maisie's voice calling Dora, Gobbles and Curmudgeon, but when she turned to look, the cottage door was closed.

Maisie's directions still uppermost in her mind, Ellie turned westward, following the earthy trace that wound among clumps of shin-high grass and then on among waist-high bushes. Soon clumps of poplar and aspen shadowed the trail. She checked her clasp automatically, but it only glowed a uniform soft green. Unable to confirm her direction, she had to rely on instructions from Maisie, who might be in danger herself.

The indistinct trail widened as it climbed into the woods. The mingled scent of trees made breathing easier than on the dusty path through the meadow. When Ellie looked up at the canopy above her, she saw many-pointed maple leaves, spear-head-shaped beech and elm, and the trembling, yellow coin-like leaves of poplars, all interspersed with dark green pines. A light wind stirred the tops of the trees with a distant faint rustle, but below on the road, it was still and silent save for the whine of the occasional mosquito. She paused to look back and recognized that she was on what had once been a substantial road that rose in a smooth curve, cutting across the bumps and hollows of the forest on either side. Ellie looked back through the tree-trunks beyond Maisie's cottage to where great oaks and maples grew beside fallen masonry that had once been walls. She saw that where Maisie lived must have been built as an outbuilding to a much larger structure, now only a ruin.

As Ellie watched, she heard the distant drumming of hooves. Half a dozen or more men on horseback rode toward the cottage. The riders slowed, milled about in a compact group, then broke up into individual horsemen, each holding a flickering torch at arm's length. They rode around the cottage, then their torches trailed smoke as they arced through the air onto the roof, against the door, through the windows.

Ellie recognized a swift-moving white patch as Dora the goat running towards the doorway, where she met a rider coming the other way. A sword flashed. A heartbeat later, Ellie saw Gobbler charge at the horseman, its long neck extended in a honking, squawking rush, cut off by another slash of the horseman's sword.

The door of the cottage swung open, revealing Maisie's russet-skirted figure and bright red hair. She threw her head back and let out a throat-tearing scream. The horseman wheeled and cantered towards her, his raised sword catching the sunlight. Ellie saw Maisie's arm whirl above her head. Something flashed through the air. Maisie's second scream, wild with rage, reached Ellie an instant later as the horse wheeled and pounded away, its saddle empty, its hoofbeats muffled by the woods between them. Ellie yelled and ran back down the path, her cloak flapping, losing sight of Maisie.

When Ellie emerged from the trees, Maisie's door was closed. Orange fire lit the cottage windows from within. Flames licked up under the roof and ran across the shingles. Horsemen appeared and disappeared in the smoke. Their torches thrown, they circled the cottage whooping and cheering in a demented carousel, trampling Maisie's garden under their horses' hoofs.

Ellie froze, horror-stricken, as flames flared out of the cottage windows, and then spewed smoke as the roof fell in. Through tears of rage she glimpsed fiery cinders and sparks rising from what had been the things of beauty and use in the cottage. Hopelessly, Ellie realized that Maisie had to be dead in the furnace burning within what was left of the walls.

As she watched, the horsemen slowed their celebration of destruction, came together into a dark knot of jostling bodies, then split up and rode slowly away. Ellie slumped onto a stump beside the path and sat hunched under her cloak, grief-stricken. She did not notice the tears running down her cheeks or feel the mosquitos biting her face and neck until it dawned on her that some of the horsemen might be hunting her. She got to her feet and set off back up the road through the woods. Gradually, the rhythm of walking numbed her memories of what she had seen. Her cloak made her sweaty and uncomfortable, but it kept her from staring at her useless green stone. The sun told her she was moving westward, but she could only guess when she would reach the north-south road Maisie had told her ran towards Charton. Dimly aware that her feet hurt, she trudged along the ancient road towards hills glimpsed in the distance.

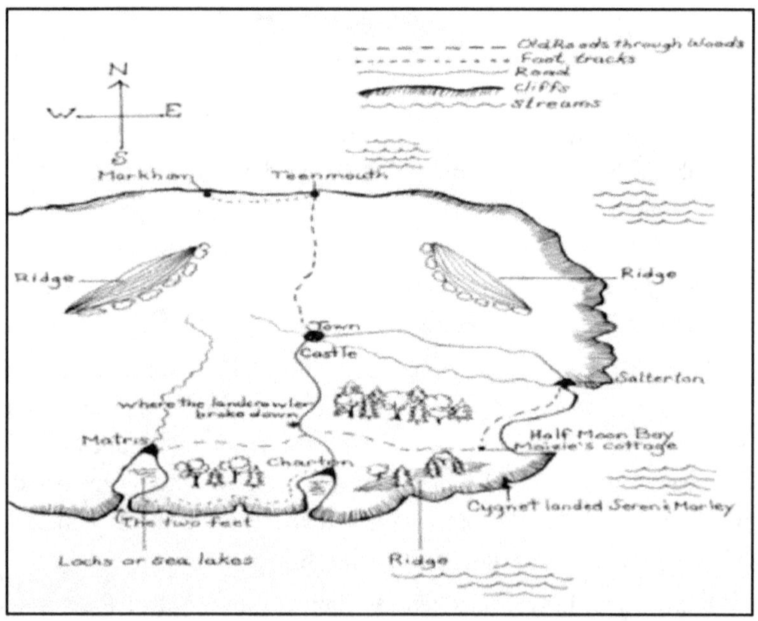

# Chapter 10: In which Astreya and Lindey divide

"Well, that was interesting," said Lindey.

She and Astreya stood facing each other in *Cygnus'* big stern cabin. Between them was the chart table, bare except for paper, pen and ink set out in front of the master's chair. From above on the quarterdeck came the mutter of conversations among the men and women who had been present in the Forbidden Room. Astreya looked quizzically at Lindey, wondering what particular aspect of the emotion-charged meeting she had in mind.

"In an unprecedented, uncharacteristic, and inscrutable act you essentially forced clasps on the three men most likely to refuse them. Cam was happy as he was, Damon believes the stones are dangerously magical, Marley thinks he's getting special privileges only because he's with Seren. You took them by surprise, making it impossible for them to decline."

Astreya's lips curled in the beginnings of a smile.

"You're forgetting Alan. He was pleased."

"Alan was flabbergasted, as you expected."

Astreya's mouth hardened into a thin line.

"It was time. They're all more than ready and capable to be navigators, and when and as we need them, masters."

"Masters of the ships that Drew is making."

Astreya nodded.

"And in the meanwhile, three men will be ready to take over should something happen to the ships' current masters."

Lindey stared at him, her blue eyes steady.

"You're planning something, aren't you?"

Astreya nodded. He stood, pulled back the master's chair from the chart table, took a step to one side, and gestured with his right hand.

"Lindey, Mistress of *Cygnus*. Your chair."

Lindey stared at Astreya in disbelief.

"That's it, Astreya? No discussion? No consultation with the other masters and navigators? Not a word to me? Whatever has come over you? It's Ellie, isn't it?"

"I'm exercising my prerogative as Grand Master."

"You're suddenly going against everything that we've been doing for more than two decades. Decision-making for the fleet is made collectively by those who wear a clasp. It's not for the Grand Master to …"

"Yes, it is, Lindey. We've met with the masters and navigators present, but when have they ever done more than agree and confirm what I invited them to do?"

"The logic of which you and I discussed beforehand. Until now."

Astreya's green eyes met Lindey's angry blue-eyed stare. He grimaced, gripped the back of the master's chair and pulled it back from the table.

"True. But let me continue. My last act as Grand Master is the re-assignment of commands. Trogen continues as master of *Elusive* with you as Grand Commander to keep him in check. Mairi becomes navigator of *Cygnus*. Seren commands *Cygnet*. All three masters are charged with training the wielders-to-be: Cam, Damon, Marley, and Alan. And you become Grand Master … er … Grand Mistress."

"Absolutely not."

Lindey subtly shifted her weight. Astreya clenched his teeth rather than flinch.

"Irrevocably so. I'm beaching myself."

"You're what?"

"Going ashore and staying ashore. Making room for you as Grand Mistress. You are the ideal person to lead the deliberations of the clasp-wearing masters and navigators."

"Piffle, Astreya, and you know it."

"Take command of the fleet, Lindey. You're the only one who can."

"This is not reasonable. Why, Astreya?"

"I journey north tomorrow at dawn. By land."

"You're going to look for Ellie."

"I have to believe that Ellie's alive, Lindey. It was my error of judgement that let this happen. One way or the other, I must find her or find out what's happened."

Lindey took a step back, startled by her own sudden realization.

"It's not just Ellie, is it? It's what Enoch said about the gun that fired at *Spindrift*. You fear that someone's going to use guns against Matris."

"Carl..." Astreya began, but Lindey kept on speaking.

"You believe that the 'Governor' is Carl, the man you fought in the library back when we were helping Gar paint," said Lindey. Then her eyes widened as she understood the implications. "Astreya, you think Carl is the person behind it all, and you're going to try to stop him. You can't sail to the Castle, so instead you're going to be inexpressibly foolish: you're going to walk. Alone. And when you get there..."

Lindey paused, blinked, and shook her head.

"I plan to ride a horse," said Astreya.

"Don't be exasperating, Astreya," Lindey snapped. You are probably going to get yourself killed finishing the knife fight with Carl that neither of you won more than twenty years ago."

"One way or another," Astreya muttered.

"You don't know if you still have your knife fighting magic..."

"No magic. Things slow down for me sometimes. That's why people think I'm faster."

"You're not sure if you still can do it — whatever it is."

"I intend to employ sweet reason."

"Then you'll need me to come with you."

Astreya shook his head and smiled.

"No, my dearest, sweetest and most reasonable person, I'm going alone."

Lindey took a step towards the chair between them and pushed it back under the table.

"There. There will be no Grand Mistress Lindey. Since you're going ashore, so am I. That miscreant Carl, if he actually runs the Castle, clearly intends to take over every part of the land … which, by the way, is the only item on which you and I agree. Meanwhile, someone has to organize the defence of Matris, and that's going to be me. So, Astreya, before you slink off to endanger your life in a foolish, selfish gesture, kindly announce … or better, write down clearly for them to read … that Mairi will be Mistress of *Cygnus*, Seren of *Cygnet*, and Trogen keeps *Elusive*."

They stood looking at each other, neither able to take the step forward that would take them into each other's arms.

"Very well," said Astreya.

Pointedly ignoring the master's chair, he sat down, pulled pen and paper towards him, and began to write. He did not see Lindey blink back tears.

# Chapter 11: In which Ellie walks westward

The road ran almost straight for hundreds of Ellie's strides, then curved around low hills, and then rose steadily on hard-packed earth that gave rooting only to grasses, wildflowers, and scrubby bushes. Above her was a canopy of green held up by the brown trunks of trees so big and ancient that their branches intertwined above the road. From time to time, Ellie had to negotiate ankle-deep runnels across the path, the result of washouts from rain or snowmelt. Occasionally, she had to detour around shards of rock that had broken from cuttings where long-dead road-builders had cleaved their way into the side of a hill.

Lulled by the rhythm of walking, she found herself thinking that Drew, the boatbuilder at Matris, would be delighted by the oaks she was passing. Many were big enough to frame a small schooner, which the tall, straight pines that grew among them could plank from stem to stern. The thought turned into a longing to be at sea, and once more confident in the lore of the shipstones and her power to wield them. Suppressing the fear that she had lost her skill that challenged Astreya's legendary ability, Ellie concentrated on putting one foot in front of the other.

At times, she had to climb over the trunk of a fallen tree that blocked the road from one side to the other. These detours broke her stride, jolting her out of reverie into the irrational fear that the forest had no end. When she stopped at a stream to replenish her water bottle and eat some of the cheese and an apple from Maisie's satchel, she teared up at the thought that they would never meet again.

As the day wore on, Ellie travelled westward with the afternoon sun slanting down the road into her eyes. She was thinking that she would have to spend the night in the woods when the road topped a gentle rise, and the big, sheltering trees suddenly ended as if she had come out of a tunnel. Aspen and poplar clumps patched a barren hillside, overlooked by the last few great maples. She reasoned that years, perhaps decades before, there must have been a forest fire that had stopped at the ridge where the road left the forest.

Ellie left the road, pushed past clumps of poplar and aspen, and scrambled up a rocky knoll. Despite sore feet and weariness, her spirits rose as she felt a breeze that had not penetrated the brown and green forest through which she had walked all day. She climbed on sun-warmed bedrock past blackened stumps and burned skeletons of once-mighty trees. Juniper bushes clung to cracks and fissures, their bitter fragrance puffing into her nostrils. The clasp on her arm tingled, but when she peeled back her sleeve she saw only a weak, milky glow, hardly visible in daylight.

When Ellie reached the top, she stood below the great bowl of the sky as if she were back aboard a ship. She scanned the way ahead. The road curved downhill into a broad valley patched with shade from afternoon clouds that were thickening into thunderheads. In the distance, a shaft of sunlight gleamed off water. Nowhere could she see anything resembling a settlement, house or even a ruin.

Ellie started back down. She was soon among pale green, flickering leaves. Despite their soft rustling, she heard hoofbeats. As she dropped to her knees, she had a momentary impression of a big shapeless hat atop the hunched figure on the lead horse, and an empty saddle on the second. Ellie crawled cautiously forward until she could peer through the fireweed and goldenrod that bordered the road. Two horses clopped towards her. She smelled horse sweat and leather. A mottled shape leaped down from the lead horse into the grass. Ellie froze, her chin almost touching the earth.

"Prrrp?"

A handspan from Ellie's nose was a pair of wide eyes flecked with gold around their vertical pupils. She blinked at the parti-coloured cat face, black on one side, golden on the other.

"Curmudgeon?"

Ellie spoke in disbelief. At the same instant as a voice checked the horses.

"Woah, there. What are you up to, Curmudgeon?"

"Maisie!"

"Ellie!"

As Maisie slid from her horse, Ellie ran towards her. They hugged.

"I thought you were dead!"

"Not dead."

"I thought I'd lost you."

"Not lost."

"Prrrp," said Curmudgeon. She wound her way around their legs, then waved a scorched tail, sat at Maisie's feet, and serenely washed herself.

"Curmudgeon," said Ellie. "What happened to your beautiful tail?"

"Singed," said Maisie. "We barely made it into the cellar."

"I watched until the roof fell in. There was no way you could survive that fire."

"You're right. Very hot and almost no air. Until I opened the trapdoor, when cool air got sucked along the passage. Then it was like walking against a wind."

"There's a secret passage from your cottage to where the big house must have been!"

"There is. Or rather, there was."

"Did you make it?"

"I found it when I took over the cottage more than twenty years ago. Whoever owned the big house dug a tunnel to his stables. I've often wondered if he managed to escape when the crazies burned down his mansion when Before turned to After. Anyway, it's where I grow mushrooms, keep preserves, brew and store my beer and cider. It's also where I keep a cache of useful things just in case I ever have to leave in a hurry."

"Not the first time you have had to 'leave in a hurry,' then?

Ellie repeated Maisie's words that hinted at twenty grief-stricken years.

"Ah… No."

Guessing at how much was unsaid behind the brief reply, Ellie left a long pause before asking her next question.

"These horses?"

"Susan's been living in what's left of the big house, munching on the grass that grows among the ruined walls. The other belonged to the accursed torch-throwing cowards who burned down my cottage."

Ellie thought of the rider at whom Maisie had thrown her hatchet.

"Maisie, I'm sorry about Snowy and Gobble."

"You saw."

Ellie nodded.

"Then you know why I won't be going back to tell Isobel I'm not dead."

"Do you think she instigated the attack?"

"Instigated. Good word. If you mean that Isobel prompted, and hinted, and cajoled, and indirectly nudged them into it, all the while protesting that she had no part in my nefarious ways, yes I do. She will no doubt be dropping the occasional timely tear over my demise even now. I fervently hope she chokes."

"Maisie, did you just …"

"Curse the bitch? Yes, I did."

"Do… Do you think your curse will work?"

Maisie threw back her head and let out a single, barking laugh.

"Ha! My curses are no more effective than anyone else's. But things do have a habit of working out as if they were. It's because I reserve my ill-wishing for people who have chosen a way that's bound to lead them to their own disaster."

Maisie's horse pecked at the ground with a forefoot and dipped her head up and down as Curmudgeon sprang onto her back. Behind her, the soldier's horse looked up expectantly.

"We must be on our way," said Maisie. "There's rain coming."

As the sky darkened over them, Maisie adjusted the second horse's stirrups and beckoned Ellie to her.

"Por side, facing aft," muttered Ellie.

Maisie looked puzzled.

"It's a sailor's joke. I have been on a horse before."

"Well, don't fall off. The ground's a lot harder than the sea."

# Chapter 12: In which three commanders talk

"So the short of it is, Seren, you are mistress of *Cygnet*, Trogen continues as master of *Elusive*, and I command *Cygnus*."

Mairi placed the letter she had just read on the chart table in front of her. Standing on the other side of the chart table, Trogen and Seren still held their identical copies. The three of them avoided each other's eyes.

"So, the late Grand Master Astreya …" Trogen began.

"He's not dead," said Mairi.

"Our hitherto generally respected father and mother have abdicated. They're beached. They've swallowed the killick. Gone lubber. They've given up, leaving the three of us to carry on the enterprise they've been controlling for the past twenty years and more."

"During which time they have educated and trained us to continue what they began," said Mairi.

"Enabling us to make further changes as need requires," Seren added.

The twins stared up at their tall cousin. Seren held their gaze long enough for their eyes to waver and then sat opposite the master's chair.

"And just what do you mean by that, Seren?" Trogen demanded.

He stood, placed both fists on the table and leaned towards her. Seren did not flinch.

"Sit down, Trogen," said Mairi sharply from the master's chair.

Trogen glanced from one woman to the other, sat, and then deliberately skewed his chair so that he could look at both of them without moving his head. Mairi copied his move, sliding her chair back and to the side. Seren did not move. Even seated, she was taller than either of them.

For a long moment, all three were uncomfortably silent.

"Further changes, Seren?" Mairi asked.

"Yesterday, in the Forbidden Room, the enterprise ceased to be exclusively composed of Astreya's family."

"What do you mean?" Trogen asked. "I still have *Elusive*. Mairi has *Cygnus*, and you are the new master — mistress of *Cygnet*."

"None of us is a Grand Master," said Mairi.

"That will have to be decided when…" Trogen began.

"At a council meeting," Mairi interrupted firmly.

"Which will not be the same as it always has been," said Seren. "Astreya has irrevocably altered the numbers of family and non-family. There's the three of us who are, and the rest who are not."

"Cam and Damon are practically family…" Mairi began.

"Count them up," said Seren. "A year ago, there were six with clasps, all related by blood. Today, three of the six are ashore and there are five more who are not related to Astreya by blood or adoption.

"Father and Mother keep their stones, and so did … does … Ellie … and …" Trogen fumbled into an awkward silence.

Mairi nodded, her eyes meeting Seren's.

"The next time all those with clasps assemble, the dynamics are not going to be the same as they were when they gave me *Cygnet*."

"And that was before you put my father's clasp on Peter's arm, and Trogen accepted him as assistant navigator," said Seren. "Now he has a voice equal to Cam, Damon, Peter, Alan, and Marley."

"That's not going to be tested any time soon," said Trogen. "And fortunately, the three of us know what we're doing and can get on with it," he added.

"Aboard ships we've always hoped to command," said Seren. "It's so perfect for the three of us that we haven't even asked why Astreya and Lindey suddenly decided to relinquish command of the ships they love."

"I assumed you knew," Mairi asked. "I found out from Mother, and Trogen's been talking with Damon. "

"Knew what?" Seren asked.

"The Castle is expanding its influence and control," said Trogen. "Matris is next. Damon found out and told Astreya …"

"A visitor did," said Mairi. "His name's Enoch. He was Damon's … what? … friend? … henchman? … when they were both students at the Castle, back before Damon decided to join with Father and Mother."

"Enoch's a strange one," said Trogen. "Mairi, can you believe that he could spend twenty years involved in, or at least observing all that's been going on at the Castle only to suddenly grow a conscience about plans to use cannons to attack Matris, and then walk all the way south to tell Damon?"

"I get the impression that Enoch easily led," said Mairi cautiously. "When Damon left, perhaps that's why he joined up with the bully who Astreya outsmarted, twice."

"That still doesn't explain if someone sent Enoch, or why," said Seren.

"There was another one of Carl's followers named Sandy, who Lindey distrusted because …"

"Too many shots to the head earned Knock his nickname," said Trogen, ignoring both of them.

"Possibly," said Mairi, "But Mother believed what Enoch, or Knock if you prefer, said about someone, probably Carl, getting hold of a cannon. And that's why she's gone ashore to take charge of defending Matris."

"And Astreya?" Seren asked.

"Has headed north to fix everything," said Trogen scornfully. "With no plan, at least none he told Damon, who is the only one who knows anything about the Castle. Ex-Grand Master Astreya might as well have slapped Damon in the face. 'Ordered me not to follow him,' is what Damon told me. Father's dumped responsibility on the rest of us. Handed out clasps all around without telling anyone what to do.'"

"We carry on," said Mairi. "We know our next destinations, and our cargo is just about all aboard. Trogen, it's your turn for the Sunny

Isles, I have the coastal circuit in heavy goods both ways, and *Cygnet*…"

Seren interrupted Mairi.

"That was the plan before the changes in command. You were supposed to take *Cygnet* to Cottontown, moor in Black Bay, and pick up the contents of Fred's workshop without letting the townies see either the ship or two unusually tall and very easily recognized people, namely Marley and me. Now if I'm to make that happen, I need more crew. Right now, there's only Marley, Alan, and me."

"You've forgotten Fred," said Mairi.

"Nobody knows where Fred is," said Seren.

"I've got a keener aboard *Elusive* you can have," said Trogen. "I've been thinking about getting him one of the ring-stones. His name's Henry."

"I wonder whether Fred knows that there was an extra clasp on the table that presumably was for him," said Mairi.

"You think?" said Trogen. "If so, then it's a damn good thing Grand Commander Astreya isn't in charge of anything anymore. Give Fred a clasp? Ridiculous. The lubber cost us Ellie."

Seren and Mairi exchanged glances.

"Where has the bastard got to anyway? Trogen demanded.

# Chapter 13: In which Ellie and Maisie make camp

Ellie and Maisie made it to the river as the rain began to fall. The horses plodded away from the road down a faint track through a stand of mature birch, which soon gave way to a grassy slope that ran down to where the river widened. Ellie slid off her horse, which promptly waded hock deep into the river to drink. Fat raindrops speckled the surface of the little lake. Maisie's face was invisible under her shapeless hat as her horse stopped near a blackened ring of stones that marked where people had camped a long time ago. Curmudgeon appeared from under Maisie's cloak, surveyed the scene disapprovingly, leaped down and stalked off to shelter under a tree. Maisie relieved her horse of its packsacks, from which she produced a roll of canvass, a ball of twine, a box of fire-starters and a hatchet.

"Shelter and a fire," Maisie said from under her hat. "Take this," she added, handing Ellie a hatchet.

"I can rig an awning," said Ellie, examining the tool dubiously.

"I cleaned off the blood," said Maisie, her face still invisible.

They went to work in silence. Maisie unsaddled and rubbed down the horses, and then went in search of firewood. Ellie cut stakes and poles from a grove of birches while Maisie fetched armloads of deadwood and curls of birchbark. Ellie rigged the frame of lean-to close to the fire-pit, and while she was securing canvass, Maisie coaxed a fire to life. Beyond the shelter the horses cropped wet grass, their forelegs hobbled.

Some time later as the sun set behind sullen clouds, they sat in their shelter, eating rosemary-scented bannock from Maisie's frypan, drinking mugs of rose-hip tea while their cloaks dripped and steamed. For the first time since they had met hours earlier, they looked at each other.

"Long day," said Ellie laconically, in the phrase she had so often used when relieving someone at watch change.

"Today the Goddess was revealed to us in unexpected ways."

Ellie stared into her mug, striving for a neutral reply to words that struck her as both meaningless and exasperatingly smug. She spoke without thinking.

"Like that soldier who unexpectedly met with your hatchet?"

Her words had an edge she had not intended. However, after only a brief hesitation Maisie replied evenly.

"You saw that happen?"

"I saw you throwing, him falling, the horse bolting."

"The horse eventually ran up the path westward, where I caught up with him and then with you."

"Unpredictably convenient for us. Unpleasant for him."

Again, the small pause before Maisie answered.

"None can predict the ways of the Goddess. We can only accept that she led you to me, Isobel to betray me, the soldier to fall off his horse, and the horse to run where I could find him for you to ride."

"Maisie, he didn't fall off his horse by arrangement from anyone. One thing followed another quite predictably. A soldier all fired up to ravage your cottage was blood-lustingly stupid enough to kill your goat and goose, which made you angry enough to throw your hatchet at him. He was responsible for what he did. You were responsible for your revenge. You can't put it all down to fate or the Goddess, or whatever."

"I don't. I'm involved. I was furious. I may have killed him. He killed Dora and Gobbler. My animals. My friends. Part of me."

Ellie heard pain in Maisie's swift reply, but could not see her face. Ellie poked the fire with a stick and added a fresh log, taking her time. When she spoke, it was in an effort to tone down the conversation.

"I'm not sure that I understand how your religion … your Goddess … works."

"Neither do I. But you need to know that the Goddess isn't a religion. Religions are for men, and men put their god or gods outside of everything, looking down at the world from a distance. Either that, or they put him … always him … inside their own heads, forever judging, condemning, and making rules that benefit men. Always men. Never women, children, animals, the totality of what lives."

"Never women?"

"Mostly, anyway. Women are an afterthought for male gods imagined by men. It's because men don't think beyond themselves most of the time."

"Men… or at least the ones I know … my father, for instance … put a lot of stock in their families."

"Their families. The families they own, lead, decide for, dominate."

"Father wasn't … didn't … He shared, same as Matris men are supposed to."

"Possibly. But that's not so for most of them. It's because men are non-branching branches. Women are branching branches."

"Not all women branch… have babies… if that's what you mean."

Maisie nodded.

"But just about all women can, whether they choose to or not."

"Do… did… you… er… branch?"

"Yes. But you might say that I'm a broken branch. My babies are dead."

"I'm sorry."

"So am I."

Rain dripped off the awning. A damp stick hissed in the fire. At length, the silence between them was too much for Ellie.

"Your Goddess, then, what is she?"

"The Goddess is just a name we give to everything we're all part of … our whole world and all that's in it, all the way through."

"The spirit of life?"

Ellie's question was sincerely spoken, as was Maisie's reply.

"And everything else that's tangled up in life. Rocks, trees, water, whatever else you can name."

"Stars?"

"Why not?"

"It would seem sensible to me that they'd have to be … tangled up … in there somewhere. Navigators call stars by name, just as people name children, and animals, and the people on whom they rely. Family. Connections."

"You see? You understand what I'm saying because of what you do. For me, connectedness is mushrooms."

"Mushrooms? Like the ones in your cellar, that's also a secret passage? Which runs to the old house that isn't there anymore, where your horse lives?"

Maisie chuckled.

"Exactly. Mushrooms come out of the earth, they feed us, some of them can kill us. They're all connected, all intertwined with rocks, trees, plants, animals that feed them and off them, all maintaining the dance of life."

"The sea's like that. Tangled. So's you can't tell what's doing and what's being done to, because everything is doing both."

"Yes, but men's religions aren't like that. They're all about tidy causes having predictable effects as if everything happens going one way along straight lines."

"At sea, everything's complicated. Some people think it's just little fish being eaten by bigger fish until the best ones get caught by us so that we can sail on top of it all as if we are in charge, which anyone who's gone through a storm at sea surely knows we're not. We use man-made maps and charts as if you can go straight from one place to another. But you can't. It's all curves and currents and tides and wind and water and you'd better not think you can control them, or you're worse than off course, you're …"

"Lost?"

Maisie's single word silenced Ellie. For a moment she was back in the ancient woods where she had run to escape the bombardment. She stared past the glowing fire. The light of a bright star pierced through a gap in the clouds and shattered into shards through her unshed tears. Maisie's hand took hers, and the moment of remembered terror no longer had power over her. After a long silence, Maisie released Ellie's hand, stood, stretched, and felt their cloaks.

"Dry enough to sleep in," she said.

She applied insect repellent to her face and hands and passed the little jar to Ellie, who copied her. Then Maisie wrapped herself in her cloak, lay down and pillowed her head on her saddle.

"May the Goddess grant you a good night," Maisie murmured sleepily.

"And you, too," said Ellie, feeling her words inadequate.

She stood, pulled her cloak around herself and stepped out of the firelight into the night. The rain had stopped, and a wind from the west was clearing the sky. Ellie stared up at the stars, cautiously slid her arm out of her cloak and consulted the green stone in her clasp. She could not be sure whether it had brightened, or if it was only in contrast with the darkness. Even though she could not see the white spear of light that should have been pointing at the North star, Ellie was strangely untroubled. She returned to the lean-to, put another log on the fire and by its light settled herself to sleep as Maisie had done, pillowed on her saddle.

~^~

Sunlight dappled through birch and poplar leaves and then flickered on Ellie's eyelids. She woke to find Curmudgeon curled up against her. When she could lie still no longer, she shoved the big cat out of the nest she had made in the cloak, and stood up. Curmudgeon kneaded the cloak and curled up again. Ellie blew on the coals of last night's fire until flames crackled in the kindling she had saved. She took the kettle to the river for water, passing the two horses as they stood nose-to-tail, swishing flies off each other. When she returned, she saw that Maisie had rolled over, revealing curly red hair and one strong brown leg. Curmudgeon had disappeared, but having seen how the cat had survived the previous day's fire and travel, Ellie was sure he was not far away and would show up before they were ready to leave.

She had no such confidence about her present or future. She hesitantly slid back her sleeve to look at her clasp. She shut her eyes, trying to reach the calm confidence with which she controlled a shipstone. For a moment, she felt the stone respond to her — as if she were plucking a single note on a guitar. It like the memory of a song, hanging in her mind almost long enough for her to guess at the melody — and then it was gone. In that fleeting instant, she had been preternaturally aware, searching, listening, groping for the other stones she knew were live and in use aboard the ships of the fleet.

She opened her eyes and stared for one, two, three heartbeats, watching the cloudy green stone fade in the morning light. Had the stone on her arm reacted to her will? Had the spear of light at its centre pulsed when her eyes were shut? Or was wish the father of thought?

The more she stared, the duller the stone became. It offered no guidance, still less the possibility of communicating with her family. What had they done when *Seafoam* returned without her? Had Mairi searched for her in *Cygnet*? Did her mother and sisters think she was dead? The only way to find out was to return home to Matris as soon as possible. Meanwhile, she staved off unanswerable questions with the practical business of combing out her long black hair and then making tea and warming bannock left over from their supper. A little wind blew smoke into Ellie's eyes.

"Tea. Wonderful."

Ellie blinked her eyes clear. Maisie stood in sunlight, plaiting her red hair into gleaming braids.

"We should reach the north-south road by noon."

"Will you come with me to Matris?"

Maisie shrugged, eloquently implying that given her situation, she had nowhere else to go.

# Chapter 14: In which Fred drinks in a pub

After a long day of walking along the cliff-top path, Fred headed downhill towards Charton with the sun setting behind him. His path joined the main road into town, allowing him to lengthen his stride downhill. He walked past a sprinkle of yellow lights coming from windows of outlying cottages, then more brightly from houses in the little town. Ahead, the lanterns of fishermen working late twinkled on the water, leading him to his destination in a dockside pub. Soon unlit warehouses and sheds near the wharf were on either side of the road. He plunged into the gloom, towards a smoky lantern flickering below a once-white board. He looked up to read "The Black Sheep" carved in clumsy letters, and walked into something big, black, and made of metal.

Ignoring a bruised shin, Fred explored the obstacle with his hands and what little light there was. Wheels. A barrel — no, a steel drum, warm to the touch. Two steps up to a wheelhouse — no, this was nothing like a ship. Levers, dials, tubes glinted in the red glow of a firebox as Fred peered through an open window. Cooling metal made tick, tick, tick sounds. Something hissed and spit.

"Steam engine!" said Fred out loud.

"Who's that?"

The voice sounded like a watchman. Fred froze, climbed silently down the metal steps, and walked towards the sign above the inn door. When there was no further challenge, Fred gripped the wrought-iron handle of a nail-studded door.

"Yer goin' in fer a beer, or y'goin' t' stand in't way all night long?" said a gravelly voice at his shoulder.

Fred hastily depressed the thumb-catch, shoved the door open, and nearly fell down two worn steps into the taproom. Lanterns hung from smoke-blackened rafters, candles stuck in old bottles burned on the tables, and a fire flickered in a huge fireplace. Two burly men in tarpaulin jackets shouldered him out of their way as a raised hand summoned them to the other side of the room. They waded through the intervening tables, receiving and giving hand-slaps and friendly punches. Fred sidled towards a dim corner near the fireplace where he found an empty table from which most of the chairs had been robbed by a nearby group of men. Seated with his back to the corner, Fred assessed the room.

His first thought was that he was probably the lightest, thinnest, weakest and most vulnerable man in the room, and he could see no women. The awareness was not new to him, so he shrugged it off by telling himself that he was certainly the most intelligent. Unease calmed by reason, he analyzed what he saw and heard.

He counted twenty tousled heads at tables closest to the bar, noted that all wore their blonde-to-mouse-brown hair at shoulder-length. He easily identified them as fishermen by their home-spun, sea-going sweaters. Most were bearded, a few of the older ones had trimmed or shaved to enhance curled moustaches. A second look and a few moments of listening made it clear that the men could be subdivided into the crews of five or six boats. Fred could not make out details, but more than a year of living with the sailors from Matris told him that they were reliving an incident from the day's fishing. Fred guessed from the exaggerated scorn, indignant defences, good-humoured teasing, and guffaws of laughter that there had been a near-collision caused by someone's inattention. Men drank, laughed, wiped their beards, then leaned back in their chairs to chuckle. One slapped the table, causing beer-mugs to be snatched up and either swigged down or raised clear of the commotion, which had no sooner begun to calm when someone overturned a jug into his mates' laps, and the whole cycle of blaming, explaining, defending and bellowing with laughter began afresh.

The five men closest to Fred ignored the fishermen. Their heads were bent towards each other, their forearms rested on the table, their hands were wrapped around glasses, and their conversation almost inaudible. Fred itemized their differences from the fishermen: the strangers all wore close-fitting, belted jackets of dark grey twill with pouch-pockets on the chest; they were clean-shaven, their nondescript hair cut severely short at the back and sides; they held glasses belonging to the pub, whereas the fishermen all used individual mugs.

"An' what'll ye be drinkin'?"

Fred looked up at a red-haired pot-boy beneath whose pug-nose were the scruffy beginnings of a moustache. Interrupting his survey of the pub's customers, Fred ordered beer and the day's stew, with bread.

By the time the pot-boy brought Fred's meal, the furor had subsided to a mumble, but the men at the neighbouring table continued to speak to each other at the same level as when the fishermen were shouting. Idly at first, and then with increasing interest, Fred listened as he ate.

"…dunno what we'll do with it."

"Can't leave it here, that's for certain."

"Whatcher goin' t' do? Push it all the way back to the Castle?"

"Maybe if we all…"

"Fat chance."

"Fact is, Charlie, you broke the handle on the steamer, and now we're stuck here surrounded by stinking fishermen."

Fred stopped even pretending to eat. Leaning one elbow on the table, he cupped a hand around his ear.

"I don' wanner walk all the way back on foot t'tell the Gov'ner we broke Sandy's steamer an' didn't find out nothin' about where the black-haired sailors come from."

"Nor even get close enough to do some damage."

"Like the gunners didn't do to the sailor-boys at Half Moon Bay?"

"Scared them off, didn't they?"

"Big whoop. Now the blackheads are all hiding."

"S' why we're here, ain't it?"

"Merely a reconnaissance," said a more precise voice. We're here to assess the terrain, report when we know …"

"Not if we can't get the steamer fixed."

"Maybe one of the fishermen could…"

"All them fishermen know is how to pull on a rope."

Fred stood, drew himself up to his full height, took two paces until he could have put a hand on the nearest man's shoulder, and announced himself.

"Gentlemen…."

Heads turned, curiosity replacing gloom.

"And who might you be?"

Fred noticed a shiny badge pinned to the pocket of the man's jacket.

"One who understands machines," he announced confidently.

"Belike a whole lot o' blather an' theorizing, like them Learneds," growled a big man whose red, curly chest-hair protruded from his unbuttoned jacket. Fred ignored him and addressed the man with the badge.

"I have considerable practical experience in making and refurbishing machinery. Particularly if it's from Before. My workshop is in Cottontown."

"Then what brought you here?"

"I took passage on one of the schooners from Matris," said Fred.

"They brung you all the way?"

"Close enough for me to walk to Charton today," said Fred evenly. "After which, my legs are tired. If it's all the same to you gentlemen, we might continue our discussion with me seated. That way, we wouldn't be attracting the attention of the fishermen."

"Get his chair, Charlie."

The big hairy man got clumsily to his feet, picked up Fred's chair and thumped it down. Fred nodded thanks, sat and looked steadily at the man with the badge, who looked back dubiously.

"So you think you can fix our land-crawling steam engine."

"Obviously, it depends how badly you've damaged it."

"Charlie here pulled on the stopping lever so hard it came off in his hand."

"We was rollin t'wards the sea, and …" the big man began.

"Charlie's very strong," said the man with the badge. "Sanderson taught him how to run the steamer, but he's at his best when it comes to a fight."

Fred contrived a smile.

"Tell me, Charlie, when you pulled on the lever, did you hear the pawls ratchet?"

"Wha'?"

"Did you hear a clack…clack…clack sound?"

"Yeah. That's right. It did."

"Then even if there are inadequate facilities here in Charton for me to fully repair your vehicle, I should at least be able to bypass the problem.

Fred smiled at blank faces.

"You're sure of yourself," said the man with the badge. "Why'd you want to be so helpful?" he added suspiciously.

"Simple," replied Fred. "I don't enjoy walking. When I've fixed your steam engine, I want you to give me a ride to the Castle."

The man with the badge blinked, frowned, and inclined his head to one side.

"Tomorrow, if you can fix it, we'll see."

"Your name is?" Fred asked.

"Militia Captain Samuel Orme."

He half rose from his chair, offering his hand. Fred saw that Orme was wearing a wide leather belt with a single shoulder strap over his grey uniform jacket, the better to support the weight of a handgun in a holster.

"Fredericks of Cottontown. Let me stand around."

When Fred climbed the stair to a room for the night, he knew more about the men, where they had come from, and their mission than they were aware that they had told him.

# Chapter 15: In which Seren heads east

A northwest wind rippled the water of the sea lake where *Cygnet* lay downwind from her buoy, preparing to make sail. The day had dawned clear, but already a high haze was building in the west. The shipyard's launch had delivered the last three junior members of the crew only an hour earlier, the water casks had been topped up the night before, the stoppers had been cast off the sails.

"All hands astern!"

Marley's deep voice brought Neil, Alan, and Henry from the halyards to the cockpit where they stood looking up at their officers. Neil's dark hair hung almost into his eyes. Carrot-red haired Alan stood beside him, his broad body contrasting with Neil's wiry frame. Henry, though the tallest of the three, looked youngest. His clothes barely reached his wrists and ankles, and he quivered with barely controlled energy. The three looked up to Seren and Marley, not merely because the two of them were unusually tall. Neil and Alan had more than two years aboard *Cygnet* with Seren and Marley when Mairi was in command, and they respected each other's abilities. Only Henry was new to *Cygnet*, but he had as many years' seagoing experience aboard *Elusive* as the other two. He stared enviously at Alan's left arm where the jewel in his new clasp glowed green in the morning sunlight, and then glanced at the ring on Neil's left hand.

Seren saw Henry's sidelong look, and briefly wondered whether he knew that the ring was Neil's consolation prize for the clasp he had expected nearly two years earlier. Feeling their eyes on her, she took a breath and let it all out before she began.

"*Cygnets*, we'll be the first through the Two Feet today, with *Cygnus* and *Elusive* not far behind us. Before we slip from the buoy, I want you all to know that we're heading east. When Ellie and Fred were aboard, we could have sailed for Cottontown. That is no longer a workable plan. Instead, our first task is to look for my sister … your shipmate. We believe she is somewhere ashore between Charton and Half Moon Bay. We couldn't find her a couple of days ago because she may have been hurt or weakened somehow. Now she's had time to recover, her clasp should be brighter and easier to locate not only with the clasps that Alan, Marley and I wear, but even with rings."

She reached into the pocket of her sailing jacket.

"In the past, rings were reserved for only a privileged few of the crew. Now that we have more stones of all sizes, they are the first step towards learning to wield a clasp. Henry, this is your ring."

Henry's eyebrows rose in surprise. A heartbeat later he stepped forward eagerly, and Seren slipped it onto his finger

"Right, *Cygnets*, it's time…" she began.

Alan interrupted her.

"As is customary, master… er.. mistress Seren," he paused to look around, then swung his arm up to bring his fist to his throat, "At your command!"

Henry and Neil copied his gesture, and their voices joined in, Marley's deeper and stronger. Seren wrinkled her nose in an unsuccessful attempt to keep herself from blushing.

"Thank you," she said, and then much louder, "Neil, you have the jib and the buoy; Alan, mizzen and foresail; Henry, you and Marley on the main, I have the wheel. Let's get to it."

Henry hesitated for only an instant, then joined Marley at the main halyards. Used to being part of a much larger and more formally-organized crew aboard the great ship *Elusive*, he was very conscious of working alongside a mate — and one who was handfasted to the commander.

"Hoist away! Let slip from the buoy! Starboard tack!"

Seren spun the wheel, Neil checked the jib sheet. Slowly at first, then as her sails caught wind, with a chuckle of water under her forefoot, *Cygnet* headed towards the Two Feet.

~^~

Later that morning, *Cygnet* was well past the entrance to the big bay that had the little town of Charton at its head. The morning's haze had turned to a light grey overcast through which the sun was a white disc. The schooner coasted along the south-facing cliffs that ran the length of the land all the way to eastward-facing Half Moon Bay. Easing along with a brisk westerly wind on the port quarter, *Cygnet's* crew had little to do. Marley was at the wheel, Seren had the mainsheet, the boys were forward.

When the stones on their arms tingled, everyone startled.

"Marley, did you feel that?"

Seren's question was sharp with surprise.

"Someone. Ellie?" said Marley.

"Alan?"

"Real faint," said Alan. "An' now it's gone."

Moments later Seren cringed as if someone had shouted in her ears.

### ELLIE NORTH NORTH EAST

"Did you both get that?" Seren asked. "That was Trogen."

Marley and Alan both nodded. All three looked astern to where *Elusive's* staysails were a white silhouette on the horizon, close-hauled on the starboard tack, heading south. As they watched, the sails seemingly disappeared, then turned into a white vertical line as the schooner headed towards them. Seren waved her hand for silence, concentrated, but before she could send a message, Trogen's aggressively powerful signal made them all wince again.

### WILL LOOK IN BAY

"If the folks with the gun see *Elusive...*" Marley began.

"They only clipped a longboat. They won't miss a great ship," Seren agreed.

She frowned as she focused her mind on *Cygnet's* shipstone.

### WE ARE HEADING INTO COVE

"Alan, take lookout and jib. Neil, stand by the mizzen, I have the main. Head her in, Marley."

### BELAY THAT SEREN I HAVE THIS

Seren glared at *Elusive,* her lips compressed. The fingers of Marley's right hand rose, reached towards Seren, paused, returned and gripped the wheel with a ferocity completely out of character with his usual delicate helmsmanship. *Cygnet* maintained her course.

## SEREN DO AS I SAY

Seren flushed, shook her head and stamped. A fresh signal joined the exchange

## BACK OFF TROGEN CYGNET BEST SHIP FOR COVE LANDING

Mairi's sending was quieter than Trogen's but no less clear. Seren reconsidered the irate retort she was about to hurl back at Trogen.

## CYGNET LAND IN COVE ELUSIVE WILL DISPATCH GUN

Now with no need to reply, and even less desire to argue, Seren took a long, calming breath and concentrated on seamanship. When she spoke it was with assurance.

"Marley, we'll put her alongside the cliff on the starboard side of that inlet. There's more than enough water under her keel. The current will help check our way. Here we go."

*Cygnet* was approaching a narrow slit in the cliffs. Ahead by two ships' length were flashes of white from where the little river splashed over rocks on its way to the steep-sided cove.

"Alan, back the jib. Good. Enough. Now prepare to take the bow line ashore. Neil strike mizzen, we'll furl later. Fenders starboard side. I have the stern line."

Seren was at the main halyards before Marley realized she was gone from his side. The wooden rings holding the sail to the mast rattled as she let go the mainsail and jumped ashore with the stern line. Alan leaped from the bow, landing beside a stunted pine that clung to a ledge in the cliff. He had the bow line around a tree trunk at the same moment as Seren secured the stern. They jumped back aboard as Marley spun the wheel to bring the stern to starboard. The collective effort was perfectly timed. The little schooner came to rest, held bow and stern to a narrow ledge below a smooth fall from the top of the cliff into the brackish water below.

"Nice spot to jump in for a swim," said Marley. "If you don't mind cold," he added softly.

"Not jump," said Seren. "Dive off the top."

"You never," said Neil, and then pressed his lips together.

Seren gave him a level, blue-eyed look.

"I had to. Ellie climbed, dived, and dared me."

Neil's eyes widened, as did Marley's. All three deliberately looked away anywhere but at Seren.

Putting aside the memory, she spoke with conviction.

"Right, I'm going ashore. We won't be able to communicate effectively through all this rock and forest, but neither will Trogen and Mairi. Be sure to slack off the lines to shore when the ebb starts."

Marley reached into a locker below the binnacle pulled out a canvass kitbag with a shoulder strap and handed it to Seren.

"Food, water, fire-starters," he said.

She took the kitbag with one hand, the other went around his neck, fingers among his dreadlocks, pulling him close. Henry, Neil and Alan stared as she kissed him, then glanced at each other to make sure that neither of them giggled. Seren slung the pack over her shoulder, poised, and leaped ashore.

# Chapter 16: In which Ellie reaches a crossroads

When Ellie and Maisie started, the morning sun was at their backs. Tiny shards of coloured light glinted in the dewy grasses on either side of the road. Their horses' hooves thudded on a wooden bridge over the stream that ran into the little lake where they had camped, then clopped up a little rise. Ahead, mist rose from the distant hills into a clear blue sky.

They rode side by side at a comfortable pace, Maisie in her shapeless hat, Ellie with her hair tucked up under the blue wool cap Maisie had given her. The horses followed two overgrown ruts made by carts that had not passed this way for months. It was not long until they were warm enough to tug their cloaks off their shoulders.

"Prrrp!"

Curmudgeon complained as Maisie's cloak rubbed his fur the wrong way. She balanced easily on the horse's rump, then sprang. Ellie glimpsed the cat in mid-air and tightened her grip on the reins in time to control her horse as the cat arrived behind the saddle.

"She's taken a shine to you," said Maisie.

Curmudgeon scaled Ellie's shoulder and leaped onto the horse's mane. As Ellie patted the horse's neck and made soothing noises, Curmudgeon half stood on her hind legs, lightly placed her front paws on Ellie's chest, and inspected where her clasp glowed faintly under her shirt. The cat sniffed, then coiled herself down in Ellie's lap.

"Curmudgeon thinks that you and your talisman are safe enough, so that should content me as well."

"My talisman?"

"The stone on your arm that you so carefully avoid saying a single word about."

"My clasp. Badge of rank."

"More than that, I'm sure. I guess it's a magic sign that gives you powers, and perhaps protection from evil."

Like all those who wore a navigation stone, Ellie had disciplined herself never to talk about what it could do. She knew that Maisie had seen her staring fixedly at the stone on her arm during the first few hours after she had regained consciousness, and she appreciated that there had been no unwanted questioning at the time. After what had happened since, she decided that Maisie deserved an answer.

"No magic. Nothing supernatural. It's a stone ... a crystal ... that resonates. Wielders, that is, navigators who can control their stones ... well, really, it's not control, it's a whole lot more like nudging ... can get their stones to find north. Working with a shipstone, which is the same only bigger, they can plot and hold a course, and also communicate with each other," Ellie paused. "And now I've told you more than I should have."

"About how the stones could be a weapon, perhaps?"

Ellie's eyes widened. An instant later she clamped her teeth angrily as she realized that her surprise had confirmed Maisie's suspicion. All her training in the secrecy surrounding the lore of the stones made her furious at herself for even hinting at a piece of family history that everyone knew, but nobody ever discussed.

More than twenty years earlier, Ellie's father, Dabih, had stood with Astreya and Lindey aboard *Elusive*. Mufrid, her commander, was a murderer and torturer who kept Dabih alive only because he was unable to navigate without him. Mufrid had been intent on eliminating both Astreya and Lindey to take over their stones. When Mufrid fell dead on the deck with a stolen shipstone in his hand there had been enough witnesses that there could be no stopping the story from spreading throughout the fleet. However, neither Astreya nor Lindey nor Dabih would speak of what had happened. Consequentially, Mairi, Trogen, Seren, and Ellie all knew there was much that they had not been told about the stones that they wore.

Maisie looked at Ellie steadily, holding her eyes. They swayed gently in their saddles, their horses' hooves thudding below them.

"Anyway, someone wearing one can know where to go," said Maisie. "That's what you mean by 'navigate,' isn't it?"

Ellie nodded, her lips pressed together. She let out the breath of air she had not realized she was holding. Perhaps Maisie had not noticed her reaction to the suggestion that the stones could be a weapon; or if she had, thankfully she has not asked for more information.

Curmudgeon stood on the horse's neck, stretched, and looked fixedly at Ellie, who frowned away the impression that the cat knew what she had been thinking. Curmudgeon curled up in Ellie's lap, and she felt the big cat purring. The sensation was curiously calming. They rode on in silence for a while, until suddenly Ellie swayed in her saddle as if physically struck.

"Something happened just now, didn't it?"

Ellie blinked at Maisie. Her fingers closed around the clasp on her arm, wanting to look at it, but arrested by the prohibition against using a stone in front of someone who was not trained in the lore. Had her stone pulsed again, as it had done earlier that morning? Was its brightness dimming to fuzzy green under her blouse?

"Um… yes."

"Tell me, Ellie, is it the stone that does the work? Or is it you?"

"It's… it's … both. The stone's just a green pebble that glows when it's close to others like it. A wielder … umm … focuses the glow, turning it from a pale green fuzz to bright green with a spear of white light at its centre."

Ellie shook her head. She should not be explaining the stones to Maisie as if she were a new-made cadet.

"Green like your eyes."

"Sort of the same colour, I'm told. Astreya's eyes are green. But Lindey's eyes are blue, and so are Seren's, and they're both strong wielders."

"It's a skill, then."

"Wielding is a bit like making music in that it can be taught and learned, but the talent is a gift. A gift that I …. that I don't seem to have any more."

Ellie's voice was tight in her throat. Curmudgeon sensed her tension and kneaded her thigh, her claws pricking through the material of the wide-legged breeches Maisie had given her. As the horses topped another low ridge and started down into a wide, shallow valley, Ellie's hand stroked the cat's soft fur, and she felt calmer.

"It's still there on your arm," said Maisie. "You didn't lose it."

"Prrrp," said Curmudgeon.

The cat raised its chin until its eyes met hers. Sunlight caught the side of the Curmudgeon's bronze eyes, momentarily turning them grass green.

As Ellie stared, her shoulder shaded Curmudgeon from the sun, and the cat's eyes went back to their usual colour and the pupil at their centre expanded.

Her calm shaken, Ellie blurted out the worst of her fears.

"My stone's gone blind. It happened in the forest. The spear of light at its centre gone … disappeared … lost."

Her last word gagged in her throat. They rode on in silence save for the sounds of the horses' steady progress. As Ellie's moment of distress faded, she heard Maisie starting to talk quietly.

"Centuries ago, in a land that may well still be there if someone is crazy enough to look for it, a man named Gregoire de la Tour, the bastard son of a noble family, followed his destiny westward to what you call the Sunny Isles to make his fortune in sugar, tobacco and rum, all of it grown and tended by Black people who he had brought there as slaves."

Maisie tipped her head back so that she could see under its wide brim. Seeing that Ellie's green eyes showed interest, she continued.

"He was White and they were Black, so it did not cross his mind that they were people until the Goddess put my great, great — many greats — grandmother in his path. She was young, she was beautiful, and he fell for her with one of those romantic passions that you read about in books. Her name was Marie-Claire."

"But everyone called her Maisie," said Ellie.

Maisie chuckled delightedly.

"Exactly. Well, the course of true love never did run smooth, so you'll not be surprised if I tell you that the seas rose, the island diminished, the trade failed, the sickness came. The Goddess, no doubt working through Marie-Claire, changed the heart and mind of Gregoire so that he no longer thought that the people of the island were his property. Marie-Claire's Black people were unexpectedly forgiving, so there was a boatload of them all who journeyed with Gregoire and Marie-Claire north to the other side of the almost-an-island where we are presently riding."

"Where they lived happily ever after," said Ellie.

Maisie shook her head.

"Where Gregoire set about proving his worth by saving the knowledge that was being squandered during the insane years between Before and After. He collected even more books than he had brought with him, built a library, founded a school, and ensured continuity of learning."

Ellie raised her eyebrows.

"Are you saying that it was your ancestor who founded the Castle?"

"Is that any more strange than your forefather who sailed for a hundred years?"

Ellie shook her head, then nodded, encouraging Maisie to continue. As they talked, their horses followed the road that ran along a curving stretch beside a sandy hill crested with pines.

"He called it the Tower. It was the people in the town beyond the wall who called it the Castle. They turned against Gregoire, Marie-Claire and the Black people who had come with them from the Sunny Isles, saying that none of them could have written the books that they had brought with them, because all but Gregoire were Black, and everyone thought they knew that Black people were incapable of anything beyond working with their hands. When this hostility was more than they could bear, Gregoire and Marie-Claire again led their people, this time westward by land to a fertile valley where they founded a community a day's travel from the Tower."

"Where?" Ellie asked. "I've seen maps ..."

"Neither that Black community nor any members of the family founded by Gregoire and Marie-Claire remain. Only me. A few jumbled stones are all that's left." Maisie's voice hardened. "The peace-loving learned folk who made the Tower into the Castle and fostered the town that grew up around it stirred up mobs of hooligans to harass the Black community and this went on for years, decades, generations. Some Black people died, some moved away, not a few were murdered, as was my husband and our two children."

Ellie's eyes widened.

"How did you....?"

"I ran. My skin is not much darker than many Whites'. I dyed my hair. I survived."

As they climbed past tall, bushy poplars, their shivering leaves yellowing with approaching autumn, Maisie looked at her and smiled.

"And then a few days ago, the wheel turned once more. Stupid White men burned my house and killed my animals. But the Goddess brought a green-eyed, black-haired girl named Ellie for me to rescue. Clearly, the Goddess is not done with me yet."

Their horses picked their way down across a dried-up stream bed and then scrambled up the gravel on the other side into the flickering leaves of young poplars. Ellie's horse was first through the rustling trees onto a broad, smooth, grassy highway. She was about to turn south towards Charton and Matris when a rumbling, clanking sound made her rein in her horse. Maisie's voice came to her indistinctly through the poplars.

"What in the unknowable name of the Goddess is that noise?"

Alone and vulnerable on the road, Ellie's horse swiveled its ears and pecked nervously at the ground with its forefoot. Around the bend came a huge, round, blunt, black shape poised between two big iron wheels. Smoke coiled up from a stack on top. The noise redoubled, the earth shook.

Curmudgeon stood on Ellie's horse's neck, her back arched, her tail high. Ellie's horse caught the cat's panic and reared. Ellie stayed in the saddle only by clutching at its mane. As the machine rattled, clanked, hissed and grumbled towards them, the cat leaped off the horse and fled back into the poplars. Maisie's horse, still in the dried stream behind Ellie, let out a high, frightened neigh. Ellie's horse reared. She slid out of the saddle, reins in hand, trying to bring the animal under control. Behind her, down the bank she had climbed, Ellie caught sight of Maisie dismounting to run after Curmudgeon. Her horse followed her and they disappeared, the little trees and bushes fluttering behind them.

Ellie's horse danced and snorted as the metal monster continued towards them. The reins went tight in her hands, almost tugging her off her feet. Her hat slid onto her back, where it hung tangled in her hair.

Then the machine was upon them, its black body looming, its tracks clanking, steam jetting from a thumping, hissing piston at eye-level. Behind the barrel-shaped body, a man's soot-smudged face stared down from a wheelhouse. A heartbeat later the whole contraption lurched to a stop. The sound diminished to the hiss of steam and the swish-and-thump of a piston idling back and forth. The wild-eyed horse shied, but allowed her to coax it out of the machine's way. She led the skittish animal past the smoking, hissing monster's shoulder-high back wheels, trying to stay clear of its hot metal. A smell of smoke, oil, and hot metal caught in her throat. As she passed below the cab, the man at the window shouted.

"Black hair! Long black hair! It's one o' them!"

Thinking to escape behind the ugly contraption, Ellie put her shoulder into the horse's side, urging it towards the far side of the road. For two or three paces, she thought she might succeed, but the horse baulked at the thick metal drawbar that blocked their way. She looked left and saw a heavy wagon that the machine was towing. Four male faces looked down at her over its curved metal front.

"Grab her. Get the horse, too."

Three uniformed men swung over the wagon's high sides, penning Ellie between machine and wagon, with the chest-high drawbar blocking escape. She grabbed for the saddle horn, tried to throw a leg up and over, thinking to mount and ride through the men, but her heel caught the strap that held her belongings. When she kicked free, she fell on her back with her pack and bedroll thumping down beside her. She struggled to her feet, desperate to try again, but the reins slid from her grasp, and all she saw was its big haunches as bolted through the men and on down the road. Before Ellie could duck under the draw-bar and run for cover, rough hands caught her arms and foul breath blew past her ear.

"Gotcher, yer little devil."

"Grab her stuff an' throw it up here. Could be in'erestin'."

"Wha' bout a little fun? Pass her round, like?"

"Don't harm her, she'll be wanted at the Castle for questioning," said an authoritative voice.

"Dont'cha want a turn?"

"And risk the Rot?" asked a fresh voice.

"Wha'?"

"They all have it, you know. Goes with the black hair. Still, if you want to see your parts turn green and fall off, it's up to you."

Ellie recognized the dissenting voice. She looked up and saw Fred looking out of the wagon at her.

# Chapter 17: In which Seren searches for Ellie

Marley still had a lot to learn about navigation, but it had taken him only minutes of his first day as an apprentice wielder to discover that he could use the stone on his arm to locate Seren. Armed with this certainty, he told Henry, Neil and Alan to mind the schooner, put a satchel over his shoulder and set off into the tangle of wind-stunted trees at the edge of the forest. He pushed aside spruce, hemlock and balsam boughs, their needles releasing scents that were still strange to him, even after many months of living further north than he had ever been before.

After he had forced his way through the first dozen strides of the forest's ragged edge, the pines stood further apart, their trunks prickly with dead twigs, their first green branches high above his head. Knowing how easy it is to lose one's bearings, he checked the stone on his arm regularly as he followed the sliver of bright light at its centre. His sailing boots were silent on the springy brown carpet of fallen needles. Occasionally, he heard a squirrel chatter or a blue-jay call. Sunlight lanced through the tops of the trees only to be lost before it could filter down to where he walked in cool shade. Marley found himself humming a lilting, circular phrase he had heard Seren sing. It was slow waltz time in a minor key, and was markedly different from the songs of his childhood in the Sunny Isles, where steel drums wove more complicated rhythms. The tune had come unbidden to his mind and was a measure of his adaptation to life at Matris.

He paused, thinking he heard the distant sound of waves from the scrubby edge of the forest at Half Moon Bay. The light brightened in the heart of the jewel on his arm. He frowned, wondering why he had not caught up with Seren. And at the same moment her hair shone like a beacon ahead of him. She was on one knee, looking under a tangled bush. A blue jay screamed its warning, she looked for the bird, and while her head was turned, he was beside her. She stood up quickly, mouth open, staring into his eyes. Then his arms were around her and her startled heartbeat was quick against his chest.

"Marley, look. That's a hood … torn off her sailing jacket."

They both bent to look into the burrow Ellie had shaped with her body during her nights in the forest. Seren plucked the torn sharkskin from a broken branch that roofed the hollow.

"Where do you think she went from here?" Marley asked.

Seren shrugged. They both stood up and consulted their clasps.

"South? The way we came?"

They looked around them at a wall of tree trunks in all directions.

"Marley, how did you sneak up on me?" Seren asked.

"Tracked your stone."

"I didn't see or hear you."

"Soft forest floor. Black sailing clothes. Black man."

"I told you to stay with the ship, you wicked man," she said and kissed him. "You didn't follow your skipper's order. My order."

"I mutinied."

"You should be with the ship."

Instead of answering, Marley pointed.

"If I was still there, I wouldn't have seen that."

A few strides away, hanging on a low broken branch was a thin hank of long, black hair, gently waving in an almost imperceptible breeze. In a heartbeat, Seren was running her fingers through the strands.

"It's Ellie's hair, isn't it?" said Marley.

Seren nodded.

"But it's north of here. In the wrong direction."

"The first thing you taught me about wielding was 'Think north'. I did, but then I thought my stone had pointed me south. Could that happen to Ellie?"

"It's possible, I suppose. It's just so unlikely, given that she's the best and strongest wielder of all of us … except for Astreya, that is."

"Let's go see."

They followed the direction Ellie had taken from her burrow to where she had tangled her hair. Soon the trees thinned and they broke out of the forest into the orchard. Before them was the path Ellie had taken. Seren wrinkled up her nose, catching the acrid smell of smoldering wood. She stopped and stared at a black shape on the ground ahead of her.

"Ellie!" Seren's voice was almost a sob.

"Only her sailing jacket," Marley said. "And breeks. Still pinned to a broken clothesline. No boots."

He picked up Ellie's torn clothes and shoved them into his shoulder bag.

His dispassionate observations steadied Seren, and she turned towards the burned-out cottage. As they drew nearer to the smoke-blackened stone walls, she almost stepped on the headless bodies of Maisie's goose and goat. Flies buzzed above the blood-soaked earth and crawled over fire-crisped feathers and fur.

"Riders," said Marley, looking at the where the horses' hooves had beaten down Maisie's garden as they circled the cottage. "Stay here."

Seren stepped back from the sad bodies and stood as if rooted to the ground, her arms wrapped around her middle. She watched Marley walk briskly to the door and give it a sturdy shove. It swung inwards from one hinge, allowing him to enter and pass out of her line of sight. From inside the stone shell of the cottage came cracking and creaking sounds that she interpreted as Marley moving roof beams or furniture out of his way.

Seren was startled by the sound of a woman's voice.

"Are you here to rob the dead? Because there's nobody there. Somehow, she escaped. Along with whoever she was hiding. I knew all along she had someone with her. She couldn't witch me into not noticing the black clothes on the line, the black hair on the couch, the extra plate, cup, knife and spoon."

"Who are you?" Seren asked.

"I could ask you the same thing, and with more reason. You're the stranger here. Where are you from?"

Seren looked down at the agitated woman who had appeared around the far side of the cottage. She wore a grey homespun dress over a white blouse with smudges of ash-grey on the cuff of her left arm, from which hung a wide basket. A scarf over her auburn hair had slipped back onto her neck, giving her narrow face the look of a small, furtive animal.

Seren waved in the general direction of Charton and Matris.

"Oh, a southerner. That's all right, then. You're obviously not one of them … the black-haired sea raiders. I mean, your hair! Did you know Maisie from before? What brought you here?"

The spate of questions gave Seren time to think.

"Maisie… the woman who owned the cottage."

"Owned? Well, I suppose she did, but I'm sure there wasn't any legal paper. She moved in fifteen or more years ago, set up shop as a potter to cover what she really was. A witch. Herbs. Potions. Poisons, too, although she was clever enough not to ever mention that. I only came here for the hair-soap she made. I always knew she was dangerous, but it wasn't until my last visit that I knew she was a traitor. Under that red dye, her hair was black. She was a spying sea pirate."

She paused, head on one side as a fresh thought interrupted her flow of words.

"You came down the old west road, then?"

Seren nodded.

The woman looked her up and down, suddenly fearful of Seren's unusual height. She blinked, pursed her lips, and took a couple of quick steps backwards, paused, and began to walk past the cottage towards the road.

"Well, I must be off home. I just came to see if Maisie had made any of her aloe hair tonic before she ran away. Be careful if you go on down to Half Moon Bay. That's where the black-haired pirates were when our soldiers scared them away with their big gun. Now they've been ordered to take it up to the Castle and I'm happy to see the back of them. I had two lazy soldiers billeted on me and my husband, just because we have a big house and no children to take up the extra rooms. It's not fair. We're upright, conscientious citizens. And we do so much for the church and the community, even the farmers whose produce we buy."

The woman talked her way past Seren, who let the stream of words wash over her, picking out facts from among the complaints. Then almost as suddenly as she had appeared, the woman turned, hurried past the front of the cottage, went around the corner, and, still talking, was gone.

Marley looked cautiously out of the door. Seren beckoned to him.

"There was soot on her sleeve. She'd looked inside. When she saw me, she was scared. Couldn't stop talking. But she thought that whoever lived here had escaped. She must have looked inside for …"

"No bodies in there," said Marley.

"So maybe Ellie and whoever lived here got away."

"I heard," said Marley.

"She also told me that soldiers were taking their gun to the Castle. They could be planning to use it on …"

"Matris," said Marley.

"We must warn Lindey, Mairi, Trogen."

"What of…"

"Marley, she's alive, and she's gone. But where?"

Seren consulted her stone and headed south along the path through the orchard. Marley checked his stone as well, as he walked behind her. When they reached the intersection with the old forest road taken by Ellie, Marley started up the incline. Grass and late-season wildflowers waved in a little breeze that flowed out of the gap in the forest.

"The ship is this way, through the forest," said Seren.

"Yes," said Marley, "We know that. Perhaps Ellie didn't. Maybe if her stone wasn't guiding her she'd take the road."

"But it's the wrong way."

"It's away from the cottage, and likely from the people who burned it."

He pointed at hoof-marks at their feet, and then at a trace of crushed and broken grasses that led westward.

"You think she got away but the riders followed her!"

Seren started up the trail, her long legs setting a swift pace.

"Wait," said Marley, and pointed at the ground.

Seren paused and looked back through the trees at the ruined cottage. Then she, too, looked down. A couple of paces from the hoof-marks Marley was examining was the tree-stump where Ellie had sat to grieve over what she thought was Maisie's death.

"Seren, she sat here. Boat shoes. Two heel-marks. Look."

"Right! Her boat boots wouldn't leave tracks on the path, but here, where there's soft earth, her heels dug in."

They both stared at the faint marks, in their imaginations seeing Ellie sitting alone, disconsolate, in danger.

"Look, here," said Marley. "Hoof prints. Horses that came after she had gone."

"Follow or return?" Seren murmured, unaware that she had spoken out loud. She stood very straight, wrestling with her decision. Every impulse was to follow her sister, but she hesitated, held back by her duty to her ship, the fleet and Matris. After what seemed a very long time, Marley could not restrain himself.

"You return, I follow?" Marley asked.

They both startled as their clasps tingled on their arms.

"Trogen!" exclaimed Seren. "But I can't make out the message. There's too much in the way — trees, hills, cliffs. He's at sea, heading east. He needs to know they've moved the gun. So must Lindey. We have to return to the ship. Together. Quickly. Once aboard, close to the shipstone, I can reach Trogen and Mairi."

They left the road and plunged into the forest together.

# Chapter 18: In which Astreya meets Maisie

"Woah, Esme."

The big carthorse plodded up the last few paces of a short slope onto the broad, green road and obediently stopped. She nodded her big head and looked around as if she was participating in the deliberations that were troubling the man on her back. The carthorse had a body designed for pulling. Her shoulders were massive, her body so wide that Astreya's legs either had to be splayed on either side or tucked up and cramped under him.

Astreya shifted in the saddle. He was uncomfortable in more ways than he wanted to consider. His backside was sore, his hip ached. Continuing to ride would be increasingly painful, but he knew that getting down and then climbing back up again would be worse.

All these physical aches and pains were as nothing compared to the tedious recital of failures that occupied Astreya's mind. His niece, his favourite niece — though he would never say so — was missing, possibly dead, because he had failed in his duty of care not only to her but also to her father, Dabih.

The name stabbed guilt into his mind. Dabih, who had been commander of *Elusive*. Dabih, who was Seren and Ellie's father. Dabih, his cousin who was more like a younger brother. Dabih, murdered by a revengeful villain. The perpetrator was dead, but that had been thanks to Ellie's courage rather than anything Astreya had done. And now another enemy he had bested in the past was intent on overcoming him, his family, and all he had accomplished in his effort to atone for his ancestors.

For more than twenty years, Astreya had felt that so long as he worked at it hard enough, he could manage the trading enterprise he had inherited. He had also felt he was gradually making up for the conduct of his piratical ancestors. But of late it was all going wrong. His son Trogen chafed at his leadership. His decision to protect the children had led to his cousin's murder. His inattention had led to the wound that took him out of action, which meant it had been his thirteen-year-old niece who saved the day, the fleet, and the navigation stones. Matris was threatened, the shipping enterprise disrupted, his bond with Lindey undermined. Until now, she had approved his choices and endorsed his plans. She often argued with him about details, stipulated exceptions, or pointed out difficulties, but she had always confirmed his course of action as reasonable. Even she had not questioned him for — what had Ellie said? 'Sitting on the spare stones like a broody hen.'

The moment Astreya heard that Ellie was lost as a result of a cowardly attack, his mind was made up. She had been right about him hoarding the power of the stones, so he gave them out to those who deserved them. Now Ellie, who had stood up to his arrogance; Ellie, the most promising member of his extended family; Ellie, the prodigy with the navigation stones; Ellie the niece he had lost, perhaps who was already dead — like her father Dabih, his uncle Gar, his aunt Meissa, his mother Alana, and the father for whom he had been named but who he had never known.

He had to find Ellie, or worse, discover what had happened to her. And then if the Governor of the Castle was indeed Carl, he had to finish the inconclusive fight begun nearly twenty-five years ago. Token shedding of blood would not be enough. This was not something in which he could involve his family or those under his command. Taking a life was bad enough without involving others in the act.

He turned, winced, rummaged in one of his saddlebags and pulled out the map of roads past and present in the hinterland on which he had turned his back years before when he decided that a seafaring life was his destiny.

"Esme, here we turn north. Soon, we will head eastward where if I have any luck left, we will find Ellie. Walk on."

The big horse obediently started up the road. Astreya hunched his shoulders in a fruitless effort to ease his mind and body. A trickle of sweat ran down his spine as his black jacket absorbed the heat of the morning sun.

~^~

Astreya's eyes closed, his chin tilted towards his chest. The steady pace of Esme's huge clopping hooves and the swing and sway of her big body had taken him past the watch-keeper's intermediary state somewhere between waking and sleeping in which his mind could wander while his eyes, ears and body stayed alert. More than halfway to sleep, he revisited fragments of thought, each a remnant from hours of indecision.

*Thought I knew best ... didn't keep Ellie safe.... didn't protect the children ... sent them away. Consequence? — Dabih murdered, children almost killed. I welcomed Walt into the family, he turned traitor. I let Mirak live, he corrupted Walt, planned Dabih's murder, nearly blew up Cygnus, almost destroyed the Village. I took the stones to Fred to be waterproofed, he made the guns that killed Walt and Mirak and his four sailors, nearly Ellie, as well. I lost my father's notebook, didn't take Carl down, the library went up in flames, Gar dead. All my fault. Always I led them astray. Astray. Astreya. Me.*

Esme stumbled, jerking Astreya awake. He blinked at the bright sunlight, and frowned in dismay. He had fallen asleep on watch. Bad enough in a seaman or cadet or junior officer, for one in command, it was unforgivable.

Astreya flipped open the patch on the arm of his jacket that concealed his clasp and consulted his green stone. As he expected, the spear of light at its heart indicated that they were no longer going due north. Before he nodded off, the ruts ahead narrowed into the distance until they disappeared into the forest on either side. Now the road was swinging west to avoid a lumpy hill and he could see only a little way ahead.

The big horse walked with the steady, distance-eating tread of an animal bred for long hours of pulling a plow back and forth across a field. She was so well trained that she could make the turn at the end of every furrow without guidance from the farmer walking behind. Her present task was even easier: compared to tugging a plow, the load on her back was negligible; there were no regular turns at the field edge, all she had to do was walk the green stripe at the centre of the grassy road. There was nothing to concern a plow horse.

Except for the cat in the middle of the road.

Esme stopped dead. Astreya nearly fell over her head. Horse and man stared down at the cat, and the cat stared back. Back arched, mouth wide in a throaty hiss, its brindled hair stood on end, doubling its size. Neither cat, horse, or man knew exactly what to do next.

Around the bend walked a woman leading two horses, obedient to the reins draped over her shoulder. She was moving with the purposive tread of one who has done enough walking to know how to conserve energy. Astreya looked between Esme's ears at the woman's hair, red as a rowan tree in autumn. Tight curls had escaped their plaits to stick to her broad forehead. Her black eyes were wide-spaced above full lips and a firm chin. Her russet skirt swayed back and forth above the tops of her boots, the top two buttons of her cream-coloured blouse were open, revealing smooth, dark skin. Her steady, evaluating stare told him that they were roughly the same age.

"Curmudgeon, will you kindly stop menacing that horse."

The cat turned its head to look at her, its fur subsided and its back lowered. Reassured that the woman could take care of the giant horse and black-haired man, it sat as if preparing to be entertained. The big horse nodded its head, the cat accepted its due and began to wash itself.

"Well, Grand Commander Astreya, you've arrived a bit late."

"What? When? How do you know my name?"

"Black hair, black beard, born to command men, perhaps not quite so persuasive with women. Ellie told me. The Goddess brought her to my door. She was lost, poor girl. Her talisman had failed her."

"Where is she?"

"Ellie was taken by a handful of soldiers from the Castle riding on a juggernaut. Her horse bolted, and they grabbed her."

"Then why…?"

"…am I headed south? Catching her horse and finding my cat."

"What about Ellie?"

"Ellie got to the road first. Her horse was spooked by a hissing metal monster. So was mine. And my cat. By the time we had straightened ourselves out, the men had Ellie, and the monster had thundered off down the road, headed north."

"I must follow, get her back."

"Yes, we must."

"We?"

"Of course, we. I'm responsible for Ellie. The Goddess put her in my care."

"She's my …"

"… niece, in a manner of speaking. Ellie told me her family history is complicated. So is mine. But later for that. Can you ride an ordinary-sized horse?"

"Ah… yes."

"Then mount up on the horse Ellie was riding. If that huge beast of yours …"

"Esme."

"Esme will be better able to keep up with us if you're not on her, and we will be able to keep an eye on each other."

"I…"

"Well then, do it!"

Astreya blinked, slid to the ground and limped towards Maisie. Curmudgeon looked at him slantwise, dashed back and leaped onto Maisie's horse, where she settled on the bedroll behind the saddle. Astreya accepted the spare horse's reins, took a moment to let it accustom itself to a new rider, and swung into the saddle with a wince. Maisie clucked her tongue at Esme, who stepped forward to meet her as if they had known each other for years. Moments later, Maisie and Astreya were riding side by side with the big carthorse plodding along behind them.

They glanced covertly at each other, back and forth, until the inevitable moment came when their eyes met. Astreya was first to speak.

"How did you and Ellie come to be on this road?"

"The Goddess brought her to my door — almost. I picked her up and carried her the last few paces into my cottage, where she recovered from spending two days and nights lost in the forest."

"Ellie lost? Ellie's always been able to find …"

"North? Her way? Well, this time her talisman … clasp … stone … failed."

"Then where were the two of you riding to? And why…"

"Why did we leave my cottage? Because the local collection of credulous idiots decided to burn it down."

"Why?"

"Because they think I'm a witch."

"Why?"

"You ask a lot of questions."

"Only way to get answers."

"True. Well, a foolish woman thought I was in league with the powers of darkness. She riled up the mayor and parson by telling them that I was also a spy for the Men of the Sea because she guessed that I was looking after someone who'd landed from the boat the soldiers had been shooting at. She then instigated — that's Ellie's word for it — a raid in which they killed my goat and my goose and then burned down my home."

For a little while, they rode in silence punctuated by their horses' hoofs.

"So you know about Matris," said Astreya slowly.

"We were going there to warn you. But we had the misfortune to arrive at this road in time for a great mechanical monster to spook Ellie's horse. They grabbed her and carted her off to the Castle."

"Why?"

"Because they saw she has black hair, which by now you must have worked out is how they identify Men of the Sea. Men like you who raid villages and kidnap young people."

"Not anymore."

"So Ellie said. But people remember. Especially if someone stirs up fearful hatred for anyone who they can call a stranger."

"Do you mean the man they call Governor?"

"So I've heard."

"That has to be stopped." Astreya saw Maisie's eyebrows rise, but he was not deflected. "First we rescue Ellie. Then I deal with the Governor. I knew him more than twenty years ago when he called himself Carl. If it hadn't been for him, my uncle would still be alive today. I should never have let him get away with … what he did."

Maisie listened to the horses' hooves and considered what she was hearing.

"You're planning to kill the Governor, all alone, just like that."

"I'm planning to talk to him."

"And if that doesn't work, which it won't?"

"I'll do what needs to be done."

"You're going to change what's happened?"

"I'm going to try."

Maisie shook her head.

"So now you've made up your mind, you think you can re-make what's been and done, all on your own. But you're not in charge of what's happened — especially not the things that come back to haunt us. Nobody is. Only the Goddess knows the hinges on which our lives turn."

"I believe we are responsible for taking what action we can against forces that threaten the innocent."

"You are used to thinking that you can do big things, aren't you, Grand Commander Astreya? That's a luxury the rest of us know we don't have. I can choose what to make for dinner, how many bangles to wear on my wrist, what to put into my potions and simples. I can choose among little things, as do we all. But none of us controls what happens, and certainly not what flows from what happened in the past. Not even Grand Commanders."

"I have to try. But you don't have to walk this road."

"We're not walking. And I do have to, because the Goddess intertwined my fate with Ellie's. I'm following the road she's on."

"So am I."

"Rescue your niece, destroy the tyrant."

"If I can."

"Alone."

"I can't ask anyone else to …"

"Grand Commander Astreya can't ask his extended family to search for Ellie?"

"It's my fault she was captured."

"Poppycock."

Curmudgeon arched her back and hissed. Astreya's spine straightened, and his green eyes fixed on Maisie's as if she were a cadet guilty of gross misconduct.

"What business is it of yours that…"

"The Goddess twined my fate with Ellie's, and now with you," Maisie answered serenely. "So I'm not going to risk her, or myself so that you can indulge in foolish male heroics. You need to think, Astreya. You need a plan."

Another pause, during which the horses' hooves measured both time and distance. Astreya's assertive mood faded.

"You sound like Lindey."

He frowned as he heard the words he had not intended to say out loud.

"Then she must be a sensible woman. Where is she?"

"In Matris. Preparing the defences."

"I'm glad to hear it, even if it's from a man who's running off to make himself into a hero. Or dead. Perhaps both."

They exchanged less than friendly glances.

"Prrrp," said Curmudgeon.

Their horses were walking up an incline so gradual that neither Astreya nor Maisie had noticed. As they reached the top, they saw smoke curling up from the black land-crawler.

"What in the name of goodness is that?" Astreya asked.

"I don't know what it's called," said Maisie. "But I am sure it's not working. However, I do know soldiers when I see them. Here, put this on."

She guided her horse close to his, reached into her saddlebag, and clapped her big shapeless hat onto his head. Astreya reached up and held it with one hand, frowning.

"Lean over this way," said Maisie.

She scooped ointment out of a little earthenware pot, rubbed it across both her palms and then drew her hands down both sides of Astreya's face. Before he could jerk back, her fingers massaged ointment into his beard and traced over his eyebrows.

"I don't have time to do your hair, so keep the hat on."

Astreya was so astonished he could not find words.

"Don't you say a thing," said Maisie. "Leave your mouth open. Good. Now if you can, squint."

Astreya did as he was told.

# Chapter 19: In which the commanders fail to agree

Seren and Marley moved swiftly, weaving their way through the old-growth pine trees, confident in the guidance from their stones. Neither of them spoke of the decision Seren had made, but both were keenly aware that she had chosen duty to Matris and the fleet over love for her sister. One moment, Seren castigated herself for being faithless; the next she felt sure that Ellie was equal to whatever challenge faced her. Marley recognized how difficult Seren's choice had been, and also knew that sympathy would only compound her distress.

It was not yet noon when they were among the scrubby, windswept spruce and balsam that guarded the forest against the storms that blew off the ocean. Short, stubby branches clutched at their clothes, until they reached the cliff and breathed the sharp smells of saltwater and seaweed. The tide had turned, and the ebb was pulling strands of kelp towards the schooner's bow. Neal, Alan and Henry were on deck, looking expectant.

"Ellie's alive. We think she's taking a land route home," said Seren.

"We'll use the falling tide to turn *Cygnet* seaward. Marley, get her ready to slip, bow and stern."

He took a breath to answer, but she had gone below to the cabin where the shipstone swung in its gimbals. Moments later, his clasp tingled on his arm as he felt her sending a message that he had not yet learned to decode.

His biceps tensed, and he rubbed his left arm in reaction to the intensity of her sending. Moments after the tingling was over, it began again. This time, he recognized the staccato quality with which Trogen snapped out orders to his crew. Next came Seren's measured answer, and then another rapid-fire retort from Trogen. Then the whole call and answer routine repeated twice more. Marley realized that he had been standing rubbing his arm throughout the entire exchange and that Alan was doing the same. Henry was staring at both of them, baffled by their behaviour. Neil scowled at his feet, knowing what was happening and resenting that he was not part of it.

Before Marley could explain to them, or set about following Seren's order, she emerged from below, her hair bright in the afternoon sun. All he could do was stare.

"*Cygnets!*" Seren's voice was sharp. "Single up! Alan, slip the bow line, Neil, hoist the jib and stand by to back it. Marley, I'll take her. You and Henry hoist the main."

Seren's crew sprang into action. In the bow, Alan tugged at the line to shore until Henry, the youngest, leaped ashore to clear where it had become caught in the bark of the gnarly little tree to which they had moored. When the end of the rope splashed down in the water, Henry ran to the stern line, checked that it would run clear, and leaped aboard again. He barely made it. Seren watched Henry's agile response, remembering Trogen calling him a 'keener.'

"Henry. You have the stern line. Steady. We don't need to be fishing you out of the water."

She spun the wheel to port. The distance from *Cygnet's* bow to the cliff face increased as the schooner started the turn toward the sea, pushed by the ebbing tide and the outfall from the stream at the head of the bay.

"Henry, haul the stern line!" Seren ordered as she brought the wheel amidships, checking their progress with a glance over her shoulder at the shoreline. Then as the schooner lay across the flow of water, drifting sideways, the jib caught wind. "Henry, ready to let go on my command." She twitched the wheel, confirmed that she had steerageway. "Let go aft!" Over her shoulder, she heard the stern warp splash into the water. "Coil down and then take the wheel."

Henry appeared at her shoulder, looking eagerly up at her, a loop of dripping rope over his shoulder. She pointed, he let it fall into the cockpit and reached for the wheel.

"Keep the wind abeam to starboard, Henry. We're headed out to rendezvous with *Elusive* and *Cygnus*."

Seren was across the cockpit in a stride, on her way below. She barely reached the chart table in the stern cabin in time for another of Trogen's powerful messages.

## ELUSIVE HEAVING TO: COME ALONGSIDE

She was still estimating the distance to *Elusive* when above her on deck first Alan and then Marley shouted "Sail!" When she reappeared on deck, they were pointing in opposite directions. Ahead, was *Elusive,* her distinctive staysails furling as she hove to, head to wind. To the west, *Cygnus* was sailing wing-on-wing downwind, her main and mizzen sails on opposite sides. Seren glanced at Marley, whose fingers were almost twitching with the desire to take over the wheel. She gestured palm down, grinned at him, and went to stand beside Henry.

"We'll gibe, drop downwind, pass *Elusive* wide to starboard, then swing around, come alongside, dowse sails and then loose furl. Marley, we'll need fenders."

Henry's eyes widened and his fists closed around the spokes of the wheel. He could feel eyes watching him. Seren was above him, looking down, Marley was in the cockpit, looking up. From their positions further forward, Alan and Neil were both snatching glances to see how he was handling the responsibility. He saw Marley's hands open, close, and then relax at his sides. Whether or not it was a message, Henry forced himself to ease his grasp on the wheel, as Seren gave the order to start the manoeuver.

"Stand by to gibe ... gibe!"

Henry swallowed with a tight throat and spun the wheel.

Cam, Damon, and Marley stood on *Elusive's* quarterdeck, looking deliberately at nothing in particular. All three had scanned their ships and made sure that lines were secure, fenders in place, sails ready for hoisting, and all those on duty were alert. Each was keenly aware that the other two had made the same careful evaluation.

Their commanders were below in the great cabin, deciding what would happen next. Trogen had curtly ordered the mates to remain on deck as he headed for the companionway, herding his sister and cousin below.

Damon cleared his throat and addressed the horizon.

"It would appear that the Grand Commander has decided on the unusual strategy of taking what's happening at the Castle into his own hands."

"Unusual?" Cam snorted.

"And even more unexpected, he took a live and fully functioning shipstone with him. I'm not a qualified wielder yet by any means, but I can tell you he had such a stone with him when he rode off on one of the carthorses."

"Flamin' stupid. He took a shipstone, but he didn't take the one man who could help him at the Castle. That's you, Damon."

"Be that as it may. Perhaps it's of more consequence that my erstwhile companion and fellow student Enoch, better known as Knock, the man who brought the information that precipitated Astreya's decision, has disappeared. Along with my shore-going poke of coin."

"Makin' it a fair guess that he went back to the people who sent him in the first place."

"Presumably."

"An' 'Streya gone off, believin' what the Knock feller said."

"Evidently."

"Leavin' our three young skippers to make it up as they go along, all the while teachin' their first mates how to use what we never asked for."

Damon scratched his left arm where his clasp made a lump in his shirt sleeve.

"Itches. Especially when my skipper has been … ah … communicating."

"Shoutin' his head off, more like," said Cam.

Marley considered. It was his turn to walk the line between respect for the chain of command and solidarity among men of the same rank. All three of them were a decade or more older than their respective commanders. Cam and Damon shared years of friendship, whereas he was the outsider who Seren had chosen to bring into Astreya's extended family.

"Search, defend or attack. Hard to choose when to do which," said Marley.

Cam's left eyebrow rose.

"S'obvious.  Seren lands to look for Ellie, Mairi helps Lindey protect Matris, Trogen mucks in with 'Streya's revenge," said Cam.

"Revenge?" Marley asked.

Cam looked at Damon, who stroked his moustache.

"Go on, Damon. He's got a clasp, like us."

"When we were all younger than … than … than the skippers who are holding a meeting in the great cabin below, I was a student at the Castle when Astreya arrived, along with a fellow who turned out much later to be both his uncle and Dabih's father, which none of us knew at the time."

"And Lindey," said Cam. "Don't forget Lindey."

"I am definitely not forgetting Lindey. Neither then nor now. Where was I?"

"Forgettin' Lindey," said Cam.

"As I was saying, I was a student at the time studying …"

"Studyin' knife fightin', I'm told," said Cam.

"…history, philosophy and after Astreya arrived, Astreya. You see, Astreya had … has an extraordinary capacity to …"

"He's so lightenin' quick, nobody can land a blow on 'im — or a knife."

"Exactly. At the same time as we all were at the Castle, a peculiarly offensive individual…"

"Name of Carl…"

"… saw Astreya's skill, ability, talent, whatever it is, and decided he had to kill him."

"For being faster?" Marley asked.

"To prove he was better, I suppose. But that went badly wrong for him. He and two henchmen …"

"Yer forgettin' to tell Marley about your henchmen, Damon."

"… who Carl brought along because he expected my friends Knock and Sandy to be present, which they weren't."

"'Cause they were useless, spineless…"

"Anyway, there was a fight. We were all in a big library. It was night. Carl grabbed Lindey, and Astreya went for him. The lantern got kicked over, the paint caught fire, Carl knifed his henchman by mistake, and Astreya's uncle Gar fell off the painting stage and was killed. Astreya blames Carl."

"'Streya blames himself," Cam corrected. "An' I'm guessin' he's all wound up about Ellie, as well."

"Especially now Carl appears to be behind the cannon that fired on *Seafoam*, which could well be used in an assault on Matris."

"Difficult decisions for our skippers now that the Grand Commander is away," said Marley.

Damon and Cam nodded.

"Family ties, responsibility to the fleet, youthful heroism," said Damon.

"Now yer makin' it all intellectual, Damon. What they're arguin' about now comes from who they are an' what makes them do whatever."

"Together or apart?" Marley asked.

"Not one of them is a pushover," said Cam. My bet is they'll each go their own way."

Before Damon could take his turn, three pairs of feet sounded on the companionway. Mairi's tightly braided blonde head appeared first.

"Back aboard, Cam. We're going home."

Cam followed her to the gangway between *Elusive* and *Cygnus*, where he paused and glanced back at the other two mates. His expression said, 'I told you so,' as clearly as if he had spoken out loud.

Seren appeared on the top step. Her eyes locked with Marley's, she nodded and strode towards the starboard rail.

"Luck, Marley," said Cam.

"Find Ellie safe," said Damon at the same moment.

Marley followed Seren to one of the warps that held the ships together. With a glance to be sure it was belayed, she swung a long leg over the rail and lowered herself hand over hand down to the deck of her little schooner. Marley inclined his head at Cam and then Damon and followed her down onto *Cygnet.*

Cam shrugged, Damon nodded.

Trogen came up on deck, shouting.

"The moment *Cygnet's* out of the way, I want the sails drawing on the port tack, heading east."

"At your command," said Damon.

His face was expressionless as his voice.

# Chapter 20: In which the land crawler explodes

The smell of smoke and hot oil caught in Ellie's throat. She shrank into herself, huddling in the forward corner of the big wagon as it was tugged along the road by the hissing mechanical monster. She knew no more about where she was going than the stupid-looking soldiers lounging in the back of the wagon, being yanked along the road to whatever might happen next. Unsettled by Fred's warning, they all kept well away from her. The four men leaned against the wagon's chest-high metal sides and tailgate, watching the passing landscape, looking bored. On their backs Ellie saw rifles, their blue-steel barrels glinting in the sunlight. Slung for comfort rather than readiness, they told her that these soldiers lacked both enemies and discipline. One of the grey-uniformed men kicked her pack towards her. She pulled her cloak out of the bundle and pulled it around her, even though the day was warm. Fred stood in the other forward corner, his shoulders hunched, his face turned away.

Ellie stared at the back of Fred's head, wishing she knew what he was thinking. His lie about her being diseased was protecting her from the soldiers, but it also kept her from asking what he was planning. She knew that he was deeply interested in all that had been lost since Before divided from After. This she understood because she, too, was curious. The shared itch to know was why they had bonded, despite the obvious disapproval of Ellie's extended family. A sneaking suspicion prowled the back of her mind.

*Was this machine Fred's new fixation? Has he only been using me until something better turned up? Is he keeping me as a bargaining chip in a deal with the Castle?*

Ellie drew her knees up under her chin and stared at the scarred wooden planking that floored the wagon. She finger-combed her hair, coiled it back into the hat, and replaced it on her head. She knew that Maisie could not have stopped the soldiers from grabbing her, but her suspicions of Fred led her to wonder whether Maisie had chosen not to intervene. Perhaps she had merely let events take their course, which she could then ascribe to her Goddess' will.

~^~

For an indeterminate time, the land-crawler pulled the jolting wagon northward. The sun scorched down, waves of heat from the steam engine washed back onto Ellie, Fred and the soldiers. They all grew increasingly hot and thirsty. Ellie watched as one of them handed out bannock stuffed with cold meat, on which they chewed with half-open mouths. They passed a stone jug of beer hand to hand, exchanging grunted words of approval. Ellie flinched as one of the soldiers kicked a metal canteen towards her, any compassion obscured by his fearful glance. She let the container lie until the man shrugged and turned his attention to Fred, offering him food and water, for which he insisting on paying. The unexpected gesture led to him being given a pull from the beer jug.

While the soldiers' attention was on getting their share from the jug as it was passed around, Ellie reached for the canteen and drank. The water revived her enough to make her aware of how hot she had become. She stood, grasped the corner of the wagon and let the breeze of their steady advance blow under her cloak. The warm material stuck to her shoulders, but the cloak helped her ignore the occasional sidelong glance from the soldiers. She stood swaying to the wagon's bumpy, jolting progress, so awkward in comparison to the rhythm of a ship at sea.

Ellie stared at trees that grew to the edge of the road as they appeared around the puffing, hissing machine ahead of her, jerked past, and were lost behind. Nowhere in the green and brown wall was a hint of a human path or even an animal track. Steam hissed, pistons thumped, the drawbar rattled and banged as it yanked the wagon forward, numbing her senses. Eventually, boredom overtook both fear and discomfort, and all she could do was endure as the engine laboured its way along a narrow passage between unending trees.

Without warning, the steamer stopped dead.

Ellie slammed against the inside front of the wagon, bruising her chest. Before she could take a full breath, an invisible sledgehammer of hot air felled her to her knees, winding her a second time. Behind her, the soldiers lost their balance, staggered and fell over each other in a tangle of arms and legs. Fred almost tumbled forwards over the front of the wagon.

Fragments of metal flew back from the engine, whined through the air, and twanged on the metal sides of the wagon, but no one could hear them because all were suddenly deaf. A soldier lay flat on his back, holding both hands to his head, blood oozing between his fingers. As she stared, numbed and deafened, two soldiers bent over their wounded companion, one of them clutching a canvass pouch marked with a red cross. When Ellie looked above them, she saw Fred's contorted, shouting face.

"Stay down!"

She lip-read the words that reached her only as a mumbled whisper. Fred ignored his own advice and peered over the front of the wagon. When he bobbed back down, Ellie saw his shock and disbelief. He stepped past the bleeding soldier and leaned towards her, hands outstretched. She drew back, unable to hear what he was saying. He pushed her satchel into her hands, grasped her arms and half dragged, half carried her to the back of the wagon, where the tailgate had fallen open. Together, they jumped down onto scorched grass, her cloak falling off her shoulders.

"Ellie, can you hear me?"

Ellie nodded as she bundled her cloak.

"Can you walk?"

Ellie nodded again and shouldered her belongings.

"Run. Hide. No. Hit me."

Ellie blinked, and then hit him in the chest with both hands as hard as she could.

Fred had been expecting a blow, but not the force she put into it. He staggered back, overbalanced, and landed on his back. Ellie sprinted past him, running off the road, pushing through the bushes, plunging into the forest.

Fred stayed down, which was according to his plan. However, had not expected to have the wind knocked out of his lungs, nor to be seeing little red flashes even though his eyes were shut. He raised his head, winced, then explored his scalp with one hand. His fingers felt blood-sticky hair. When he opened his eyes, he saw captain Orme looking down at him.

"Mr. Fredericks, are you all right?"

Fred nodded, winced again, and answered in a genuinely unsteady voice.

"I'm … I'm shaken. And I appear to have cut my head. What happened?"

"The steamer blew. Charlie's dead. Head taken clean off him. And Barney — private Hamble — has a nasty cut to the head, like you, but I'm thinking it's a mite worse, 'cause his eyes don't look right and he's not taking things in."

"Possibly a concussion," said Fred.

"Agreed," said Orme. "Good to know you're thinking straight."

"Give me a hand, Captain Orme and I'll take a look at him. I have some knowledge of emergency medicine that may be … thank you."

Moments later, they were both bending over the injured soldier, who lay with his face to the sky, his eyes open, blank, and unfocused. Blood was seeping through a clumsy bandage above his eyebrows and was running down his cheek. He did not even try to speak when Orme called his name, and his eyes did not follow when Fred waved a finger in front of his eyes.

"Not good," said Fred. "We need to get him to somewhere he can be looked after by a physician."

He stood up, lurched, and was grateful for Orme's steadying hand.

"Where's El … Where's the black-haired girl?"

"Run off after she knocked you onto your keister. I've got a man looking, but it's like she's vanished."

"Hey, there. Do you need any help?"

Orme spun around. A red-haired woman was striding towards them. Behind her stood a man in a shapeless hat, holding the reins of three horses. Orme's right hand reached for the revolver at his belt.

"Make ready, men!" he shouted. "You just keep going, miss, mistress, ah… Citizen. I have the situation in control."

"It certainly doesn't look like it. You have one man down, the one beside you has blood on his collar, your infernal machine is leaking smoke, steam, and water, and your two remaining soldiers are pointing their guns every which way. Kindly tell them to put them away, because right now it's anyone's guess who's going to get shot first — perhaps even you."

Militia Captain Samuel Orme did as he was told.

# Chapter 21: In which Ellie's stone flares

Ellie ran through the overgrown verge of the road toward the forest, part of her mind telling her that escape was futile. Maybe she should be running in zig-zags to confuse the soldiers' aim. Perhaps she should throw herself flat and crawl. Possibly she should just stand still and let the soldiers take her.

*No! Not that.*

Ellie stopped thinking and ran faster. Her loose trouser-like riding skirt caught on tall grasses, then thigh-high bracken nearly tripped her. She kept going between head-high aspen and on into a thicket of cedar trees. Their trunks were close as a hedge, but she shoved her way between intertwined branches that plucked her cloak and shoulder bag from her grasp. She fell to her hands and knees and crawled. Twigs scratched her face, and her hands sank to the wrists in fallen debris. Then suddenly, she was in the deep shade of huge pines and she and there was nothing to slow her staggering, lurching, desperate running.

*Run blindly, Ellie, and you'll be lost. Again.*

The warning was as clear as if spoken at her ear. She looked around wildly, expecting to see someone behind her, but she was alone. Tree trunks around her and branches above sucked up all sound except for her throbbing heartbeat and the rush of the air she was panting into her chest. Soon her heartbeat no longer thudded in her ears and pulsed at her throat. Ellie was able to think again, and with the return of awareness came the need to know what was happening back on the road. She turned around, and near-panic redoubled her pulse because the trees were the same behind her as they were ahead and on either side.

Ellie pushed up the sleeve of her blouse to check her bearings with her clasp as she had done so often at sea, but halfway through the gesture, she flinched.

*Think north, Ellie.*

Again, it was as if someone had spoken at the back of her neck. She held her breath and closed her eyes, focussed on her stone, miserably expecting failure. When she opened them, her stone flared bright green, glowing in the forest gloom like a tiny green fire. Across its domed centre was a thin, bright line.

Ellie took a long breath, deeper than she had taken in days. Her neck muscles unclenched, she stood to her full height. Slowly, deliberately, her clasp held high, she followed the pointing line back towards the road. She strode past reddish-brown trunks until the branches above her were in sunlight. Then she was among the cedars at the forest edge, their fronds glinting as they swayed in a light wind. Ellie peered cautiously out at the road.

A soldier stood thigh-deep in bracken. He was scanning the forest edge, turning slowly, rifle at his shoulder. Ellie waited, transfixed, as the weapon swung to point at her. The foresight caught the light. Below it was the round black muzzle in which lurked the shot that would end her. She held her breath. Then she was looking at the side of the rifle as the soldier continued his scan. She exhaled.

A shout and the soldier's rifle swung to point back along the road. A second soldier beside the wagon, aimed at two people on horses, a third huge horse following behind. She heard a distant "Woah!" as all three came to a halt. Bright red hair caught the light.

"Maisie," Ellie breathed.

Maisie dismounted and walked towards the back of the wagon, where Ellie saw two more figures. One she recognized as Fred, the other, holding a pistol at waist height, must be the officer.

Ellie strained to hear, but a little wind down the roadway blew the words away, and she could only guess at what was being said. Evidently, the captain had given an order. Rifles were lowered, but the officer still held his pistol.

*That big horse looks like our Esme, but who's on the horse I was riding, wearing Maisie's hat?*

The captain gestured with his pistol, the man stepped back to cringe beside the big horse.

*It's Astreya! No, the beard's wrong. It's grey. And this man is old, and short.*

The man shambled towards Maisie, who patted his arm as if he was a nervous horse. Her hair gleamed as her chin came up in that determined look Ellie had admired from their first meeting. The captain holstered his pistol, the soldiers' rifles pointed down.

"Wha' 'bout the girl?" called the soldier in the bracken.

"Let her go. Come here."

At the captain's terse order the soldier closest to Ellie waded back to the road. Both soldiers now held their rifles at the hip, more relaxed but still threatening. Maisie and the captain conferred inaudibly. After a little while, Ellie saw that they had come to a decision. Maisie led the big horse forward around the wagon, with the man who surely couldn't be Astreya shuffling behind her.

At first, Ellie thought the captain had let them continue on down the road, then they stopped between the wagon and the land crawler, where the captain gave more orders. The soldiers put their rifles into the wagon and set to work unhitching it from the engine and fitting a wheel on the draw-bar. The old man led up the cart horse and unloaded tackle from its pack. Ellie felt recognition bloom inside her head.

"Astreya," she whispered, and instantly doubted herself.

The moment passed, and Ellie wondered whether she had imagined it. Most likely, the Grand Commander was working the shipstone aboard *Cygnus*, heading south, far too far away for anything but a dim echo to reach her. The man beside Maisie was shorter and older than Astreya; besides, the master of *Cygnus* always stood to his full height with his green eyes level and steady, while this man was stooped and dejected-looking, his head tilted towards Maisie, waiting to be told what to do next.

Ellie watched the complicated process of equipping the big horse to haul the wagon. Maisie stood, pointing and giving instructions. Eventually, everyone climbed into the wagon, with the two saddle horses tied on behind. For a moment, Ellie lost sight of the man wearing Maisie's hat until he appeared at Esme's head.

'March!"

As the captain's order reached Ellie, the man stood to his full height and strode forward. Again, she was sure he was Astreya, and she held her breath, fearing that he would be recognized. Then the man stumbled, and again was an elderly, half-witted servant, limping along beside the horse's big head. Ellie parted the spruce-boughs to watch the horses and people pass by the stranded land-crawler. She thought she saw Fred look back along the road to where she knew he could not possibly see her. As the procession shrank into the distance, she became aware that mosquitos were raising welts on her neck and wrists. Remembering Maisie's little pots of ointment, she retraced her tunnelling way through the cedars and rescued her cloak and satchel.

When she was no longer tormented by flies, she pushed back her sleeve and looked at its green light and the thin line at its heart, but as she watched, it faded to a dull, mossy green. Pushing down the panic rising in the back of her mind, she strove to think.

*Had it really been Astreya? Had nearness to the master wielder somehow revived her stone?*

"Only one way to find out," she muttered and set off down the road.

# Chapter 22: In which Cygnet sails to Charton

Seren and Marley stood on the foredeck of *Cygnet*, balancing easily as the bow lifted to a moderate swell. Wind rushed across the jib and foresail beside them, blowing their words to leeward. Alan was below, starting to prepare a meal, Henry was at the wheel, and Neil was standing at his shoulder, making him nervous.

"We can make Charton if we come about soon," said Marley.

"You agree, then," said Seren.

"Of course. But just to be clear, how much do we share with the crew?"

"We're presently heading south because that's where I want Trogen to think we're going … and also because, with this west wind, we have to hold our course until we can reach straight into Charton."

"And then?"

"North, looking for the forest road we know Ellie took. It has to meet up with the road to the Castle."

"And then?"

Seren hesitated.

"Matris."

Hearing doubt in her voice, Marley answered confidently.

"Could be she's already on her way south."

"Best case."

Marley glanced astern, and seeing Henry and Neil looking up at the tell-tales on the stays, took Seren's hand, pulled her close and kissed her. She responded instantly, then pushed him away, blushing.

"That wasn't seaman-like conduct."

She spoke earnestly, but her blue eyes were laughing.

"Oh yes it is," said Marley, and then in a voice loud enough to be heard astern, said, "Make ready for a course change northward."

"At my command," said Seren.

She stared ahead, letting the wind cool the blush on her neck and cheeks, before turning to follow Marley astern, where a few minutes later he took over the wheel from Henry.

"Stay to starboard of the passage between the headlands," said Seren. "Then when the wind's no longer blanketed by the high land, swing to port, well clear of the centre of the bay."

Marley nodded. His long-fingered hands were light on the wheel, sensing the wind-shift as they entered the big bay that had Charton at its head. Alan tended the mainsail, Neil had the jib and Henry the foresail. The little schooner lost way as she entered the bay. The regular swing, sway and rush of water along the hull that came from sailing on a comfortable reach at sea gave way to softer sounds as the wind became patchy, and then eased so that *Cygnet* no longer heeled to starboard. Seren stood with one hand on the port stay.

"There's a shoal east of the middle, but otherwise there's deep water all the way in. We'll run downwind past the boats at the wharf and take the space alongside the finger quay, port side to, facing south. Prepare to dowse the main and foresail."

The sails that had sagged in the wind-shadow of the headlands, firmed again as the schooner found the wind across the land.

"Ready to jibe … jibe ho!" said Seren.

There was the purring rattle of rope through blocks as the crew sheeted in the sails, followed by a succession of flapping thuds as the sails swung over the centre line and caught air on the other side.

"Ease sheets!"

*Cygnet* slid past the outfall of a stream, past a straggle of cottages, along a line of sheds, past half a dozen fishing boats bobbing at the wharf, towards the finger quay.

"Strike the main and foresails, let fly the jib."

Mast rings clattered, blocks whirred, and canvass flapped as the crew stripped the main and foresails down their masts, then tugged the spars into the centre line.

"Hard over, Marley," said Seren. "Bring her just short of head-to-wind."

Marley spun the wheel. The schooner turned, lost way, then stalled. Seren bit her lip during the anxious moment that would tell if her manoeuver was successful.

"I have the stern warp," said Seren. "Henry, get ready to check her way with the bow line. Marley, midships. Alan, back the jib. Neil, fenders."

With the wind on her bare poles, and her jib pushing her astern, *Cygnet* slid sideways towards the finger quay. When the black wooden pilings were close, Seren leaped, the stern warp in one hand. A heartbeat later so did Henry. They both threw three turns around the nearest bollard. *Cygnet* still surged ahead, as if unwilling to be tethered to the land. Cordage creaked, taking the strain. Seren and Henry checked the schooner's way, and then hauled her alongside the wharf.

Marley left the wheel to help fold and put stoppers on the mainsail. He glanced at Seren, whose blue eyes showed relief that her approach had been successful. His eyebrows went up and down, and his teeth flashed in a smile.

"Well done, everybody," said Seren. "Let's have her neat and tidy. I'm off to pay the publican for the use of his quay. Shore leave for everyone. When Marley decides *Cygnet's* properly squared away, we'll have a meal at The Black Sheep."

As the most frequent port of call for the Matris fleet, Charton was familiar to Seren and her crew, except for Marley, who was only on his second visit. When he had overseen *Cygnet's* harbour furl and coil down, he led the three boys to the inn whose sign swung over the door of a two-storey oak-and-brick building only a dozen strides away.

Marley pushed the heavy, nail-studded door open, and paused on the step down into the taproom. Henry ducked under his arm. The low-ceiling room was cool and shadowy. Only a little light came from the small windows; lanterns hung from age-blackened beams. There was only one customer, sitting with his elbows on a small table littered with the remains of a meal, a thatch of brown hair falling across his face.

Marley's gaze passed over him and focussed on Seren's blond curls. She was concluding arrangements with the inn-keeper, a burly man with a wide smile. His hands were eloquent with welcome, but his close-set, flint-black eyes missed nothing that happened in his pub.

Seren shook his hand and started towards the door. As she passed the table of the man with the shaggy hair, he leaned back, swung a long arm, and grabbed at her backside. As Marley took his first step to intervene, Seren snatched up the man's beer mug and poured it over his head. Spluttering an oath, he stood up, overturning both chair and table. As he lurched drunkenly toward her, Seren side-stepped, her right fist drawn back to flatten an already misshapen nose. She hesitated. It was as if the man had grown an extra head. An instant later, Seren saw that the second face belonged to Henry, who was on the man's back, holding on by his fingers, which were clawed into the man's mouth, distorting his face into a grimace. He clutched at the arms over his shoulders and staggered into the upturned table.

A black fist thudded into the man's midsection with all of Marley's weight behind it, felling him to the floor with Henry still on his back. A heartbeat later, when the publican arrived with a short club in one hand, it was all over. Henry was getting to his feet and wiping his fingers on his breeks, a look of triumph in his eyes. Alan and Neil stood close by, disappointed that there was nothing for them to do with their clenched fists.

"Matthew," Seren began.

"I seen it all," said the publican. "You an' yer crew ain't t'blame fer nothin'. Fact is, they saved me the trouble o' straightenin' the bastard out meself."

"Who is he?" asked Henry, still triumphant.

"His name is Enoch," said Marley, as he turned the groaning body over with his foot. "He's been drinking what he stole from Damon's shore-going poke."

He bent and pulled a purse from Enoch's belt. Made of highly polished red leather with the letter D fine-tooled onto its top flap, it did not belong near Enoch's cracked leather jacket and grubby, food-stained shirt.

Matthew the publican nodded.

"I had 'im pegged for a wrong'un from the beginnin', but he showed me coin enough for me to serve 'im, so what could I do?" His eyes scanned all of their faces, lingering on Seren's frown. "Miz Seren, gimme a chance to tidy up a bit, and mebbe you'll all be takin' something to eat an' drink."

He summoned a stout man in a cook's apron and the red-haired pot-boy. The cook took Enoch's shoulders and the boy his feet with practiced skill, and they headed for the door with their groaning burden sagging between them.

"Ah… what are you planning to do with …" Seren began.

"What about him?" Henry chimed in. "He's thinkin' o' getting up again. What if he…"

"Ain't goin' to happen," said Matthew. "They'll plonk him down on the wharf, or if you like, sling him into the harbour. Your choice, miz Seren."

"The wharf will do, thank you," said Seren.

Matthew gave instructions and then continued to ply them with seemingly innocent chatter that was belied by the searching glances from his cunning black eyes. He herded them away from the wreckage to a table with five chairs.

"We bin gettin' strangers through here lately, Miz Seren, an' I don't mean folks like your fam'ly an' crew from Matris, what we all like to see bringin' us good thing to buy an' spendin' yer coin here at Charton. No, we bin getting' sojers from up country at the Castle, an' they was ridin' this great mechanical contraption. 'Twern't all that reliable, 'cause no sooner had it got here than it broke down. Sojers aboard it was fair scuppered. Sat here in me pub drinkin' an' blamin' each other 'til a spry young feller told 'em he could fix it. An' he did, right enough, next mornin', an' they was away back north. 'Markable feller he was, too. Well spoken, coin comin' out o' his purse right generous."

"Where did he come from?" asked Seren, as they took chairs around one of the larger tables.

"Dunno. Came on foot, out the west," said Matthew, with judicious lack of precision.

Seren mouthed 'Fred' at Marley, who nodded.

"'E was sharp, right enough. All smilin' while 'e was askin' questions. Kept the sojers drinkin' an' talkin' til right late in the evenin'."

"He went north with them?" asked Marley.

"Too right 'e did. Ridin' on the wagon what was pulled by the great engine."

*Cygnet's* crew glanced at each other and said nothing.

"Nar then, what can I get for all you folks to eat and drink?"

Seren sat silent during most of the to-and-fro of the ordering process. When Matthew bustled off to the bar and kitchen, and the three boys began reliving the dispatch of Enoch, she spoke quietly to Marley.

"We have to be on our way, and soon. I'm guessing that it'll take at least a day for Ellie to reach the road to the Castle, maybe more. I don't want her meeting the soldiers in their machine."

"Specially if there's someone aboard who can recognize her," said Marley.

"Do you think Fred would turn against her?"

Marley shrugged.

"He likes machines. Parlayed his skill for a ride to where there's a…"

"Cannon…"

She breathed the word quietly, her eyes on the publican and his pot-boy as they neared the table, laden with mugs, plates, and bowls. Before Matthew could begin his soothing chatter, Seren intervened.

"Matthew, I'd like you to take charge of the man your people carried outside a few minutes ago. Put him in a room, give him food to eat and water to drink, and don't let him go for at least a day. Keep score of your costs. Marley, give him an advance payment."

"Right you are, missus."

Matthew slid plates onto the table, nodded and withdrew. Seren waited until her crew were silently chewing their first bites of food before she spoke in a low voice.

"Here's what's going to happen. We'll finish up here, sleep aboard tonight, and soon as it's light Marley and I are heading north on foot — horses if we can find someone willing to …"

"My uncle's got horses," said Henry eagerly.

"See what you can do. Marley will go with you to arrange things after we've done eating. Now, which of you has been along the cliff path to Matris recently?"

Neil's hand went up a little faster than Alan's

"Neil, tomorrow you'll take a message to Lindey that I'll write after the meal. Alan, you're leading hand while we're away. Keep Cygnis in good shape, snugged down harbour-fashion, watered and ready to sail, one person aboard at all times. We'll leave you coin, but only one drink each per day. Now, enjoy your meal."

The boys looked at each other and simultaneously decided their best course of action was to eat now and talk later. Marley and Seren contrived to spoon stew and chew bread with their hands clasped together under the table. Matthew covertly watched all of them. When Marley reached for Damon's depleted purse, the innkeeper sidled across the taproom, hands folded ingratiatingly in front of him.

"Miz Seren, I hate to tell yer, but that feller we dumped on the quay … well, he ain't there no more."

# Chapter 23: In which Astreya enters the Castle

Astreya's feet hurt. They were more bruised than blistered, but he could not make up his mind which was worse. He no longer led Esme the carthorse so much as he half-leaned, half-hung on her neck, gripping the hame of her horse collar.

It had taken time to get Esme into her intricate hauling harness. As Astreya pulled the collar out of the big saddlebag, along with its many straps, chains, buckles, and rings, the stone on his arm tingled. The sensation was both incoherent and numbingly strong, causing him to drop a jingling handful of chains on his feet. He stood, expecting a message, but the sensations faded away. Doubly confused, he went back to a task he had never done on his own.

His bumbling alerted Maisie not only to his unfamiliarity with the gear, but also how his ineptness could be turned to advantage. She guided him through the sequence in which collar, back pad, hip straps and britchen were positioned to support the traces from the hames to the drawbar of the cart. She gave each element its name and function in a tone of voice suitable for instructing a child or lackwit. Astreya nodded dutifully as he fumbled with leather straps and buckles. Esme stood patiently, lowering her big head for him to position the nose and browbands, the crown, and the throat latch.

Equipping the big horse from nose to tail took time, and Orme was in a hurry to get on their way. When Maisie explained that they would have to lengthen the reins for them to reach the extra distance to the wagon over its long draw-bar, his patience ran out. He ordered Astreya to guide Esme by walking at the horse's head. Before she climbed into the wagon, Maisie shot Astreya a covert apologetic glance. He stared at his feet, imitating Esme's unquestioning acceptance of fate. He had not gone more than a few paces before he heard Maisie introduce herself to the soldiers in the wagon.

"Gentlemen, I'm Marie Louise de La Tour d'Auvergne… but you can call me Maisie. Please don't step on my cat."

Astreya, strode out, remembered, and went back to his old-man shuffle. She had known his name when they first met, but she had not offered hers. The string of words that he had just heard was pretentious, but nobody laughed. He was sure that none of them were about to call her anything except miss, ma'am, or a respectful mumble. She had taken control of the situation with the same note of command that had completely overwhelmed him when they met. Now that her voice was directed at someone else, he could appreciate her ability.

As he walked at the head of the slow-moving procession, Astreya heard Maisie explain why a man, a woman, two riding horses and a cart-horse should be on the road to the Castle. She spoke of sailors who had come in a black ship to pillage and loot her homestead, from which only she and her lack-wit servant had escaped. At first, Astreya was piqued to be characterized as slow-witted, even if it was to keep his identity secret, and for a few plodding paces, he ignored how she was embellishing her lie. However, as she went on, he heard a catch in her voice as she spoke of men throwing burning torches through the windows of her home. He detected a shudder as she told of the cut throats and headless bodies of lifelong servants. He wondered what and how much was true. Some of what he was hearing was consistent with what she had told him earlier, but now the facts behind her story had changed. Her account of running from a fire to a stable held the ring of truth and was consistent with what she had told him of riding west with Ellie. But what of her lie that she had led her plowman and horse to the road along which they were making their slow, laborious way?

Throughout her story, none of the men in the wagon said a word. Astreya was not surprised by half a dozen men letting a talkative woman run on until they no longer heeded her, but he was curious why he had not heard anything from Fred. Had Fred recognized him? Was he biding his time until he could be helpful? Or was he waiting for the chance to unmask both of them as enemies of Carl and the Castle? Astreya walked on, pondering the disturbingly flexible story told by 'call me Maisie.'

And as he tramped along beside Esme he wondered what could have happened to Ellie. He had heard a soldier ask about a girl, and the captain's reply. But was the girl Ellie? And if so, how had she escaped? Had Fred seen her? Where could she go? As he grew more and more tired, he began to question whether Maisie had indeed been travelling with Ellie, and even wondered whether somehow Maisie had deceived her into talking about him, and then silenced her. That was worse than the thought of Ellie left behind in the forest. Astreya gripped Esme's harness to ease the pain in his hip. Absorbed in unpleasant possibilities, he stared ahead, seeing nothing but the strip of grass down which he and the big horse plodded.

They stopped briefly to water all three horses at a stream where a fierce spring run-off had washed through the road's surface right down to its gravel base. Perhaps fearful that Esme would not be able to pull the wagon back up to the other side of the gully, Orme had shouted "Keep going!" but the big horse had other ideas. Esme was thirsty, and she was going to drink, no matter who said what.

Astreya drank as gratefully as the three horses. He stayed near Esme partly from tiredness, partly to maintain his role as Maisie's servant. However, he was close enough to hear Fred gravely reporting to Orme that the soldier who had been hit on the head was still unconscious. Whenever Maisie looked in Astreya's direction she avoided meeting his eyes, deepening his worst suspicions. When horses and people were ready to move forward again, Esme leaned into her collar and forged on through the water and back up to the roadway as if to reprove Orme for doubting her strength.

An afternoon of hot, almost windless hours passed slowly. Unbroken forest crowded the road on both sides. The pain in Astreya's hip worsened. Late in the day, he started to notice the occasional logging track. Later still, he trudged past rough side-roads leading into cut-over scrub. Eventually, they left the forest behind, and he was able to look past split-rail fences at fields that stretched out on both sides as far as he could see. The two wheel-marks in the road between which he plodded divided into four, the ruts deepened, and countless hoof marks scarred the grassy strip between them. Eventually, the four brown traces blurred into a wide bare-earth road.

Esme slowed and snorted dust from her nose. Astreya rubbed his eyes. The haze that had hung in the distance resolved into a smudge of smoke from many chimneys above a tangle of roofs. It would soon be supper-time for the people who lived in the town beside the Castle.

Sensing that their journey was almost over, Esme quickened her pace, and Astreya hobbled faster. To his right, glimpsed under Esme's chin, he saw a rough, red-stone wall that appeared and disappeared into the distance as the land lumped and hollowed. Soon, it was only a narrow field away. Astreya saw flint shards gleaming on its top, higher than a tall man could reach, and his tired mind recognized the same wall he had climbed by moonlight with Lindey, Eva, Damon, and Gar, more than two decades earlier.

On his left, well-spaced slate-roofed cottages crouched in their gardens, some of them overgrown and abandoned. Then before Astreya could wonder which was the Widow Amy's home where he had stayed so long ago, he was between two-storey brick houses set side by side, some of them crowded close up against the wall to his right, which was now more than twice its out-of-town height. The day had been waning as they approached the Castle, and the road was in shadow, smudged by smoke. Esme's pace slowed once more, her head lowered, and she huffed air out her nose. Astreya smelled wood fires, food, and a mixture of less pleasant smells from many people living close together. Through open windows, he heard voices raised to quiet children, argue, order, or complain. Tired, uncomfortable, and made stupid by weariness, he puzzled why there was nobody in the road. They came to an intersection offering four or five alternatives.

"Sam! Hey! You with the horse! Keep to the right."

Orme's voice recalled Astreya to the role he was playing. He nudged Esme with his shoulder, and they trudged on, past a continuous line of houses that leaned against each other, with the wall looming over their roof-tops. Then as the road widened again, Esme stopped, awaiting instructions. Astreya peered past her big head.

There, built into the tall red wall, exactly as he remembered it, was the Castle's gatehouse. It towered higher than any of the houses, its gabled roof frowning down on the intersection of five narrow, shadowed roads that wound into a town so over-built that the houses looked like a single, jumbled building. Piercing the middle of the gatehouse was a red brick arch, its wooden doors swung back, the whole structure framing a spire that gleamed in the last light of the sun.

Astreya stood transfixed by memory. He mumbled the words Gar had spoken two decades earlier.

"They got the composition right. Must have been an accident."

Astreya thought back to that summer when he had learned to paint, fallen in love with Lindey, discovered he could prevail in a brawl, but then failed to fight off Carl when the hall caught fire and Gar fell to his death. His fingers felt for his stone in its clasp under his shirt, as if he were feeling its power for the first time.

Maisie's voice jerked Astreya out of his reverie. Her tone was condescending.

"Sam, you stay with the horses. Captain Orme gave Mr. Fredericks and me directions to the inn where he's staying. The Jug and Bottle, wasn't it? Sounds so enchanting."

Astreya grunted an acknowledgement in keeping with his role of simple servant. Orme's voice came from the wagon.

"Hurry. The watch will be making their rounds any time now."

"Have Sam look after my cat, Captain Orme!" said Maisie in her splendid lady voice. "Come then, Mr. Fredericks. Let us make our way to the inn."

There was still enough light for Astreya to see Maisie's hand on Fred's arm, graciously accepting accompaniment.

Orme's voice startled Astreya as he stared after them.

"Through the gate, old man. We're almost there."

Astreya clucked his tongue to Esme, who lowered her head and took the strain with a reproving grunt. As they entered the tunnel through the gatehouse, the steady clopping of her big hooves echoed many times louder. They emerged into a huge grassy area cris-crossed by brown-earth paths to and among large buildings that were only dark shapes in the failing light.

"Go left, down to the stables."

Esme responded quicker than Astreya, swinging in a wide turn to allow for the wagon to follow her. Behind them, the clopping sound redoubled as the two horses behind the cart entered the tunnel.

The ground sloped downwards under Astreya's feet. He almost fell, saving himself by grabbing Esme's harness. He had staggered for a dozen or more paces when the big horse abruptly stopped.

Astreya almost fell into a horse trough, in which Esme was already slurping up the water that she had been craving for too many miles and hours.

Astreya splashed water into his face, almost lost his hat, then cupping his hands at the pipe that was feeding the trough, he drank until he had to stop and gasp for air.

"Prrrp!"

A weight landed on his shoulder. Orme's voice was at his ear.

"That's her cat. Take it with you to the stables. There'll be someone there who'll help you unsaddle. Now move out of the way; there's two thirsty horses waiting."

# Chapter 24: In which sisters meet

Ellie had been walking steadily for more than two hours since the wagon disappeared ahead of her along the road to the Castle. Occasionally, she shifted her satchel from one shoulder to the other. Once or twice, as the road climbed over one of the low hills along the way, she thought she glimpsed two horses tied to the back of the wagon, but at the next rise, the road ahead was empty. As she walked, Ellie tried to organize the questions that rattled around her mind like loose peas in a pod.

*Was that Astreya? If so, why was he pretending to be an old man? What was he doing this far ashore in the first place? What was Maisie thinking? Didn't she notice his limp? Had they been taken prisoner? Or had they contrived a passage to the Castle? And if so, why? What was Fred planning? Why had he helped her escape? What were all three of them hiding from her? How much further was the Castle?*

"Well, if I'm to find out, I'll have to rescue them first," said Ellie to the road ahead of her.

When Ellie reached the stream where Esme had stopped to drink, her stomach told her that it had been a long time since the bannock and tea that had started her day's journey. Gravel crunched under her feet as she took the last few strides down to the water, where she drank from her cupped hands, then sat and rummaged in her satchel. She found a fist-size loaf of bread, densely packed with dried fruit. It was chewy but astonishingly satisfying.

Ellie lay back and gazed up at a sky so blue that her eyes watered. She did not know where she was going, or what she would do when she got there, but her stone had responded to her will, however briefly, and though all was not as it was, the moment had somehow retrieved her confidence. The past few days receded into memory, her eyes closed and she dozed. Ellie daydreamed of a green stone, horses' clopping hoofs, and voices.

"Slow down, Marley. There's someone beside the stream. Maybe they can tell us how far we are from … ELLIE!"

Seren's long legs took her down the rattling gravel in two huge strides. Ellie stood up, bewildered by a dream turned real. Seren picked her up and hugged her so tight that when Ellie said Seren's name it came out in a breathy hiss. They would have fallen into the stream had not Marley thrown his arms around both of them. The three stood linked together, swaying, unable to say anything except each other's names. Then all three asked the same question:

"How did you get here?"

Ellie stifled a sob.

*I'm not going to go all mushy and cry on their shoulders. I'm not.*

"I walked," said Ellie firmly. "Then I rode a horse. Then I rode a steam-driven chariot, until it blew up. Then I walked."

Seren and Marley gave her puzzled looks.

"No, really," said Ellie. "I'm not crazy."

"Of course not," said Marley.

*Thanks for trying, Marley, but you don't know what to think, neither does Seren, and I can't find words to tell you.*

"This morning we were in Charton," said Seren brightly.

*You didn't even look for me before that?*

"Wow," said Ellie. "You were quick."

They did not hear the sarcasm in her voice.

"We rode," said Marley, pointing at the two horses, which were already drinking at the stream.

"We followed your stone," said Seren.

Ellie stepped back out of Seren's arms, frowned, and bit her lip. When she spoke, her voice was deliberately flat and emotionless.

"My stone hasn't worked since I fell out of *Spindrift*," she said, avoiding their eyes.

"But Ellie, Marley and I could feel you, off and on. You know, the way a stone gets blanketed behind cliffs or thick trees or…"

"Seren, my stone's not working. No spear of light," said Ellie. "Nothing, except for the occasional prickling feeling on my arm."

"Oh, Ellie," said Seren, her blue eyes wide. "What happened?"

*Now I have to tell her. But I don't want to.*

"I… got lost. Couldn't control my stone. Nothing but a greenish fuzz, with occasional tingles," she said, wondering as she spoke if she had imagined them.

"When did the tingles happen, Ellie?" Marley asked.

"There was one about two hours ago. I thought I saw Astreya. There was a man leading a horse that looked like Esme. They were headed north pulling the big wagon that had been behind the land crawler — the big, black engine that blew up.

"We saw it," said Marley. "Abandoned. We passed it on our way here."

"It must have been Astreya's stone you were following," said Ellie.

"That explains it," said Marley. "Damon saw Astreya as he left Matris aboard a carthorse. He was sure Astreya had a shipstone with him. He must be ahead, on the way to the Castle. Damon said…"

Ellie interrupted him.

"A shipstone? One of the big ones I found at the Village? I asked him what he was planning to do with them. That was two … three… oh, many days ago."

"He handed out clasp stones to Cam, Damon, Alan, and Marley," said Seren. "There was one for Fred, too, but he'd disappeared."

"Wow. What a turnaround. When I told him that's what he should do, he fobbed me off with 'all in good time.'"

"You spoke to him about handing out stones beyond the family?" Seren asked.

"Yes I did. He wasn't a bit pleased. I asked him why he hadn't done anything with the stones I found, and he got all stern and reprimanded me for asking him. That's when I took Fred to Half Moon Bay."

Marley looked thoughtful.

"You must have got him thinking. Then when we couldn't find you, he must have changed his mind."

*He came to look for me. And when I saw him, I didn't even know him.*

"Damon's friend Enoch turned up with news about the cannon that fired at you. After that, Astreya reassigned the ships and headed north on his own," said Seren.

"He did what?"

"Mairi commands Cygnus, Trogen keeps *Elusive*, I have *Cygnet*," said Seren. "Lindey takes charge of defending Matris, and the three of us commanders are charged with teaching our first mates the lore of the stones."

Ellie looked from one of them to the other.

"Then it really was him and Esme on the way to Charton," said Ellie slowly. "What was he doing with Maisie? And how did Fred get aboard the wagon?"

"Fred left Matris before Astreya handed out the stones," said Marley.

"Who's Maisie?" Seren asked.

"Maisie's the person who found me, two days after the attack on *Spindrift*. I'd been walking around the forest, and I was … I was a mess. She put me back together, and then her cottage burned down and her animals were killed, all because of me having black hair."

"We saw the burned-out cottage," said Seren.

"Maisie knew the soldiers would come looking for me, so she set me on an old forest road. I saw them burn down her cottage and kill her goose and goat. I thought she was dead, too. So I walked west, hoping that I'd eventually be able to head south to Charton. But Maisie wasn't dead. She caught up with me, on horseback, along with her cat. And she even had a second horse for me. Eventually, we got to this north-south road and were all set to head for Matris, when along came the land crawler. It spooked the horse I was riding, and … and the soldiers caught me."

Seren and Marley stared at her.

"You were captured?" Seren asked.

Ellie nodded.

"It was weird. Fred was with the soldiers. He pretended he didn't know me, and then when the crawler blew up, he helped me escape."

"We heard from the landlord of The Black Sheep that Fred left Charton after fixing the soldiers' land crawler," said Marley. But how and when did Astreya get mixed up with the soldiers, the crawler and the woman — Maisie?"

"And what's Fred up to?" asked Seren.

"I don't know," said Ellie.

They fell silent. Ellie looked at the horses, which had finished drinking and were standing in the stream as if waiting for instructions.

"Only way to find out is to follow. You can ride with me," said Seren.

"Not too quickly," said Marley. "We can't just gallop up and demand answers from everyone."

"Then let's mount up and follow at a distance," said Seren.

*You both distrust Maisie because you don't know her, and Fred because you do. The trouble is, so do I.*

Wondering if she had spoken out loud, Ellie let herself follow her sister's plan. Seren added Ellie's satchel and cloak to her saddlebags, she and Marley mounted their horses, and as Ellie took Seren's hand to get up behind her, they both hesitated.

"Did you feel that?" Seren asked.

Ellie nodded. Her arm tingled from her clasp to her finger-ends. For a moment, they both wondered whether the prickling came from one or both of them. The sensation faded before either of them could decide.

"Up you get," said Seren, tightened her grip and hauled Ellie up behind her.

"What's happening?" Marley asked. "It feels like messaging, but ... louder."

All three pushed up the sleeves on their left arms.

"It's back!" Ellie exclaimed. "And it's pointing north! What did you do?"

"Nothing," said Seren."

Marley shook his head, setting his ropes of hair swinging. All three stared at the green jewels on their arms.

"A bit east of north," said Ellie. "Steady, strong, but sort of muffled — like a shipstone that's been shielded."

All three spoke at the same time.

"Astreya."

*I didn't believe it ... me... when I was near Astreya. But just now, I was first to feel the shipstone!*

~^~

Through the rest of the afternoon, they rode on towards the Castle. As the shadows grew longer, they saw the red wall on their right in the distance. All three had been consulting their stones from time to time, so when the road curved towards the northwest to avoid the wall, they knew they were no longer aiming at the signal from the shipstone and Astreya. They conferred, and decided to cut cross country directly towards the Castle wall. The land was neither fenced nor tended, allowing them to make their way without reference to anything except the guidance from their stones.

The ground undulated irregularly. They were soon out of sight of the road, with only intermittent glimpses of the wall as they topped one of the many low rises. Soon one of these ever more frequent views revealed a spire and the tops of buildings within the wall. Eventually, they found themselves on a rough track running in its shadow, which they followed southwards looking for a gate, or a break in the head-high red stone.

Because she was riding behind Seren, Ellie was able to concentrate on her stone, growing more and more confident each time she consulted it.

"Astreya's over to our left now," said Ellie. "Ride closer to the wall and then stop. I think I might be able to see over if I stand up."

Seren coaxed her horse closer to the rough stone. With her feet on the horse's rump and her hands on Seren's shoulders, Ellie peered over the jagged flints set into its top.

"It's… oh, I don't know … a few minutes' walk from the wall to the first of five or six big buildings. They're two or three stories high, I'd guess, and one of them has a spire. There's light in a few of the windows. I can't see any people, but it's getting harder to see anything but shapes and shadows. The sun's almost gone."

"The track by the wall is no better than when we joined it," said Marley. "It doesn't look good for finding a way in — other than wherever the main gate is."

His horse huffed air out its nose and bobbed its head up and down. As if agreeing, so did Seren's. Ellie's feet wobbled, and she sat back behind her sister.

"They smell water," said Marley.

"I think I saw some," said Ellie. "A gleam as the sun went behind the buildings."

They gave the horses their heads. With the reins slack, the two animals followed the track down into a gully. The clatter of their hooves tapping their way downhill mixed with the sound of water running over stones. They slid from their horses' backs and let them drink. Marley spoke quietly, his voice barely audible over the sound of the stream.

"There has to be a …"

"…hole in the wall."

Ellie finished his thought as she scrambled alongside the stream towards the wall.

"Ellie, be careful. It's dark and…" Seren whispered.

"I can see just fine, Seren. There's a tunnel. When I stoop over, I can see through. It's shallow enough to wade. I'm going in. You two stay here, look after the horses, maybe make camp for the night."

"Ellie!" Seren began.

"Don't fuss, Seren. I'll be back. As soon as I find Astreya I'll message you."

"Are you sure …?"

"'Course I am. My stone's working again."

Ellie shouldered her satchel, stepped out of the riding trousers Maisie had leant her, and into the water. The first step took her calf deep. She gasped at the cold, and then her second step brought the water to her knees. The stream got no deeper, although it tugged at her legs. Holding her shoes and the loose-legged garment bundled in her arms, she let her toes find their way on the sandy-smooth bottom, feeling her way forward in short steps. The arch loomed over her head and the rushing water was louder in the tunnel. Green light from her clasp flickered on the water's surface and was lost in the rough stonework overhead. When Maisie's wool hat touched the invisible roof, Ellie almost dropped her clothes and shoes. After two more cautious steps, she was past the lowest point of the archway. Soon the sky was above her and was able to stand up straight. She looked through the grasses at the top of the stream's banks across a rolling meadow to the cluster of buildings she had seen from the other side of the wall.

"I'm in!" she called softly into the dark mouth of the tunnel.

Hearing no answer, she waded out of the stream, up the steep bank, then pulled on her loose trousers and shoved her wet feet into her shoes. Then she consulted her stone and followed the bright line at its centre.

# Chapter 25: In which Ellie finds Astreya

As the light of gloaming faded from the western sky, Astreya sat in the doorway of the Castle's stables. He was exhausted. He rubbed absent-mindedly at his hip, where the pain that had stabbed him at every step was diminishing to a dull ache. Behind him, three horses were making small sounds as they settled in for the night. A hoof pecked on the floor; straw rustled; steady champing told him that at least one of them was still pulling hay from his feeding basket.

Two soldiers had helped him unsaddle the riding horses, and undo the many buckles on Esme's harness. Then they shared the tasks of watering, feeding, and rubbing down before putting the horses into stalls for the night. Now the soldiers were lounging on bales of straw, putting off their return to barracks. They ignored Astreya, no doubt thinking him too stupid to matter.

"Dunno how long t'will be afore we can be goin' home."

"Don't be sayin' that sort'a stuff, Dick. It ain't healthy. 'Sides, we get paid right well."

"More coin, but it don't go as far as it did. Everything costs more. No point in a full purse if it don't buy you nothin'."

"You got all y'need for beer, an' then some."

"But if I were only back home, I could be usin' it fer seed, and me animals, and mebbe some cloth fer the wife."

"Y'still don't get it, do ya?"

"Watcher mean?"

"We're sojers now, Dick. We're stuck. No goin' home 'till them blackhead sailors is dead an' gone."

"They never bothered me. Far as I'm concerned, they can sail up an' down as long as they like, s'long as they let me plow me field and tend me animals."

"You'll be in a whole lot o' trouble if they hear you talkin' like that."

"Listen, I don't hold with all this defendin' our people stuff. Look what it got Ernie. Big hole in the head, an' it weren't from no foreigner, neither. Wouldn't want to be the one what's got to tell his missus he was killed by Sandy's steamer. Happen I'll bugger off home afore I'm next."

"You do, an' they catch you, you'll wish you hadn't."

"Horsefeathers."

"By rights, I should report you fer plannin' desertion, offerin' comfort to th'enemy, an' stuff like that. Stuff they could really work you over for, just fer havin' said it."

"Like to see some o' them bully-boys try it."

"Hold it, Dick. Someone comin'."

A yellow light bobbed towards them. A boy appeared at the stable door with a lantern in one hand and a large covered basket in the other.

"Lookin' fer the ol' man, name o' Sam, what came wi' the big horse."

"Over here, lad," said Astreya.

"Beer, bread, an' stew," said the boy. "Y'can thank the lady wi' the red hair. An' Cap'n Orme, too, he what gave me the pass t'get through the gates. They said for you to be ready wi' the big horse termorrer. Now I has to be back t'pub right quick."

As he put the basket beside Astreya, one of the soldiers spoke from the shadows in the stable.

"What'cha got fer us?"

The boy spoke over his shoulder as he headed back towards the gatehouse.

"Cap'n ordered 'nuff fer three"

Astreya rummaged in the basket. His fingers discovered three lidded bowls, three stone bottles and six thick slices of bread. The two soldiers joined him at the stable doorstep. While he listened to the sounds of them chewing and swallowing, Astreya devised a question that would make him sound like a simpleton.

"What's it like bein' a sojer?

"He's thinkin' o' joinin' up," sniggered the soldier named Dick.

"'T'aint too bad. The cap'n is whatcher call reasonable. Not like some. 'E does what he's ordered t'do, an' so do we. Like we were when bein' hauled around by that damn steamer."

"That ain't goin' to happen again very soon," said Dick with satisfaction. "Mebbe we jus sit around here in barracks fer a while."

"Not likely. I heard they're bringin' the cannon back here."

"An how're they doin' that, without their great machine?" Astreya asked.

"Horses, o'course. Same as before Sandy got the crawler goin'," said Dick.

"Fat lot o' good it all did fer Ernie. 'E ain't goin' t'make it back to his wife an' kids."

"Hush there, Will."

"Get stuffed, Dick. Nobody here but Simple Sam, an' he ain't tellin' nobody nuffin'."

"Finish up yer beer. We gotta get back to barracks afore it's so dark we can't see."

"You hankerin' after Ernie's corporal stripes? Risin' in the ranks, like?"

"Don't you put me down, Dick. Happen Orme will recognize me merit an' loyaty to the cause."

"Happen he'll notice you kissin' his arse."

"Up yours. I'm out o' here"

Will stood, brushed crumbs off his uniform, and strode off towards a building with light coming from its ground-level windows. Dick watched him go, leaned back against the doorpost, crossed his ankles, and belched.

"Good beer," said Astreya.

"Better'n what we get over there in barracks. Seems there ain't never enough fer all, even wi' half of us away east wi' the cannon."

Grunts and swearing came from the direction taken by the ambitious soldier. The other chuckled, crossed his ankles, and took a pull at his beer bottle.

"So keen t' be back, ol' Will fell in the hole where they dug out the crawler."

Astreya chose his words with care.

"Someone find that great machine under the earth? Don't seem likely to me."

"Believe it. When they dug it up, it were all in bits, but Sandy — Colonel Sanderson, that is — fixed it up hisself, workin' away in the cellar for weeks. That's where he found the cannon, too. An' its ammunition. An' all kinds o' other stuff, as well. Hidden it all was, back in the Before."

"Go on. They never found a thing like that there," said Astreya.

"'Deed they did. Seems they was fixin' up the big old building what burned down many a year ago, an' someone fell through the floor into a hidey-hole bigger'n a house, all filled with stuff from Before."

"Y'don't say," said Astreya slowly.

Out of the darkness came the sound of Will's voice calling for help and cursing his luck.

"That were Will we heard fallin' into the big ditch they dug to get the cannon an' the crawler out from under. I'd better go haul him out now, or I'll be 'splaining to the cap'n why he's missin' another sojer. A few more casualties, an I'll be the only one left."

He tipped back his bottle to drink the last drops, stood, put the bottle into the basket, and patted Astreya on the back.

"Night, now, old feller. Don't go lightin' no lanterns. We don't want all that straw n' hay to burn, an' all the horses wi' it."

Astreya made an affirmative grunt and watched Dick walk away. A short while later, the cursing redoubled, then all was silent. Astreya thought back to when he and his uncle had painted birds, animals and people under the dome of what had been the library. Then, the Castle had been filled with the green-gowned Learneds and Healers, along with their retinue of students, scholars, and apprentices as well as a contingent of servants, cooks, gardeners, and ostlers to serve them, not to mention the company of women tucked away in one of the big buildings where they were taught their 'women's role' as nurses. Looking out into the darkened Castle grounds, Astreya could see only a few lighted windows — not enough to account for even a fraction of those who used to live within the walled community.

A shadow moved among the shadows. Astreya frowned, stared into the gloom, but saw nothing. Deciding that he was mistaken, he got to his feet, flinching as the weight came on his bruised feet, travelled up his leg and was amplified by his hip.

"Astreya!"

He looked around, saw nothing, and shook his head.

"Astreya!"

"Who is it?"

"S'me, Uncle. Ellie."

"Eliana!"

"Shh…"

"They're gone."

A slim figure appeared beside him. Hesitantly, he held out his hands towards her, but she stepped between them and hugged him tight. He patted her back awkwardly, one hand bumping into her satchel. Sensing his hesitation, Ellie stepped back and looked up into the shadows of his face.

"Are you all right Uncle? Everyone's looking for you. Where's Fred and Maisie? Why haven't you messaged? Are you hurt?"

She heard what might be the beginnings of a laugh.

"Ellie, it's you we've been looking for. What happened? Why didn't you message?"

"Couldn't. My stone failed on me. Or I failed it. Or something. Anyway, I was lost."

"You lost your clasp?"

Even in the semi-darkness, Astreya saw hair gleam as Ellie shook her head.

"It's working again now. It … I don't know … it pulsed a few times when I thought I saw you. But it wasn't until I met up with Seren and Marley …"

"Aren't they aboard *Cygnet*?"

Ellie shook her head again.

"They're outside the Castle wall, beside a stream. I waded in."

"The wet way," Astreya murmured, remembering the night when Lindey and he had fled after Gar died.

"Only up to my knees. I had to stoop to get through the tunnel. Listen, Uncle, we can find it by heading towards Seren and Marley's clasps. You'll have to keep your head down when you wade through. Then we can ride double, get you home …"

"It's you who should go back. I can't leave."

"Why? What are you planning to do?"

"I have to return Maisie's cat."

*For sure, that's not the reason.*

"Uncle, we can take Curmudgeon with us."

Ellie felt a warm pressure below her knees. She frowned.

"Prrrp!"

"Where's Maisie?" she asked.

"Prrp, rrrrp,"

*I didn't ask you, cat.*

"Maisie's in the town at an inn. Fred, as well."

"Then let's get them. We can leave by the stream, ride around to the town. Do you know which inn?"

"Ellie, no. It's you who must leave. There are things I have to do here." His voice fell lower than a murmur. "I have to make things right."

Ellie heard the words Astreya had not meant her to hear. She stood very still, trying to reconcile her respect for her uncle with a sudden awareness that what he was planning was so dangerous that he did not want anyone involved.

"Things are going to be all right now, Uncle. I'm fine, everyone's safe. Let's go home."

"Everyone won't be safe unless I …"

Then Astreya's hand pressed down on her shoulder as he lurched forward, almost falling. She staggered under his weight.

"Sorry. Sitting too long after walking a bit too far for a sailor. Eliana, there's a couple of bales of straw inside on the left. Could you lend me your shoulder while we…"

Astreya's voice, which had been tight with pain, trailed off. He took shallow breaths through clenched teeth as they shuffled through the stable door into the dark, where he turned, felt for the bales, sank onto them and leaned against the wall. He sat in silence while Ellie listened to his breathing gradually returning to normal.

"Thank you, Eliana. Back out on the step, there's a basket that still holds some bread and stew. Probably cold by now, but if you're hungry, please help yourself."

Ellie felt her way back out the door by trailing her fingers over the rough wood of a wall. She found the basket and the bottle of beer beside it and brought them back to Astreya, who refused the food but accepted the beer. The stew was cold, but Ellie was fiercely hungry, so she used the bread to scoop up what was left. As she ate, she worried about how Astreya had evaded, hinted, and avoided her questions. Remembering how he had shut her down when she had talked frankly about what he should do with the stones, she looked for an inoffensive opening.

"Why did you dye your beard, Uncle?"

"Because they hate us for what we've done."

*That's a mighty strange answer to my question.*

"We haven't done anything to them."

"Oh yes, we have, Eliana. We're the black-haired Men of the Sea who steal children, pillage and burn."

*Does he want to be guilty?*

"You never did those things. And anyway, it's long ago."

"Not for him," Astreya muttered. "He's fired them all up with old tales retold, elaborated, and embellished."

"Who?"

Astreya did not answer.

"Uncle…" Ellie began.

"That's enough, Eliana. When you're done eating, you have to leave. If they see your black hair, they'll… well, just make sure they don't. Seren, and Marley mustn't go anywhere near the town. They'll stand out, attract attention, set off … unfriendly reactions. So all three of you should head back to Matris as soon as it's light enough to see where you're going."

*That's not going to happen. Not as long as you're not yourself.*

Ellie considered how Astreya's voice started firm and commanding, then shaded into anxious concern. She tried not to sound as if she was arguing.

"Uncle, in a little while, when you're feeling up to it, you can tell me where Maisie and Fred are, so I can fetch them. Then we'll all cross the open ground to where the stream tunnels under the wall. I'll help you through. In the morning, we can take turns riding the horses, and we should be able …"

"That's not going to work, Ellie. You must go. Please don't argue with me."

Ellie was taken aback by the pleading note in Astreya's voice, so unlike his firm, quiet way of speaking. He was almost beseeching her, which was even more difficult to disobey than a direct order. Words tumbled out of her mouth.

"There's plenty of time yet, Uncle. Let me make you comfortable first. Do you have a cloak with you? No? Surely there's a blanket around here somewhere…"

Conscious that she was babbling, Ellie started to feel along the wall in the dark. Then realizing that she need not grope blindly, she peeled back the sleeve of her blouse and looked about her in the wan green light from her stone. She recognized Esme's big rump in the stall closest to the door and guessed from the sounds of breathing that two more horses stood in the shadows. Two steps further, and she saw a ladder running up to an attic overhead. Two more steps revealed big iron hooks and rails from which hung saddles, bridles, tack and … *oh good!* … horse blankets. Ellie pulled the nearest down into her arms and returned to where Astreya lay. She saw that in her brief absence he had slumped down sideways, and was now almost reclining on the straw. His eyes were closed, his face slack. Ellie lifted his legs onto the bales and covered him with the horse-smelling blanket. The slow rhythm of his breathing did not change.

Ellie sat down to think. If she used her stone to message Seren and Marley, Astreya would undoubtedly wake, and they would likely ply her, and then him with questions.

*What to do?*

She closed her eyes to concentrate, and as she searched for possibilities, she felt the silver band around her arm thrilling to a sensation like that of an opening door, a growing light, a positively sensuous pull that was not any single wielder's stone but rather …

*The shipstone Astreya brought! Of course!*

Had she spoken out loud? Astreya had not stirred. She bent over Astreya, close enough to hear him breathing. Her awareness of the shipstone did not increase, if anything it faded.

*Not on him, WITH him! It's on Esme's harness.*

She stood, and moved silently to where she had seen the saddles and bridles. She saw the big horse collar, and the complicated straps and brass fittings that allowed Esme to apply her strength to pull a plow, a wagon —

*— or a cannon!*

The thought came unbidden and with it, disturbing speculations about Astreya's state of mind. He seemed changed, diminished, obsessively focussed on his own secret plan. Why had he brought the stone with him? To trade it? But to whom and for what? Was he planning to destroy it? Use it? If so, against whom? Or what?

*He's got to be planning something … the cannon?*

All she knew about cannons was from having been a target. Perhaps Astreya, who never revealed all he knew, might have some way of using his stone to … what? Was it a person he was aiming to kill? Like everyone in the fleet, Ellie had heard the story about how Mufrid had fallen dead without anyone having touched him. Any way she imagined Astreya's plan, she could not avoid the strong possibility that he did not intend to survive.

*And for what? No. I can't let him do that.*

Now if she only could find where the shipstone was in all the tack that hung on the shadowy wall. Rather than fumble gear that would surely jingle and wake Astreya, Ellie closed her eyes and concentrated as she would have done when navigating at sea. She turned so that her left arm was closest to the wall, and shuffled sideways. As she moved closer to Esme's tack, there it was, glowing green in her mind's eye. She stood and shuffled into the gloom, her eyes tight shut.  She smelled leather and sweat … felt leather straps … stroked canvass … touched even, tight stitches. She slid her hands down one side of the U-shaped collar to its thickest part, which took the weight of the horse's big chest.

*There it is!*

A flap the size of her palm, held tight by a drawstring, neatly fastened by a seamanlike reef knot. Her eyes still shut, she plucked, pulled, then slid her fingers into the pocket built into the padding, and touched the cool metal case that protected the shipstone.

Resisting the temptation to grab and run, she carefully pulled the egg-shaped case out of its nest in the horse collar, slid it into her satchel, and re-tied the drawstring. Then she tiptoed to the ladder, climbed until she bumped her head against a trapdoor, shoved it open, and climbed into a loft half-full of hay. She quietly lowered the door, lay down in the hay, sighed, and was instantly asleep. She did not notice when Curmudgeon curled up against her.

# Chapter 26: In which Fred and Maisie talk

When Maisie and Fred left the wagon at the gatehouse, she whispered "Keep going. Talk later," to Astreya, her voice tight. Then she patted him on the shoulder as if he were a pet, then handed Fred her saddlebags, took his arm firmly and strode across open space of the five-ways. When the looming gatehouse was behind them, Maisie's fingers relaxed. After a few paces, they were in the deep shadows of a narrow alley. Houses stood side by side, their doors at the edge of the cobbles. They were the only people abroad. Ahead, occasional patches of yellowish light escaping from windows only emphasized the gloom. Their footsteps echoed back from the close-packed houses.

"You know who that was, don't you," said Fred.

"Astreya."

"Why didn't you …? Fred began.

"What, call him by his name, maybe get him to take his hat off so that the captain could see his black hair and know he's a Man of the Sea?"

Her voice was sharp.

"How do … You know about Astreya, then."

"Enough to want to keep him alive."

"I'll go along with that."

"Glad to hear it, Mr. Fredericks. Now, tell me why you abandoned Ellie."

"She was safer on her own."

"Watching her uncle Astreya walk into danger?"

"You made him walk."

"I had to."

"So it would fit the lie you told."

"You don't believe I'm Marie-Louise de La Tour d'Auvergne."

"Not for one minute," said Fred cheerfully

"Well, you're wrong, because I am. Or rather, I was. Until that man in the Castle incited the hooligans to murder my husband and children," said Maisie.

They took several steps in silence while Fred revised his opinions.

"That's ... that's awful," he stammered.

"Yes it is," she replied.

They took a few steps further. Fred's tone of voice changed again.

"If that's so, then you know more than I do about what's been going on behind those walls."

The alley came to an abrupt end. Above, the sky was still pale blue in the gloaming, but they could hardly see where they were walking. To their right, darkened houses leaned against the Castle wall like a huddle of drunk men. To their left, wan yellow light from two upstairs windows lit a sign painted with a jug and a bottle. Fred stopped walking, took Maisie's hand off his arm and held it with exaggerated formality.

"Madame de La Tour, do me the favour of your company as we investigate what manner of food and drink this establishment has to offer. Then we can decide how to find Ellie and get Astreya out of the fix in which he has landed himself."

Maisie inclined her head in an aristocratic nod. It was too dark for Fred to see the expression on her face, but he hoped she might be smiling. He gallantly replaced her hand on his arm, and grasped the door handle to usher her in ahead of him. The door was locked. Chagrinned, Fred knocked enthusiastically.

"Taproom's closed. Curfew," said a deep male voice within.

"How about lodging?" Fred asked.

Bolts snicked back and the door opened to reveal a tall man wearing a long green apron over a white shirt and black trousers. The light of his candle gleamed on ivory-coloured hair; bushy eyebrows overhung sepulchral eyes.

"We require food and wine if you have it, beer if you don't, then two rooms," said Maisie. "Our luggage will be delivered shortly."

"Rupert, at your service. Enter."

~^~

An hour or so later, Maisie and Fred looked at each other across a table for two on which were the remains of an unexpectedly good dinner. Fred's elbow was on the table, his feet were crossed alongside it, and he wore the expression of a man who had eaten and drunk well. He reached for the dusty green bottle. A faint ringing came from the two glasses as he tipped the bottle.

"Don't pour the sediment in the heel," said Maisie.

"Wouldn't dream of it," said Fred. "Who would have thought we'd find an inn this far north that offered wine?"

"My family grew grapes a day's walk from here," Maisie spoke musingly, almost to herself. "Looking toward the sea in a valley shielded by hills that protect it from the worst of the winter. There we used to grow rich, red grapes, espaliered against a south-facing wall, growing on stony soil so the vines had to work a little harder to produce a vintage significantly better than what we're drinking now."

Fred rolled the wine around in his glass and looked at her through quarter-closed eyes. He spoke gently, but with an intensity that demanded answers.

"So, Marie-Claire de la Tour, where exactly was your tower?"

"Over the sea a long time ago, a man named Gregoire lived in the Sunny Isles, where his slaves made his fortune in sugar, tobacco and rum. He styled himself de la Tour."

Fred sipped his wine, looking at her skeptically over the brim of his glass.

"My great, great grandmother was young, beautiful, and even though he was White and she was Black..."

"Let me guess. Her name was Marie-Claire," said Fred solemnly. "And it was true love at first sight."

"Yes, it was. When the seas rose and the crops failed, her White husband freed them all and took them north in Gregoire's ship."

"Where they wished it wasn't so cold in the winter."

"Where Gregoire collected books, built a library, founded a school, ensured a continuity of learning."

Fred raised his eyebrows.

"The Castle? I'm having a little difficulty assembling the details of your story. How do we get to the part about the grapes grown in a sheltered valley a day's walk away?"

"Time, Mr. Fredericks. It all took time. Time for Gregoire's grandson, my great grandfather, to be ejected from the Tower, chiefly because he was Black. He went back to the community of people a day's journey from here who traced their ancestry back to those who had accompanied Gregoire and Marie-Claire when they fled the Sunny Isles."

Fred leaned both elbows on the table and stared at Maisie as if seeing her for the first time.

"Passing by that gatehouse cost you some serious effort."

Maisie nodded.

"Yes. And since I have come so far with my story, let me finish by saying that neither the community nor any members of my family remain. Only me. A few stones are all that's left of the wall where the vines grew." Her voice sharpened. "The peace-loving, learned men who renamed the Tower into the Castle made sure that they were all and only White. Over the years they incited the town thugs to harass the Black community. Some died, some moved away until there was only me, my husband and our two children. Who they murdered."

Fred stared at her, shocked.

"How did you....?"

"They saw me first, knocked me on the head, left me for dead. When I woke, I saw the bodies of my husband and two little ones."

Fred stared at her with wide eyes.

"How did you...?"

"I ran. I hid. I survived. I lived alone with my grief for many years. Then four days ago Ellie came to my door and I rescued her. Then more stupid White men tried to burn me as a witch. So I ran, again, this time with a black-haired, green-eyed girl."

"Um…" said Fred. "This rescuing business must be catching. You could say that Ellie rescued me. Now I suppose I have to do the same for her."

"Yes you do, Mr. Fredericks. So how do we go about it?"

"First of all, we have to get into the Castle and find out who's up to what with cannons and land crawler steam engines."

"Carl, who calls himself Governor."

"We get him to help us find Ellie and Astreya. And dissuade him from his campaign against the people of Matris."

"And request restitution for the years of evil done to me and my people?"

"That, too."

"And how do you propose to accomplish these miracles?"

"Talk persuasively, showing him the error of his ways."

"You're relying on your skill with words."

"Well, actually, I was hoping you'd do the words. My expertise is with machines."

Maisie's eyes narrowed and her lips compressed.

"Then we must trust in the ways of the Goddess."

~^~

"It's been ages since she left," said Seren.

She was pacing up and down the side of the stream from the wall to the horses cropping at a patch of grass.

"There are a great many possible reasons…" Marley began.

"Some of them deadly," said Seren, her voice tightly controlled.

"I don't know anyone more able to take care of herself than Ellie," said Marley. "Except for you," he added as Seren stopped pacing and looked down at him.

Marley sat in the shadow of the wall, leaning against his saddle. One arm rested on a bent knee, his long-fingered hand hung loose. He looked up at her and smiled, his teeth gleaming in the fast-fading light. His calm only irritated Seren. She had an urgent need to do something, now, which was exactly balanced by the knowledge that there was nothing she could do.

"Why doesn't she message? Perhaps her stone's gone dead on her again. She could be lost. Something could have happened to …"

"Most likely, she can't send because there are other people close by."

"Do you think she's in danger, or…"

"Or perhaps what she wants to tell us is not something Astreya needs to hear."

"You think he's gone crazy? I'll ask her…"

"We shouldn't message her until she does."

"Do you think she may be captured, or…"

"I don't know, Seren. But I trust Ellie's judgement."

"But not mine."

"I did not say that."

"You implied…"

In one smooth motion, Marley stood and took both of Seren's hands in his. She almost pulled away, then threw her arms around his neck and hugged him tight. The sky still glowed in the west. The horses chomped grass, the stream made faint gurgling sounds. Eventually, Seren relaxed, so did Marley, and they looked into each other's eyes in the last remnants of daylight.

"If Ellie were here, she'd say I am embracing you in a decidedly unseamanlike fashion," said Seren with a wry smile.

Marley laughed quietly and kissed her.

"Right, Mr. Mate," said Seren. We wait. But if she's not here very soon after first light tomorrow morning, we ride around to the main gate and go find her."

"At your command," said Marley.

# Chapter 27: In which Curmudgeon catches a mouse

A distant explosion woke Fred. Muffled by distance and the inn's walls, he recognized a thump like that from the cannon that had fired on *Spindrift*, only a few days earlier. A sound of a second, longer-lasting rumble made him hesitate, puzzled by what he heard. An insistent knocking rattled his bedroom door. He swung his feet out of the bed, pulled on his breeks, and was tucking in his shirt with one hand as he opened the door. Maisie swept into his room, resplendent in a long, brilliantly multicoloured nightdress, her red hair a loose cloud around her face. Fred's jaw dropped and he stared.

"Mr. Fredericks, that was a gun, wasn't it?"

Fred nodded, swallowed, and belatedly engaged the higher functions of his brain.

"I'm not certain. That was … how shall I say? … a bigger, deeper, longer noise than a cannon shot. Something exploded, for sure. Maybe even the cannon itself."

"Well then?" Maisie demanded.

"I want to know for certain. If the cannon is still serviceable, then …"

"If it was the gun from Salterton, and it's on its way here, then it …"

"Introduces an element of uncertainty."

Maisie stared at him, agitated, her dark eyes intense.

"An element of uncertainty? It's a calamity in the making! And you're not going to talk it away with fancy words."

"Very well, what would you have me do?"

"Put your clothes on. Meet me downstairs. If you get there first, order food sent to the stables for Astreya — Sam. Ask questions. Apply yourself!"

Maisie turned in a swirl of coloured fabric and was gone.

~^~

"Wake up, old man. Cap'n says to get that big horse of yours into its harness."

The shout woke Ellie in the hayloft above Astreya. Momentarily bewildered by the memory of a dream in which she was running away from an earth-shaking explosion, she sat up, listening. She heard footsteps; one set disappearing into the distance, another shuffling in the straw on the floor below. Astreya must be awake and doing as he was told. Her first impulse was to climb down and help him, but then she hesitated. A soldier might still be there, or nearby. She started picking stalks and seeds of hay out of her hair and from her clothes. As she shook out her long black hair and then stuffed it into the hat Maisie had given her, she became uncomfortably aware that Astreya might not have thought to cover his head. She crawled silently to the trapdoor and gently opened it enough to peer down into the stables below. Almost the first thing she saw was the shapeless, floppy hat. Astreya was standing beside Esme, who was obligingly lowering her head to let him fit the horse collar around her.

*The shipstone that I took from Esme's collar — will Astreya notice it isn't there?*

Ellie watched Astreya as he harnessed the patient horse. She eased the door fully open so that she could see more of the stable floor, hoping that the jingle of chains and buckles would cover the sound.

A shadow fell across the floor as a man came through the main door.

"Who're you an' whatcher doin' in me stables?"

Ellie drew back hastily. She heard Astreya's voice answer, and a back-and-forth discussion began that started dire, then shaded to accepting, finally achieved companionable. Without abandoning his role as Sam, Astreya had drawn the man into working with him. Ellie heard the scratch of a shovel. The newcomer — probably the ostler — was mucking out the stalls. Then came the jingle of chain links and the creak of leather drawn tight in a buckle. Ellie risked a quick look through the trapdoor. A wheelbarrow came into view, pushed by a hunched figure.

A hay stalk drove into her knee, and she drew back in sudden fear.

*They're about to feed the horses ... and the hay is up here.*

Resisting the impulse to move quickly, Ellie crawled until she reached the back wall, where she wriggled down into the dry, prickling hay until she judged herself invisible. Her nose twitched with dust, threatening a sneeze. She forced herself to breathe through almost closed lips.

Heavy feet thumped up the ladder. She heard the man's voice muttering to himself, then the hiss of a pitchfork thrust into the hay. A forkful spilled down to the lower floor with a sound like flowing water.

"Ere! Who's there? I hears yer, yer little divil. Whatcher fink yer doin'?"

Ellie held her breath, imagining the four shining tines of a pitchfork poking, prodding, stabbing into the hay where she hid.

*Best I talk to him while I still can.*

She half-rolled to get her feet under her, but before she could emerge from the hay, she heard a guffaw of laughter.

"Well then, look at you there little miss kitty! Gave me quite a start, yer did, hidin' there in the hay. Right. Out o' me way, I got a bit more to toss down, an' then we'll go below an' get acquainted. An' yer got yerself yer breakfast, too!"

"Prrrp!"

Curmudgeon's speech-like sound was somewhat muffled by a mouse in her teeth. Ellie felt the fear-tightened muscles in her neck and shoulders relax. Several more forkfuls of hay slithered to the floor below. The heavy footfalls receded down the ladder.

"Come on, kitty! That's a clever girl."

Ellie tried to swallow with a dry, dusty mouth. She stayed crouched in the hay, listening to the sounds made by men and horses below her. Big teeth crunched, hooves tapped. Ellie heard the irregular clopping sounds of a horse turning and being led out the door to the water. When she could no longer hold her position, she pushed out of the hay into the space near the trapdoor, and sat, wrapping her arms around her knees. The ostler led another saddle horse out to drink. Ellie stretched like a cat and peered cautiously down in time to see Astreya's hat and shoulders, then the top of Esme's big head, the horns of her collar, then the reins, the shafts and traces secured to the back strap, and finally the white, rippling hair of her tail.

Ellie watched as the big horse's hooves clopped out of the stable and thudded towards the horse trough. Then very cautiously she climbed down the ladder.

"Prrrp, Prp," said Curmudgeon.

~∧~

Sunlight sparkled from the flints at the top of the wall around the Castle, then crept down the red stone until it reflected off the little pool where the stream escaped. Marley opened his eyes. Bedazzled by the light gleaming on Seren's bright hair, he slid his arm very carefully from around her shoulders and wriggled regretfully away from her. She stirred as he covered her with his cloak, but she did not wake. He tiptoed to the creek, splashed water into his face, and went in search of wood for a fire.

A little while later, Seren's nose twitched. She opened her eyes to see Marley crouched beside a little campfire whose flames were barely visible in the sunlight. As she watched, he poured a pannikin into a mug and brought it to her. She ran her fingers through her hair, pushed herself up to lean against her saddle and smiled at him.

"Tea! Marley, you're a wonderful man. And I'm an unwashed, uncombed mess."

"Not to my eyes."

Seren put down the mug and held out both her arms. When she picked up her mug a little while later, her tea was almost cold. She drank looking over the rim at Marley, who smiled back, entranced

"Finish your share of the apple and cheese."

"You're pampering me," said Seren. "And I like it a lot!"

Marley chucked.

"I'll fetch the horses."

A rumble of sound echoed against the wall beside them.

"Explosion of some kind," said Marley. "Cannon fire?"

"Ellie!" Seren exclaimed. "We have to go look for her. Now!"

They broke camp swiftly, saddled the horses, and followed the track around the wall.

After they left the stream, a scruffy-looking man emerged from the brush near where Marley had gathered sticks for a fire. He yawned, scratched, walked to the where the stream tunneled under the wall, sat, took off his shoes and waded in.

# Chapter 28: In which Astreya's day begins early

Astreya stood beside Esme at the water trough, watching the ostler lead the two saddle horses away towards a fenced paddock. As the man disappeared behind a cluster of buildings, Astreya tried to recall an unpleasant dream. He vaguely remembered a thumping sound, like a ship's keel striking bottom. But he was on land, so that could not be. He still felt as if he was not fully awake. Sleep had overcome some of his physical exhaustion, but fatigue had rendered him almost as simple-minded as the role he had been playing. He recalled asking Ellie to leave him, but could not remember if she had gone before sleep claimed him. Hoping she was safe, he ran his hand over Esme's shoulder, stroking her smooth hair as she drank what seemed an impossible quantity of water.

The sun was barely above the horizon. The light streamed across a landscape of rolling fields, glowing on their low crests, leaving the hollows between them dark and mysterious. The flints at the top of the Castle's eastern wall twinkled above the meadow they protected. To his left was the stable, which backed against the northern wall; away to the south were the three-storey soldier's barracks. Beside them was a single, shadowed shape made of two or three close-built buildings, blended into one by the level light. He walked around Esme, checking that her harness was snugged into position with the shafts braced up.

A flash of reflected light made him turn to look at the spire of the building he had seen through the gatehouse arch the previous night — as well as more than twenty years ago. Against the deep blue of the western sky the steeple glowed as if lit from within. Astreya experienced a curious double vision: what he saw in the present blended with memories of when he had been seventeen, learning to paint from Gar and falling in love with Lindey. And along with those two pivotal events he recalled his knife-fight with Carl as the library burned and Gar fell to his death.

The library still stood, a blackened hulk only a little more than a stone's throw away. He stared at the building, seeing it as it had been when Gar had said, "Whoever built that wanted to impress. What he achieved is impressively hideous."

Massive stone walls rose out of the ground and curved inward almost imperceptibly. That was as Astreya remembered it, but the windows in the stonework were now gaping holes, smoke-darkened at their pointed tops, above which was empty air. Where there had been a bulging, multifaceted dome supported by encircling stone walls, there was now only a broken skeleton. Heavy oak beams that had held up an arched roof were now blackened and splintered shards, pointing skyward. Where there had been a squat, square patched-on entrance, Astreya saw a wide trench slanting down into the earth towards the foundations. Astreya's feet carried him towards the trench without him having decided to move. He peered at rough-hewn tree trunks around big, heavy double doors.

"What'cha doin' over here, old man? The gatehouse is back there, an' Cap'n Orme's waitin' for yer."

Astreya walked back to where Esme waited patiently, her chin still dripping water, and led her towards the gatehouse. As he walked, he noticed that the paths radiating out from the entrance to the Castle were mere narrow traces, unlike the wide and well-trodden ways they had been two decades earlier. Where were the many green-gowned scholars and Learneds who once walked to and from their studies, sleeping quarters, and meals? Wondering the changes, Astreya led Esme toward the gatehouse where militia captain Orme stood waiting.

"Your horse fed and watered?"

Astreya nodded.

"Right then. There's an item of ordnance that …" Orme paused, and rephrased for a simple plowman. "I need your horse to drag a cannon out of where it's stuck, and bring it back here. Follow me."

Astreya nodded again, before taking up his position at Esme's side. They walked under the gatehouse, entered the five-way intersection and followed Orme along a road that headed eastward. The golden moment of dawn was past, but almost level light was still in Astreya's eyes. Esme's hooves clopped on the cobbles, her harness jingled, and the sounds echoed back from houses on either side of the narrow road. They passed men on foot, singly and in groups of two or three. Thinking to stay in his character as a simple countryman, at first Astreya either nodded or raised a hand in greeting, but none of them responded. His memories conflicted with what he saw. He recalled a crowded, bustling little town, alive with people intent on the imperatives of their lives; what he saw was a few dispirited individuals trudging along a street of close-packed houses, many of which were vacant. Human and animal feet had kept the cobbled street clear down its middle, but rubbish filled the gutters. At every third or fourth house, drifts of debris had risen up the steps to doors that were ankle-deep in trash.

At first, Esme's big neck blocked Astreya's view ahead. Then the road curved to the right as it left the town. He saw houses separated by hedges, beyond which he glimpsed fields.

"We're here," said Orme.

Esme stopped so suddenly that Astreya almost fell. She lowered her head and blew a rattling gust of air past her lips. Her skin shuddered under Astreya's hands. He looked past her head to see what distressed her.

Three steps ahead were the bloody remains of a severed human arm.

~^~

The narrow street was still in deep shadow when the innkeeper unbolted his door, stood aside to let Fred pass and began sweeping off his front steps. His heavy eyebrows concealed the attention with which he watched Fred, who was pacing back and forth outside the inn. He paused under the sign of the Jug and Bottle to look up at what he guessed was Maisie's window. Above the pitched roof, morning sunlight turned the smoke from cooking fires into golden threads spiraling upward into cloudless blue. While he still had his head tilted back, the inn door opened.

"Mr. Fredericks. There you are at last," said Maisie.

Fred frowned at her with the exasperation of a man who has been kept waiting by a woman. He reconsidered his sarcastic reply just in time, and instead spoke formally.

"Good morning, Madame La Tour."

Unnoticed by either of them, the innkeeper leaned on his broom, listening.

"Never mind the fripperies. I'm Maisie. You're Fred. Now, let's get on with it."

Fred took a step back and looked at Maisie, his head tipped to one side. Her clothes looked smarter and more sophisticated than she had been on the journey, but today it was her self-assured manner that was askew. One hand fidgeted with the scarf at her neck, and the other brushed back a tendril of her bright red hair. A musical ringing sound puzzled Fred until he saw the bangles at her wrist.

"Well? Did you find out anything?"

Fred shook his head. Maisie's bangles jingled as she gestured impatiently.

"Then what have you been doing?"

"Waiting for you," Fred answered evenly.

"Then let's be on our way. No, wait."

Fred's exasperation was obvious. He turned to go, and almost fell over a boy in a grubby apron, who danced back out of his way.

"Watch where you're…" Fred began.

"It's Pat," said Maisie. The boy who took food to Astr … to my plowman. How is Sam this morning, Pat?"

"Didn' see the old man, mam. One o' them green-gowned Learneds tol' me t' leave the basket, 'cause he'd be back right soon."

"A Learned, in the stables?"

"Yeah. An' a cat."

Fred and Maisie exchanged glances.

"The Learned, what did he look like?" Fred asked.

"Couldn't see much more than his green gown-thing. 'E was in the shadows, like, an' the sun were in me eyes. But 'e spoke t'me right nice, not the way his kind usually do. Y'know, like they're all high and mighty an' I'm only here to serve 'em."

"Well done, Pat," said Maisie.

Her bangles rang as she plucked at her purse, but Fred was quicker. A coin appeared in his fingers with magical swiftness and disappeared under Pat's apron equally quickly. Brown hair fell over the boy's eyes as he nodded his thanks. He tried to scamper inside, but the innkeeper handed him the broom.

"Do you think the Goddess seen fit to…" Maisie began.

"I don't know about any Goddess, but I can tell you that Ellie has an amazing ability to show up when you least expect her," said Fred. "Shall we find out if it was she who the lad saw?"

Maisie's hand closed on his forearm. They left the shadow of the inn in a few paces, felt the sun on their backs and saw their shadows precede them on the cobbles. They did not notice the innkeeper staring after them.

The sounds at the start of the town's day were around them, spilling out of open doors and windows in a murmur of indistinct voices, punctuated by the occasional shout. A little girl appeared in a doorway with her thumb in her mouth, her eyes big as she watched them pass. A man with a tool bag came out a door and slammed it behind him. Opposite, another man holding a pick-axe did the same. They greeted each other in grunts, and strode ahead of Fred and Maisie, grumbling to each other about their wives.

"Ah, the happy life of the married working man," said Fred.

Maisie did not respond to his sarcasm. She noticed that save for the two small children, the street was almost empty and there were boarded-up windows in many of the houses. Their footsteps were disconcertingly hollow.

As they entered the five-ways open space in front of the gatehouse. Maisie tightened her grip on Fred's arm. The big doors scraped open and thudded against stone stops on either side. Maisie hesitated. Fred slowed, observing how she deliberately placed one foot in front of the other, her jaw set and her lips compressed.

Behind them, horses' hoofs clopped on the cobbles and echoed off walls. A voice shouted orders over the rumble of wheels. They turned to see the cart horse lean into the turn towards the gatehouse.

"Is it…? Maisie asked.

"Cannon," said Fred. "Towed backwards. And we're in the way."

As they stood aside, they saw Astreya's feet, his body invisible behind Esme's shoulders. Head down, her muscles rippling with effort, the big horse pulled the cannon up the slight rise towards the wall and gatehouse. She clopped closer, the sound of her hoofs amplified by the tunnel through the gatehouse. The cannon rumbled past them, its barrel almost horizontal.

"I was thinking I'd have to send for you. Glad you're both here."

They turned to see Captain Orme. His uniform jacket was buttoned to his throat, his leather belt was polished, the butt of his pistol gleamed at his side, but his hat was askew on his head, and a muscle twitched his cheek.

"What's been happening, Captain?" Fred asked. "We heard explosions."

"And why is my horse pulling that … thing?"

"I'm very sorry about that, Missus … um … Madame la Tour. There wasn't time to ask you. Y'see, the cannon and its ammunition were being hauled back here by two horses, and when they were at the edge of the town, they blew up."

"The horses exploded?" Maisie asked.

"They and the men leading them were killed," said Orme. "The officer in charge, too. They'd been followed, stones flung at them, holes dug in the road."

"The explosions … were they attacked?" asked Fred.

"Maybe. Made a good-sized hole, I can tell you. The ammunition's all gone. Not much left of the horses and men, either. Only one man left alive to tell what happened."

He grimaced and gestured them to follow him. They walked through the archway behind the cannon, uncomfortably aware that they were looking at the muzzle.

"Old ammunition. Unstable. Banging about in saddlebags. Recipe for disaster, I'd say," said Fred.

"Major Sanderson said it worked fine in Salterton," said Orme.

When they came out the other side of the gatehouse, it was as if the town had vanished. The spire gleamed in the sunlight ahead of them, and the sky was no longer confined to a strip of light between tall, close-packed houses.

Two men walked towards them. One wore a purple cape that rippled from his shoulders, catching the light. He strode importantly, ignoring the scruffy man at his heels.

"The Gov'ner," Orme whispered. "Listen, Mr. Fredericks, he's going to be some upset when he hears what's happened. I need you to tell him you can fix the crawler."

"Maybe, if I have the services of a good blacksmith. But I can tell you right now that it's not something that can be done overnight."

"But you can try."

The gatehouse behind them, Orme led them past Astreya, who was uncoupling Esme from the cannon with the help of three soldiers. Orme led Fred and Maisie a few steps forward and then motioned them to wait. The Governor stood as if posed for a picture, staring haughtily, ignoring the man talking to him. Fred recognized the same clumsy, ill-educated voice he had overheard in Astreya's big family house.

"So… Enoch was a spy," Fred murmured.

# Chapter 29: In which Ellie goes exploring

Ellie followed Curmudgeon down the ladder. Sunlight on the doorstep beckoned both of them out of the stables into the morning. The brindled cat chose her spot carefully, and in one fluid motion lay down on her back, wriggled like a kitten, stopped, sat up suddenly and stared at Ellie, who was looking around warily.

"Where is everybody, Curmudgeon?"

The cat turned her head and looked past Ellie's shoulder, the end of her tail twitching. Ellie followed her slit-eyed gaze. Hurrying towards them was a boy carrying a basket.

Ellie tried to adjust her hat, but her fingers felt only her long black hair. She nipped back through the door and stood, irresolute. There was not enough time to climb up to find her hat and satchel. She was about to hide in Esme's loose box when she saw the blanket she had tucked around Astreya. In two steps she was pulling it over her head and draping the horse-smelling folds around her body.

"Hey, Sam! You in there old man?"

Ellie did her best to deepen her voice.

"He's exercising his horse."

"Oooh, 'scuse me, Learned. Didn't see yer. I got the old feller's breakfast."

"Put it by the door, please. He's helping the soldiers. He'll be back shortly."

"Righty ho, then."

Ellie peeked out of the hood she had improvised. Curmudgeon strolled to the basket and sniffed the red-and-white checked cloth that covered its contents. She looked at Ellie.

"Prrrrrrp."

A little while later, Ellie and Curmudgeon were sitting on the blanket with the basket between them. They were back up in the loft, in sunlight that streamed through the big loading window that Ellie had not noticed the night before, and had just propped open.

"Let's see what we have here, Curmudgeon," said Ellie. "Jug of tea. Milk. Bread, with butter, even! Some kind of preserve … strawberry. Want some? Oh, you smelled the cold chicken, didn't you? Well, here's your drumstick."

For a little while, they concentrated on eating. When Curmudgeon grudgingly accepted that Ellie would not let her investigate what was left in the basket, Ellie turned out her satchel to check that Astreya's shipstone was safe. She found a comb, socks, underwear, a colourful scarf, a nail file, the little pot of mosquito repellant, and … *oh joy!* … a bar of lavender-scented soap. She climbed down the ladder, snuck out the door, washed at the horse trough, and returned to join Curmudgeon in the attic. They prepared themselves for the day. While the big cat groomed behind her ears with an expert paw, Ellie combed out her long black hair.

The warm light dimmed as the sun rose into a band of cloud. Not far from the stables, a group of soldiers assembled in front of their barracks, and then marched towards the gatehouse. Two were out of step, but the sergeant either failed to notice or did not care. As he led them up the path, two green-gowned figures were coming the other way. The sergeant waved them contemptuously aside. Ellie and Curmudgeon watched as the two men gathered up their gowns to keep them from the dew-wet grass.

"Learneds!" Ellie exclaimed.

She ran her fingers over the horse blanket. It was almost the same shade of green as the Learneds' gowns.

"Well, Curmudgeon, the colour isn't quite right, and the texture's completely wrong, but from a distance…"

Ellie watched the pair of hooded figures walk towards the building with the steeple. Their green robes were too long for her to tell whether they were men or women, but she noticed that they walked with their heads bowed, looking fixedly at the narrow path. Curmudgeon licked the paw with which she had been washing her left ear, and looked at her.

"If you're done primping, Miss Kitty, we're going exploring."

Ellie climbed down to the doorway where she settled the satchel on her shoulder and drew the green horse blanket around her. Curmudgeon jumped down beside her and sniffed at the hem.

"It smells of horse, I know. "I'll have to make sure nobody gets close enough to take a whiff. Here I go. You coming?"

Ignoring the spiderweb of narrow footpaths among the buildings, and resisting the impulse to walk at her own swift pace, Ellie pulled the blanket into the shape of a hood, bent her head, and walked towards the trench that led into the basement of the ruined building. With her vision restricted to only a stride ahead, she followed a hoof-marked earth track from the stables to where it divided into two cart-rutted tracks, one heading for the gatehouse, and the other for the trench. Shadow moved up her legs as she walked down the sloping cut in the earth toward a pair of heavy doors reinforced with iron. A padlock dangled where they met. She was about to turn around when she saw that the hasp was open.

Cautiously, Ellie unhooked the padlock, then creaked the doors open and stepped inside. She pushed back her improvised hood and looked into almost complete darkness that smelled of burnt wood, spilled oil, dust and decay. She shrugged off the blanket, and green light seeped out from the stone on her arm, revealing dark stone walls several strides away on either side. She was standing on a grey floor, patched with black oil stains, thick with dust, in which she saw the print of big wheels with hoofmarks between them.

*Room enough for a team of horses pulling ... a cannon? a steam crawler?*

The basement was full almost to the shadowy beams overhead. At first, all she could see was the occasional gleam off shards of glass or metal. Then as her eyes accustomed to the light from her clasp she saw a waist-high pile of dark green metal boxes that blocked the way into the rest of the cellar. They reminded her of the foot-locker below her bunk aboard *Cygnet*, but were longer and deeper. There were more than two dozen of them, most of them piled five high, some resting on the floor. Behind the stack, she glimpsed dim shapes of wheels, pipes, spindles, rods, and tubes heaped up higher and higher until they disappeared against the back walls of the cellar where the light from her stone faded into darkness.

Ellie investigated cautiously. Four of the boxes on the floor had their fasteners undone. Ellie crooked her fingers under a lid and lifted. Ancient hinges squawked. She saw rows of gleaming brass and steel.

*Bullets. Bullets for rifles, like the ones the soldiers were carrying.*

She raised the lid of another box, which opened quietly on greased hinges. Inside were longer, larger shapes, each about the length of her forearm, but thicker.

*I wonder what ... just a moment, there's writing inside the lid.*

"DANGER EXPLOSIVES," she read out loud, and instantly remembered what Fred had said, years before. 'If they're old, they're probably unstable, certainly unpredictable. They could be inert, but they could detonate at a feather touch.'

Ellie closed the lid very gently and backed away. She would have left the other boxes where they lay, but curiosity was stronger than fear. The contents of the next box she opened glinted brassy and white.

*Really big bullets. Cannon shells, for sure.*

Two boxes were piled one on top of the other. The top one opened with the same squawk as before. At first, she could only see something glinting a hand's width below the brim. She leaned forward, reached in and gasped.

*Coin! Silver ... no, wait, it's gold!*

Shin high, and close beside her, two eyes eerily reflected her stone's green light. Ellie jumped and nearly cried out.

"Prrrp?"

Curmudgeon blinked and the twin reflections vanished and reappeared.

"Prrrrp."

Ellie watched the big cat circle around her, felt a muscular tail brush her legs, and saw Curmudgeon pick her way forward, leading the way further into the gloom. Not to be outdone by a cat, Ellie followed her around the boxes, and along a narrow path between seemingly random pieces of ancient metal. The cat stayed a couple of paces ahead, occasionally pirouetting to ensure she was being followed. The bewildering piles of junk on either side grew higher until Ellie was following Curmudgeon along a head-high aisle that she guessed was dangerously close to collapsing. Forty or fifty paces from the doors where they had entered the cellar, Curmudgeon stopped, sat, and looked up. A ladder leaned into shadowy beams above. The cat put a paw on the bottom rung, turned her head and looked a question at Ellie.

"Prrrrp?"

"Really, Curmudgeon? You want me to carry you?"

Far behind her, the big doors creaked. Ellie clapped her hand over her glowing green stone, crouched and peered back to where two soldiers were silhouetted by the light from the door. Their voices echoed in the darkness around her.

"Watch it with that cart. You near knocked me over."

"Sorry 'bout that. Here, what's this on the floor?"

"Stinkin' horse blanket what some idiot left when we had the team in here pullin' out the gun an' the crawler."

"Kick it out the way. Don't want to trip when when we're carryin' the ammo."

"'S'why we brung the cart."

"Box with a C on it, right?"

"Right. C for cannon. R for rifles. E for explosives an' slow match to set 'em off. You can leave them right where they are. It were more'n likely a couple o' them what blew while they was bringin' back the gun."

"Hey, c'mere an' take your end. This is heavier than last time."

"That's not a C, it's a G, so leave it."

"This one's a C for sure."

"Move it real easy. Don't want to go like Jonesy and Sanders."

"That were enemies what done that."

"So you say. But it were Jonesy what had the 'splosives in his saddle-bags."

"Hurry up. Guv'nor's waitin' t' see us blast them sailor-boys on horses."

"Mind you aim better'n they did at that sailboat."

"Teach yer grandma to suck eggs. Riders ain't bouncin' around like boats on the waves. It's a clear shot over the wall."

"Take an end. Easy now."

Ellie heard metal scrape and then a soft thud.

"I said easy, you numpty!"

More scraping, but no thuds. The men's voices faded as they left the basement. Then hinges creaked, doors slammed. She took her hand away from her stone and looked up the ladder by its green light.

*They need to know! But I can't message from here, underground. So up we go.*

"You'd better be right, Curmudgeon. Get on my shoulders."

Ellie could see only two rungs above her before the dark wood faded into the blackness behind it. As she climbed, she counted out loud: "Ten rungs… eleven… twelve…Ouch!" Curmudgeon's claws dug into her skin as the cat crouched lower. She held her arm so that the stone shone above her head, and saw a trapdoor.

"Maybe we're in luck, Curmudgeon. There's a rope. Now if I'm right, and I pull it hard enough…"

Above her head, a slit of light widened into a shoulder-width square as a trapdoor swung open. Ellie took two more cautious steps until her eyes were just above floor level. Curmudgeon sprang off her shoulders.

Ellie clenched both hands on the top rung of the ladder. Reaching into the mental state in which she could control her stone, she sent:

**SEREN MARLEY QUICK HIDE GUN FIRING AT…**

A sound like a blow to the head stopped her from completing the message. Deafened, she hauled herself up onto the floor and lay still.

# Chapter 30: In which the cannon roars

Astreya stood beside Esme, absently stroking her big neck. They were inside the Castle walls, watching soldiers cleaning blood off the cannon. The smell of blood, dust and smoke was still in their nostrils. Together, they had picked their way among severed pieces of horse and human flesh to get to the cannon, hitch onto its drawbar, and haul it out from among what was left of the bodies of horses and men. With the bloody horror of the blast hole behind them, both he and Esme fell into passive inattention. Calmed and comforted, Esme acknowledged his touch by bobbing her head. Gradually, they both relaxed.

In more than twenty years at sea, Astreya had dealt with ugly scenes aboard ships when men and women had been injured and even killed. His blood had stained the deck of his ship after an explosion from which he still carried a scar and the limp he tried to conceal. He had left his ship, his home and his family to avert such atrocities before they could be brought to Matris. Now his assumption that he could make things better seemed hopelessly naive.

What had Maisie said? 'None of us controls what happens.'

Now he was trapped in the role Maisie had given him. Astreya had become Sam, the lack-wit old plowman, a mere cog in the machinery of death, no more in charge than the big horse he tended. Lindey was right. He had walked away from the trust they had shared since the day he first saw her indomitable, blue-eyed, gaze to go in search of what she had called his 'foolish, selfish gesture.'

Esme fidgeted, pecking with a forefoot. Her hoof narrowly missed Astreya's foot, jerking him into awareness of his surroundings. Walking deliberately towards the cannon was a figure resplendent in a red military-style jacket, blue breeches tucked into knee-high boots, a purple cloak turned back on his shoulders to show off his finery, the whole outfit topped by a boat-shaped hat.

"Carl," Astreya muttered.

Astreya stared at the man he had last seen when they both were twenty years younger. Carl the self-styled Governor was no longer the lithe nineteen-year-old knife-wielding student with whom Astreya had fought: he had bulked up, and with the extra weight he had become arrogant, pompous, and used to having his own way

Esme's head went up and down, momentarily blocking Astreya's view. When he peered around the big horse again, he saw Carl stride to a halt and stand, one shoulder disdainfully raised. Orme marched up towards him, stopping a deferential pace away, and spoke in a voice too low for Astreya to hear. Orme raised a hand shoulder high and beckoned. Fred and Maisie stepped forward beside him.

Until that moment, Astreya had not noticed them. Shocked by his inattention, he also realized he was standing tall. He let his body slump and again became Sam the halfwit. Hunching his shoulders so that the hat obscured his face, he stared at them, feeling suspicious of their motives. Astreya saw that they were both tense: Maisie's lips were tightly compressed and Fred's thin shoulders were raised almost to his earlobes.

A scruffy-looking man plucked at Carl's cloak

"Enoch," Astreya murmured.

"Gov'ner, I got sump'n to tell yer."

"Not now, Enoch," said Carl, waving him away.

Enoch spoke louder and pointed.

"Spies, Gov'ner. Look! T'other side o' the wall. Black feller, an' the tall woman. There they are, Gov'ner! See?"

Carl stared imperiously at the distant wall. His face twisted as he grasped the situation.

"Orme, shoot them, immediately,"

Orme shouted orders. Soldiers swung the cannon around and dug in the tail anchor. Two men ran towards the ruined library.

"Where are those men going, Orme? I ordered…"

"Getting ammunition, sir." Orme stood a little straighter and spoke louder. "As I was saying, sir, I came back to the Castle when …"

"Yes, yes, when Sanderson's land crawler blew up."

"Yes sir. While Sanderson was following your orders to return the cannon to the Castle, I …"

"When he ran away."

"No, sir. When he was killed."

"So, Orme, what was your part in this the second catastrophe in less than two days?"

"Getting the gun back after the explosion, sir."

"What incompetence allowed this to happen?"

"Don't know, sir. The men think it was the Men of the Sea, sir. They followed Sanderson and the cannon, making it difficult for them. At one point they got ahead and dropped a tree across the road. When Sanderson's men tried to clear it out of the way, they threw stones at them. And…"

"Are you telling me a handful of stone-throwing sailors stopped them from bringing the cannon here?"

"Not stopped, sir. Slowed. They were nearly here. The enemy got ahead of them last night. Dug up the road, sir, and blocked it with a tree, just outside the town. Sanderson tried to push on. The gun stuck. He …"

"He ran away. Go on."

"If so, sir, not fast enough. When I heard the explosion early this morning, I went to investigate, and found … um … what was left of him."

"What explosion?"

"Ammunition, sir. At least that's what I thought when I heard the sound. So I went to look, then returned and commandeered this woman's horse to fetch the cannon here."

"What are you talking about, Orme?" Carl demanded irritably.

Astreya realized that Carl had not been listening.

"I was explaining about the crawler, and the big horse, and the cannon…"

"They're gettin' away," said Enoch. "Prob'ly headin' fer them other sailors what…."

Astreya saw the heads and shoulders of two distant figures above the top of the east wall.

"Fire the damn gun!" Carl shouted.

Two soldiers appeared from behind the library, pushing a cart. Moments later, Astreya heard metal click as one of them slid a shot into the breach.

"Wait! Don't shoot!" Fred shouted. "The tampion's still in!"

The soldiers paused. Fred ran to the muzzle of the gun, reached up and unscrewed a round wooden plug.

"Fire with that still in, and … boom!" said Fred.

"T'weren't me," the two soldiers said at the same time.

"Enough of this incompetence!" Carl yelled. "I said immediately!"

The breech-block snicked shut. A soldier rotated two aiming handles, pointing the cannon towards the red wall. Fred sprinted back to Maisie, hands over his ears. She copied him, as did Orme. Carl continued to stand as if having his portrait painted.

**SEREN MARLEY QUICK HIDE GUN FIRING AT…**

Ellie's message reached Astreya as one of the soldiers yanked on the trigger rope. Astreya looked at the muzzle, expecting a flash, a roar, and a cloud of smoke. For almost a heartbeat, nothing happened. Then he saw the entire cannon leap off the ground, hang in the air and disappear in a cloud of black smoke. A gout of orange flame rolled skyward. Then the shock wave tossed him against Esme in a cloud of smoke and flying debris.

Seren received Ellie's message as she and Marley rode around a bend in the track. It was so blindingly loud in her mind that for a moment, she could only cling to her horse's mane. As the sensation faded, she saw the last houses of the town to her left. Ahead of her was a hedge hiding the road to Salterton.

Seren kicked her horse, and with Marley close behind her, galloped towards the road. She risked a glance over her shoulder and saw people clustered around the gun.

"Faster!" she yelled.

They thundered down the track, the wall on their right, an open field on their left. The track swung away from the wall, then turned again to avoid someone's vegetable garden. Seren clutched at her horse's neck as it rounded the bend, its hooves throwing up clods of earth into Marley's face.

The cannon roared.

Half stunned by the sound, they crouched lower in the saddle, clinging onto their horses as best they could. Then both animals balked in front of a wooden gate, and Seren nearly flew over her horse's head. Marley swayed in his saddle, barely recovering as his horse danced in circles, huffing and snorting. Seren started to coax her horse back to where she could see over the wall.

"No, wait, Seren, don't go back! They'll see…"

"Something went wrong. They're all dead!"

## UNCLE I HAVE THE SHIPSTONE

They swayed in their saddles a second time, their heads ringing with the intensity of Ellie's sending.

"It's Ellie! Again! We have to go to her."

"The horses can't jump the wall," Marley began.

"Use the road," said a voice behind him. "We'll follow."

Trogen pushed the gate open, revealing Damon and eight sailors from *Elusive* standing in the road.

"TROGEN!" Seren shouted. "The Castle! Hurry!"

# Chapter 31: In which Ellie can only listen

Dust, dirt and debris rained down onto Ellie through the burned skeleton of the library dome. When she raised her head, she saw Curmudgeon, claws out and hair on end, regarding her accusingly.

This time it was Ellie who took the lead. She got to her feet, brushed herself off, and headed towards a shattered window with Curmudgeon following her cautiously. They passed a big library table, its legs in the air, half-leaning against a bookcase that leaned on another bookcase and so on toward a windowsill higher than Ellie's head. She clambered up scorched pieces of shelving that had been piled into the semblance of a stair. When her head was high enough to see out the window, she saw the gun lying on its side, smoke still oozing from a split in its barrel. Beside it, two bodies lay tumbled on the ground, their legs and arms grotesquely twisted. Ellie felt her stomach turn. Fearful of what she might see next, she scanned the area, fixing on the familiar big horse and the black-haired man with his arm around its neck.

*Astreya's alive!*

Closer to her window, she saw more bodies, one getting to his feet. He flapped dust off his purple cloak with his hat and replaced it on his head. His face was heavily handsome, dominated by black eyebrows, one of which was contemptuously raised.

"Orme? Knock? Where are you?"

*The Governor. Not impressed.*

They moved, and bright red hair caught the light.

"Maisie! Fred!" Ellie shouted, her voice sounding distant in her ears.

They did not hear. Two strides from them, more bodies stirred. The Governor continued to shake dust off his blue cloak. At his back, a man staggered to his feet and broke into a shambling run. Astreya, completely oblivious, was fumbling with the horse collar.

## UNCLE! I HAVE THE SHIPSTONE

Ellie screamed soundlessly, and her stone warmed against her arm as it sent out her message. She saw Astreya wince and stare in her direction. Aghast, she watched a man circle to come from behind, a knife held low.

*No! Instead of warning Astreya, I distracted him!*

For such a big horse, Esme's kick was unbelievably quick. Her huge hoof took the man in the chest, hurtling him into the air. He fell onto his back and lay still. Esme swung her head around to regard her victim. Apparently satisfied, the horse nodded and stood still.

*Oh, well done, Esme!*

Ellie took another step up the rickety bookcase and peered over the windowsill. She saw Astreya draw himself to his full height, set his shoulders, and stride towards the gaudily dressed man. Someone shouted an order, and three soldiers ran from the gatehouse, their rifles at waist height, bayonets fixed and gleaming.

## ASTREYA!

She saw Astreya hesitate, frown, and then stare past Carl.

*Oh my goodness, I messaged him. Again!*

Maisie and Fred followed his glance and looked at the library. Ellie crouched lower. Astreya started to walk past Maisie and Fred, towards Carl and Orme.

"Cover them!" Orme ordered.

As she ducked out of sight, Ellie glimpsed bayonets only a pace from Astreya's chest.

*No, don't shout! You'll distract him again!*

Maisie stepped around the soldier and eased Orme's hand away from his head to explore his bloody hair with her fingers. Ellie heard her speak to Fred.

"Scalp wound, Lots of blood. Skull intact."

"Orme, what happened?" Carl demanded.

Orme swayed on his feet. Maisie steadied him.

"Answer me!" Carl shouted.

"For goodness sake, he's wounded. Let him be," said Maisie crisply.

Carl looked curiously at Maisie, who was pulling a scarf from her neck to wind around Orme's head.

"Well, well, well. A red-haired woman. Very much alive."

"And under my protection," said Astreya, taking a stride towards them.

Ellie saw a bayonet barring Astreya's way.

*Careful, Astreya!*

Carl's voice was as arrogant as his wide-legged stance.

"Astreya," Carl drawled. "The man who left the Castle like a thief in the night, more than twenty years ago. Now, you're back, sending your little black-haired spy ahead of you. And here's the woman who took her in. Or was it you who was taken in, Maisie the witch? Did that spying girl talk you into joining Astreya's covert attack? Or were you already part of it?"

"What have you done with my niece?" Astreya demanded.

*I'm all right! He hasn't got me.*

Maisie pointed the index and little fingers of her left hand into Carl's face. Carl flinched, but instantly recovered.

"So, Astreya, still letting your women protect you?"

"This is between you and me, Carl," said Astreya. "They are not involved."

"Oh yes I am," said Maisie. "And so is Ellie. Your filthy cannon shot at her. Your soldiers burned my house."

"When you have apologized to her," said Astreya, "then you and I can resolve the issues between us. Starting with you producing Eliana, immediately."

Carl snorted.

"Return the girl? Apologize? Resolve the issues? After more than a century of plundering, looting, and kidnapping by the Men of the Sea, where would you like to start?"

**HE'S BLUFFING HE DOESN'T KNOW WHERE I AM.**

This time, Astreya barely blinked.

"That was ..." Maisie began.

"...a long time ago," Carl completed her sentence. "That's what they told you, is it? Well then, shall we begin with the library that he burned?"

"You were there. You know that it was ..." Astreya began.

"...not your fault? Nothing to do with you and your spying uncle? Please."

"He wasn't a spy. We were hired to embellish the library with images...

"Insulting daubs and scrawls. I knew. It was I who reported your offensive drawings. It was I who discovered your little book of coded secret instructions. I nearly had you to rights, but I had to care for the man you wounded before you fled into the night."

"That was you. You knifed your friend, Carl."

"Nonsense..."

The two men glared at each other, oblivious to their surroundings. Seeing Maisie shake her head, Ellie rolled her eyes.

*This is irrational. They're winding each other up for a fight.*

People began coming through the gatehouse and from the buildings within the Castle walls. Some were in grey uniforms, some in green gowns, and some were townspeople curious about the explosion. Ellie frowned.

*We're outnumbered. This isn't good.*

Carl's lips curled in an orator's practiced smile. He spread his arms in welcome. His voice rose, rounded, reached out towards the growing crowd, turning them from individuals into an audience. His smile broadened. He pointed dramatically at Astreya.

"Here he is, my good people. This is Astreya, the one who began all the terrorism. Astreya, the black-haired knife fighter, the Man of the Sea, who stole into the Castle with his blonde witch and the priest of evil. They burned down the library. Learneds, you know of these black-haired Men of the Sea. Townspeople, you recall the man who bewitched the mayor. Here he is, the man who infiltrated the Castle, drew spells on the library walls, and then set fire to it."

"We made drawings of flowers and birds," said Astreya disgustedly. "It was done at the Learneds' request." He raised his voice. "Not many of them left now, are there Carl? Not like it was when…"

*Uncle! You're playing his game.*

Carl talked Astreya down.

"That was then. Now I have my soldiers and my missionaries, my champions who combat your evil. My Learneds study and teach. But not only here. The men who are fully and truly Learned, I send back to their villages and towns and farms. They preach the good news how my army protects them from the Men of the Sea who raid, rape, kidnap, plunder and loot. Then honest citizens come to the Castle to learn the arts of war with which my Army of Retribution will soon wage against all the Men of the Sea, who, led by this man Astreya, invaded the peaceful community known as Matris, corrupted the settlement, made it a harbour for piracy, and a base for expansion into our lands."

"That's simply not …" Astreya tried to interrupt.

*No, no, Astreya! Don't try to reason with him!*

Carl's oratory flowed on.

"Astreya's people cut down our forests to build more ships with which to surveil our coasts, probe our bays and inlets, searching for where next to kidnap our girls and boys. And when we warned them away, he landed spies and Astreya himself came to lead an attack on the Castle. But he failed. Here he is, surrounded by you good people of the Castle, the town, and my army who will not rest until his hateful presence, together with those he has corrupted, are swept into the sea from which they came. And now, I command my army to …"

A commotion at the gatehouse momentarily distracted everyone. Carl's harangue faltered. He reached both arms skyward as if to bring down help from above.

"I command all members of my Army of Retribution within the sound of my voice to…"

Two horses clattered through the archway, scattering Learneds and soldiers alike. Carl's torrent of words fell silent as two tall riders reined in beside him, ignoring the soldiers who pointed their rifles uncertainly at them.

*Oh dear. Seren and Marley, you've arrived in time to be overwhelmed by sheer numbers.*

"What are you doing here?" demanded Astreya. "Why aren't you at sea?"

*Independent judgement by officers in command. That's how you trained us, Uncle.*

Carl watched the two tall people dismount, frowning at Marley, who held the reins of both horses.

"Going to let your tame savage do your fighting, Astreya?"

"Oh do be quiet," said Maisie.

Incredulous that a woman had interrupted him, Carl refocused on her. His chin still held high, he squinted down his nose at her.

"Does this woman speak for you, Astreya?"

"You fired your cannon at his niece," said Maisie.

"An unprovoked attack," said Astreya. "It nearly cost Eliana her life."

"Spies…" Carl began.

"Lies," Astreya interrupted. "Lying is what you do, isn't it, Carl? Making people believe what isn't so. Give a dog a bad name, and then everyone wants to kick it. Make them believe. Change their world by twisting words. Turning what is until it's upside down and people believe what is not."

*True. But your words won't change him.*

"You're getting old, Astreya. Your mind is wandering. So I will tell you what's going to happen. I will give you and your people safe passage back to your village, but with conditions. First, you will promise never to attack our shores again. Next, you will pledge the Castle a regular tribute. And to make sure this all happens, I will keep the black-haired girl. She's a little young, but I'm an experienced and vigorous man in full command of my faculties. She will soon learn obedience."

*You don't have me, and you never will.*

For a heartbeat, Ellie stood ramrod straight, feeling her face grow hot with anger and revulsion. Then she climbed down from the window in disgust.

*There's not going to be a solution. They're just talking at each other, neither listening. They're on the edge. Any moment now, words won't be enough. They've given up looking for what's possible. There's nothing either can say that the other will accept. Neither can afford to fail, and any chance of success is long over. Astreya can't back down, Carl won't. There's no third way.*

*Except that there is. It's me.*

Ellie's heels thudded on the wooden floorboards as she strode towards the trapdoor. She paused before climbing down, focused her mind and used her stone to message:

**SEND HIM TO THE LIBRARY**

# Chapter 32: In which the Library explodes

Seren drew back her fist, Maisie's fingers clawed. Two bright blue and two jet black eyes fixed on him, threatening.

Carl took a step back from the two women.

"No more, Carl," said Astreya. "Send your soldiers to their quarters, I will withdraw my people. Then we can negotiate."

Carl forced a dramatic laugh and shook his head.

"You're inside the walls of the Castle, Astreya, and hopelessly outnumbered. Haven't you noticed?"

The crowd at the gatehouse seethed and parted as Trogen, Damon and a dozen men and women in seagoing uniform charged through the half dozen guards at the gatehouse. The defenders, who had learned nothing from Seren and Marley's arrival, were all watching the confrontation in the courtyard. Hit from behind, they staggered into each other, dropping their weapons and falling.

"Shoot those invaders!" Carl shouted.

Soldiers scrambled to their feet. Some pointed their rifles' bayonets at the newcomers, some at Astreya and the four around him, all hesitated lest they harm the crowd or each other.

"Belay!" Astreya commanded. "Stand down, all of you."

His tone compelled obedience. Trogen, Damon along and more than a dozen sailors halted their charge. The soldiers' weapons wavered. Trogen continued a purposeful walk towards his father. The soldiers' bayonets swung from Astreya to Trogen to the other sailors and back.

"Shoot them, Orme!" Carl screamed. "Why aren't your men shooting?"

"No loaded weapons in the Castle," said Orme. "Your standing order."

Carl's voice shrilled, like a spoiled child. "Well, have them get them! They're surrounded. Take them down!"

"Let's kill him," said Trogen. "Simplify things."

Belatedly recognizing that he was no longer in control of the situation, Carl forced another imitation of a laugh, and attempted sarcasm.

"Your son, Astreya? Simple as you are. None of you have thought this through. You're inside my castle. Your only chance is to do as I say, because I alone have the power here. All your men and these deranged women will back away from me now, or none of you will go out the gatehouse, I promise. It's up to you. Fight, and there will be blood."

### SEND HIM TO THE LIBRARY

Astrey's right hand twitched towards the stone clasped to his left arm. He looked past Carl at the library. Trogen, Seren, Marley, and Damon all did the same.

"What's happening?" Maisie asked.

"Eliana is in the library," said Trogen. "Let's go get her."

"Well, that's all right then," said Maisie, approvingly.

"Well, that's all right then," Fred said sarcastically at the same moment. They stared at each other, each bewildered by the other's reaction.

Carl's expression went from puzzlement, to understanding, to satisfaction.

"So… now that we all know where Eliana is," said Carl, raising his voice to reach not only the sailors from *Elusive* but also the crowd of soldiers, green-gowned Learneds and people of the Town. "I will fetch the girl and we can complete an agreement in which you, Astreya, will return to your village, pledge never to harass our ports and shores, and agree to send an annual tribute, all of which will be guaranteed by your niece Eliana's continued presence here with me at the Castle. Orme, keep them where they are. I will return shortly."

Carl turned and walked away like a man with a purpose. No longer obsessively arguing with Astreya, he strode towards the basement entrance to the library, pulling a key out of his pocket as he went. Seren clutched Marley's hand, closed her eyes and sent the strongest message she could.

### ELLIE! HE'S COMING TOWARDS YOU!

"We can take them…" Trogen began.

"Meanwhile," said Astreya to Orme, let us have our people sit."

"Their guns aren't loaded, we can take them…" said Trogen.

 Orme thought for an instant, then nodded.

"Sit!" Astreya ordered sharply, and sat down.

Everyone looked confusedly at each other.

"What are we, dogs?" said Trogen incredulously.

"Hmm… Sitting is not usually considered an ideal state of preparedness," said Damon as if to himself, "However, since we do have a cessation of hostilities…"

He folded himself into a cross-legged position. The sailors closest to him did likewise, then those behind them. Seren and Marley, the tallest people within the Castle walls, glanced at each other. Marley's hand took hers, and they sank down side by side. Fred looked down at the tops of all the heads around him, shrugged and joined them. Only Trogen and Orme still were standing.

"Trogen, please continue to stand," said Astreya. "And cooperate," he added.

Trogen glanced at his father, took three slow steps toward Orme. They faced each other and impulsively, shook hands. Trogen folded his arms and stared at the crowd of soldiers, Learneds and townspeople who were standing a cautious distance from the Men of the Sea, muttering to each other.

"Order arms," Orme commanded. "We have a truce. At ease. Sit down."

The soldiers guarding Astreya lowered their rifle butts to the ground and began to sit. Before they were down, others joined them, their rifles in their laps. The townspeople and Learneds watched and conferred, then gradually copied. Soon, all but a few townspeople were on the ground in a variety of sitting positions.

One of the Learneds remained standing. He turned his green gown back off his shoulder in a gesture calculated to attract attention. Trogen glared in his direction, causing those around the would-be orator to stare. The Learned glanced over his shoulder at Trogen, who shook his head, uncrossed one arm, and signalled 'no' with one wagging finger. Their eyes locked. Trogen's finger stopped wagging and pointed downwards. For a moment, neither moved. Then the Learned lowered himself into a sitting position, his green gown flouncing around him. Trogen nodded and re-folded his arms. Another green gown fluttered, and then another as the last few of the Learneds sat.

The guards and the guarded heard a murmuration of voices from the crowd. Some who had come to see a fight expressed disappointment, others encouraged their neighbours to be still so that everyone could see what would happen next.

"So, we're all going to sit here until he comes back with Ellie and tells us that we can go away and leave her as his hostage," said Fred incredulously.

"Ellie would never … She must have a plan…" Seren began.

Booted feet echoed in the tunnel through the gatehouse. Three men ran out, shouting, their bayonetted rifles hip-high. Seated figures rolled out of their way.

"Stop where you are!" Orme shouted. "We have a truce. Return your weapons to the armoury. Lock them down, lock the door."

The two men halted, looking about them in confusion. For two, then three heartbeats, nobody moved. Then the rifles pointed skywards, the two men turned and slowly walked back into the gatehouse. There was an audible sigh of relief as everyone let out the breath they had been holding.

"Start by picking up casualties?" Orme asked.

Trogen nodded.

While Orme and Trogen gave orders, Astreya's attention turned to Maisie, who was looking at him thoughtfully.

"You're making it up as you go along, aren't you?" said Maisie.

"Ellie's negotiating with Carl," said Astreya.

"You let her endanger herself?"

"What else?" muttered Fred.

They all sat quietly as three soldiers and three sailors began to carry the bodies of the fallen towards the building with the spire.

## DIVERSION IN TEN...NINE...

Astreya, Seren, Marley, Trogen, and Damon looked at each other, unconsciously continuing the count-down. Their sudden head movements caught the eyes of the onlookers, who started to speculate. A few of them started to get to their feet. The soldiers looked to Orme for orders, and he looked at Trogen for an explanation.

"What's happening?" asked Maisie.

"It's Ellie," Seren began.

Everyone felt the thud of a subterranean explosion. A grey cloud spewed out of the basement entrance. The horses jerked the reins from Marley's hands and bolted. Trogen lunged for the soldier nearest him, grabbing his weapon. People were getting to their feet when a thunderclap second explosion felled everyone to the ground. The first had been a mere preliminary tap: the second heaved the earth under them, toppling anyone standing, disorienting those still sitting.

A second even more powerful shock wave belched out the basement, blew up through the floor, tossed bookcases, beams, and floorboards into the air. The library shook to its foundations. So much dust filled the air that almost no one saw a pillar of black smoke rise above a gout of flame. People coughed, wept, and struggled to breathe in air thick with dust and ash. Still more explosions rocked the building as it collapsed into itself. Nobody heard the rattle of rifle bullets or the crash of metal inside the stone walls, because they were all imprisoned in their own distress, gagging, coughing, deafened, and almost blind.

The soldiers and townspeople suffered the most. Many abandoned themselves to gasping panic, unable to scream for coughing. The men and women from Matris were made of sterner stuff: they endured. Gradually, relief came to eyes scratched by dust and throats hoarse with ash as the sailors shared water bottles from their march. The entire landscape was grey with dust. It clung to clothes, hair, faces, and hands. It puffed up into the air at the least movement. It turned everyone grey, instantly ageing them into a community of ghosts.

"When you can speak, say your name," said Astreya, his voice a croak.

Maisie spat, coughed and responded, fitting her name in between answers by Trogen and Seren, Marley, and Fred. She heard a creaking sound that might be Orme's voice, and then a succession of names from Damon and the sailors from *Elusive*. She reached out a hand to touch Seren, who turned from staring into Marley's eyes to look at her.

"Can you …? Did she …? Is Ellie…?" Maisie stammered, her throat half choked with dust.

Seren shook her head. Dust flew off the grey wig that had replaced her bright curls. Tears cut streaks through the ash on her cheeks. Astreya's eyes were clear even though his hair was now as grey as everyone and everything around. Trogen clambered to his feet, half supporting Orme, whose eyes streamed tears down his cheeks. They had turned away from the dust cloud in time, as had most of the sailors. Such was not the case for the soldiers, almost all of whom faced the source of the shock wave. The few who had still been standing had all been knocked over, some of them tangled with their comrades. All had lost their weapons.

Astreya set off unsteadily towards the basement entrance to the library. Seren and Marley helped Maisie to her feet and followed. Esme plodded after them, shaking dust from her mane and tail.

# Chapter 33: In which Ellie copes with Carl

Ellie started down the ladder into the library basement. The stone on her clasp threw a dim green light on her hands, but when she closed the trapdoor above her head, darkness pressed in on her from all sides. Step by step she felt her way downwards until her foot touched the floor below. She stood, one hand still gripping the ladder.

"Need more light," she muttered.

Something brushed her arm on its way to land with a soft thud on the floor by her feet. Stifling a yelp, she forced herself to speak calmly.

"Curmudgeon?"

"Prrp, prrrp."

"Glad you're here, cat. But don't do that jump-down-from-above thing again, please?"

"Prrrp."

She rummaged in her satchel.

*Clasp knife, a box of fire-starters, egg-shaped metal box .... The shipstone!*

She flipped open the clasps and darkness retreated. She stood in a sphere of green light, holding the stone in the bottom half of its hinged egg. Her heart no longer pulsed in her throat. Curmudgeon looked up at her questioningly, her eyes glowing, then started down the alley between the piled-up scrap metal. Ellie followed.

*We need a diversion. Something to shut that awful man up.*

When they reached the pile of boxes, Curmudgeon jumped onto the highest. Her eyes gleamed as Ellie held up the shipstone. As she had expected, the door was locked from the outside.

*I have to get him down here so that I can ... what? Stab him with my clasp knife? Threaten? Bargain? With me the cost of peace? No thank you. But maybe...*

Ellie remembered what she had heard the soldiers say as they loaded ammunition for the cannon, and returned to the metal boxes by the door.

*Shells for the cannon, bullets for rifles. Not helpful. Gold. Not now. Explosives. More than enough to blow me and Curmudgeon into smithereens. What else?*

She cautiously opened the box of explosives. Light from the shipstone showed her a coil of what looked like black rope.

*Slowmatch! .... Might make time for me to get away before ... but the door's closed, and the lock is on the other side.*

Curmudgeon jumped off the boxes and walked towards the door.

*I could maybe hide behind the pile and blast it open but what would happen to Curmudgeon? I need someone to open it!*

**ELLIE! HE'S COMING TOWARDS YOU!**

The message was faint, like someone shouting into a pillow. For an instant, Ellie stood stock still, wondering if she had imagined Seren's sending.

"Prrp?"

"It's Seren," said Ellie. "We're getting out of here."

Her mind made up, she went swiftly to work. She set her satchel on one of the boxes, balanced the shipstone on it, picked up the coil of rope-like slowmatch, and saw that it was marked with twists of white string a finger's length apart. She cut off a section with her clasp knife. Then she gingerly removed one canvass-wrapped charge and laid it carefully on the floor. She poised her knife to make a little hole, but Fred's words 'at a feather's touch' came back to her, and instead, she gently rolled the canvass sausage onto the end of the slow-match.

Ellie stood and surveyed what she had done, then as she was scooping the shipstone into its metal egg, its light gleamed on the open box of gold. She grabbed two hands full of the heavy coins and thrust them into her satchel, along with her knife and the shipstone in its egg. Then by the dim light from the clasp on her arm, she crouched beside the slow-match, her box of fire-starters in one hand, listening.

Footfalls.

A rattle from a chain.

A key scraped in a lock.

Now!

Ellie struck a fire-starter. Once. Twice.

Orange flame flared.

The lock clicked.

Ellie touched the flame to the slow-match.

It fizzed sparks and went dark.

She lit it again.

The door hinges creaked.

Ellie stood, blew out the fire-starter, took a breath to send a message

## DISTRACTION IN TEN

## NINE

And then she screamed. As the thin line of light widened Ellie ran towards it, still screaming.

Light flared around the silhouette of a man.

Ellie flung herself at him. With her arms tight around his waist, she turned her scream into a wail.

"Oh thank you, thank you, thank you!" said Ellie, between forced sobs.

His hands clumsily patted her back as she pressed herself against him.

"You're all right. Don't worry, little girl. I got you."

*No you haven't. Eight ...*

"There's something in there!" Ellie shrieked. "It's alive! It's coming to get me!"

The something streaked out the door. A muscular tail slapped against her leg.

"It's a cat. Nothing but a cat. Look, there he goes!"

*Seven... Now I've got YOU...*

She unwound her arms from his waist, grabbed his jacket and pulled him away from the doors. He tried to hold her, but she had him off-balance. Rather than falling, he followed her up the sloping ramp to ground level.

"It's all right now, little girl. Let's go talk with …"

"No! I won't! I hate him," Ellie howled. "He only wants me 'cause I'm … I'm … I'm … I want to be free of all of it … the boats … the sea … the family…"

*…six …*

Carl slapped her, hard. She let go, turned and ran, her cheek stinging, away from the library, away from her family, away to where the meadow was edged with rushes, far ahead of her.

*…five … he's behind me, he's gaining…*

Ellie slipped her satchel off her shoulder, caught it in her left hand, pivoted, and as it swung at arm's length, let go, almost fell, staggered, ran to where spiky green leaves poked higher than the grass underfoot.

"Bitch!"

*GOT YOU! …four,*

"You stole my gold!"

*Oh, great. The idiot's stopped. …three...*

Ellie skidded to a halt, turned and faced Carl.

*…two…*

"Yes I did, you nasty man. Go on. Count it. Two hands full. How much is that worth to you?'

"Bitch, you're going to wish you'd never…."

Ellie waved her arms, taking a taunting step towards him.

*…one…*

"You can't catch me. You can't stop me. You're a soft, fat, bag of guts, you're …

Carl lunged towards her, clutching the satchel. Ellie held up both hands, middle finger raised, screamed, turned, and ran.

The ground softened under her feet. The rushes were close. Something caught her ankle, she waved her arms, fell feet-first down a steep ditch, felt her back strike the stream bank, saw sky through waving rushes, took a deep breath and held it, closed her eyes and tried to send the strongest message she could. But before she could frame the words, the ground shook under her shoulders. Carl loomed above her on the lip of the bank down which she had slid.

*Any moment now!*

"You little bitch, you didn't just steal, you blew up what you couldn't carry. But it didn't work, did it? You're lying in the mud, you conniving black-haired slut, and you are going to be so sorry, for so long that you'll wish ..."

*Well, it was a good try.*

Ellie stared up into a cloudless blue sky, trying to accept the inevitable. Then Carl's body flailed through the air above her, propelled by a shock wave that flattened the rushes and troubled the stream into hillocks of splashing water, into which Carl fell, face down, and lay still, the satchel in one hand.

# Chapter 34. In which Ellie assesses the outcome

Two days later, Ellie sat looking at a room full of people. To her left Seren was holding hands with Marley; to her right, Maisie was talking to Astreya. If she leaned forward, Ellie could see past them to Fred and Orme, who were talking like old friends.

They sat at tables arranged in a circle so that everyone faced inward. Opposite her, the men and women from *Elusive* had pushed back their chairs, crossed their legs, and were sampling the bottles set before them by servers who were clearing away the remains of a feast. Trogen sat among them, a glass in one hand, encouraging his crew to drink freely — advice none of them needed. Damon watched him, smiling and preening his moustache.

*They all look so ... ordinary. Am I the only one who's changed?*

"May I offer my congratulations, miss Eliana."

"Thank you, Innkeeper. I don't know your name."

"Rupert, publican, recovering academic."

"You're a Learned!"

"I was, until the decimation of the Learneds orchestrated by that unlamented man who perished in the Castle brook."

"How is it…?" Ellie began.

"That I didn't get purged or banished to a village? I left before the self-styled Governor could force me out of my position as dean of historical and philosophical studies. I was able to stand up to that poisonous individual because I had money of my own with which to buy this inn."

"And if you wish, you will be at least a dean again," said Astreya. "Maisie and I have been planning the return of learning to the castle, hereafter to be known as the Tower."

"Sit with us, Rupert," said Maisie. "That is if you are interested."

"Are you sure you want a de-gowned Learned?"

"We need a learned man with practical experience," said Astreya. You represent both."

Ellie, Maisie and Astreya stood up to make room. Rupert produced a chair, removed his green apron, and sat beside them.

*Carl's dead, Astreya's taking charge, Maisie's fast becoming Marie de la Tour again... I've disappeared.*

As if she had heard Ellie's thoughts, Maisie was beside her.

"The Goddess must love you something special, Ellie, 'cause she's been working overtime looking after you," said Maisie. "Last time I saw you, you were covered in dust and dirt ..."

"...wet and muddy from the waist down," said Ellie, smiling despite herself.

"... leaves and grass in your hair, and you'd lost the hat I gave you."

"It was a wonderful hat. I kept it on all the time. Until ..."

*Until I engineered Carl's death.*

"... the big bang," Maisie completed.

"Which one?" asked Fred, turning his chair to join them, a wineglass in one hand. "The massive earthshaking explosion that finished the library? Or the warning shot you so cleverly arranged, Ellie, or the one that blew up the cannon?"

"Or the one that blew a hole in the road," said Trogen.

*And here's Trogen, afraid he might get left out.*

"That was your cunning ambush, Trogen," said Fred.

"All we did was drop a tree in their way. It spooked the horses, they danced around, banged into each other, and ... well ... that's when we found out they were carrying explosives," said Trogen. "It was ... it was ... a mess," he added.

"I want to know why the cannon exploded," said Fred. "I took the tampion off, but even if it had still been in, the barrel shouldn't have split."

"I poured three hats-full of gravel down the barrel and screwed the bung back in," said Trogen. He frowned, tight lipped, repressing a shudder. "I didn't expect that it would do so much damage."

*"He's shaken! He didn't know what would happen, either.*

"You did the right thing, Trogen," said Astreya quietly. He put a hand on Ellie's shoulder. "You both did."

For an emotion-charged instant, the three of them looked at each other, the rest of the room forgotten. Fred broke their shared moment with a cheerful question.

"So, from what you've told us, Ellie, the library is now a gold mine," he said.

"I've placed a guard on it," said Orme.

"Good idea," said Fred. "So long as you let me pick over what's there — other than the gold, of course."

"Join us, Captain Orme," said Astreya. "We need your knowledge of the Governor's army."

"To demobilize it," said Orme.

"Just so," said Astreya.

*Fred's found his next project.  So has Maisie.  They don't need me. I don't have any part in what they're planning.*

Behind Ellie's back, a chair scraped the floor and fell over. She turned to see Seren hurrying out the door. Marley stood, looking after her, concern in his dark eyes.

"Is Seren all right?" Ellie asked.

Maisie's bangles rang as she patted Ellie's arm and drew their heads close together.

"She's gone to throw up. She's pregnant."

"How do you …" Ellie began and fell silent.

*Of course, she knows. She's the only one here who's had babies.*

"Does anyone else know?" Ellie asked.

Maisie caught Astreya's, eye, pointed at Seren's empty chair and then at Ellie.

Astreya joined the two of them, leaned forward and whispered.

"Seren and Marley told me last night, while you were getting some well-deserved sleep. Seren's eager to carry on as long as possible, but when her time comes, they both want you to take command of *Cygnet*. Meanwhile, *Cygnet* will have two skippers. That is, if this is what you want, Ellie?"

"That would be fine, Grand Commander," said Ellie.

"Then, soon-to-be-Commander Ellie, I'll bring your promotion forward at the next Council of Wielders. Of course, the decision will be up to them. You know it's the way it should be. And now, so do I. So does everyone, though they probably won't say it for fear of your green-eyed stare, Ellie."

"At your command," Grand Commander," said Ellie.

Astreya solemnly winked at Ellie, and she nodded.

~^~

Next morning, Rupert the innkeeper stood outside his inn, preparing to bid farewell to three of his guests. Astreya was already sitting on Esme's broad back. Pat the pot boy held two horses for Seren and Marley to mount.

Ellie was waiting beside Seren's horse as Maisie came out the inn door.

"Come to Matris," said Ellie impulsively, knowing as she spoke that this would not happen.

"Some day, perhaps, if the Goddess wills it, I will meet the women of Matris."

"Come now, Maisie. The future is sneaking up on us and everything changing."

"Ellie., you transformed both our lives when you came to my door, and now we must go do what's next."

"I'm afraid, Maisie. I think my future has been planned without me."

"Neither fear your future nor anyone's plan for it," said Maisie. "Choose your star, Navigator, and follow it."

With a jangle of bracelets and a flourish of red hair, Maisie enveloped her in a hug that lasted until Curmudgeon pushed between them and sat at Maisie's feet. First Ellie and then Maisie stooped to stroke the big cat's head.

When they looked up at each other, they both were blinking back tears.

## About Old Salt Press

Old Salt Press is an independent press catering to those who love books about ships and the sea. We are an association of writers working together to produce the very best of nautical and maritime fiction and non-fiction. We invite you to join us as we go down to the sea in books.

Visit the website for details of all Old Salt Press books: www.oldsaltpress.com

# About the author

I was born in England in 1941, during an air raid. My father was a British naval officer, my mother a singer from New Zealand. In 1949, we immigrated to Canada. After acquiring degrees in English literature, I taught at Canadian universities and then worked as a writer/editor for government and industry.

I retired in 2003. Having written and edited other people's work for many years, I completed *The Astreya Triology* in 2001.

Next I wrote *The Laughing Princess*, a collection of 12 interrelated stories that concern dragons. It is beautifully illustrated by Ottawa artist, Shirley MacKenzie.

Back in the 60s, I was a little too old to be a hippie, but I visited folk who were on the North Mountain of Nova Scotia in those years, and have kept in touch with some of them. For them (but not about them) I wrote *The Hippies Who Meant It*, published in 2016.

I 2020 I returned to the world of *The Astreya Triology* to write *River of Stones*, a stand alone story which takes place 20 years after the conclusion of the Triology.

Then as a lockdown project, I wrote *Angel's Share*, a novella set in the same world, chronologically a century before the Triology. It, too, is a stand alone story that is also an introduction to all five books.

In 2021, I published *Ellie*, which continues the story three years after the close of *River of Stones*.

# The Latest Great Reading from Old Salt Press

## Rick Spilman

### Evening Gray Morning Red

A young American sailor must escape his past and the clutches of the Royal Navy, in the turbulent years just before the American Revolutionary War. In the spring of 1768, Thom Larkin, a 17-year-old sailor newly arrived in Boston, is caught by Royal Navy press gang and dragged off to HMS *Romney*, where he runs afoul of the cruel and corrupt First Lieutenant. Years later, after escaping the Romney, Thom again crosses paths with his old foe, now in command HMS *Gaspee*, cruising in Narragansett Bay. Thom must finally face his nemesis and the guns of the *Gaspee*, armed only with his wits, an unarmed packet boat, and a sand bar.

## Linda Collison

### Rhode Island Rendezvous

Book Three, The Patricia MacPherson Nautical Adventures.

Newport Rhode Island: 1765. The Seven Years War is over but unrest in the American colonies is just heating up… Maintaining her disguise as a young man, Patricia is finding success as Patrick MacPherson. Formerly a surgeon's mate in His Majesty's Navy, Patrick has lately been employed aboard the colonial merchant schooner *Andromeda*, smuggling foreign molasses into Rhode Island. Late October, amidst riots against the newly imposed Stamp Act, she leaves Newport bound for the West Indies on her first run as *Andromeda*'s master. In Havana a chance meeting with a former enemy presents unexpected opportunities while an encounter with a British frigate and an old lover threatens her liberty – and her life.

# Joan Druett

## Finale

The year is 1905, and the heyday of Thames, in the goldfields of New Zealand.  Back in 1867, Captain Jake Dexter, a flamboyant adventurer and pirate, and his mistress, the actress Harriet Gray, invested the fortune they made during the gold rushes of California and Australia in a theatre and hotel called the Golden Goose, which has become an internationally acclaimed tourist venue, famous for its Murder Mystery Weekends. Guests gather, and a fake murder is staged, and it is up to them to find the killer.  But this hugely successful venture is now at great risk. Timothy Dexter, an American of dubious ancestry, threatens the inheritance of the Golden Goose Hotel, and the Gray family gathers to hold a council of war, interrupted when a real murder intervenes. And a young tourist, Cissy Miller, entrusted with a Harlequin costume and a very strange mission, may be the only one to hold the key to the mystery.

# Antoine Vanner

## Britannia's Innocent

The Dawlish Chronicles: February – May 1864.

Political folly has brought war upon Denmark. Lacking allies, the country is invaded by the forces of military superpowers Prussia and Austria. Cut off from the main Danish Army, and refusing to use the word 'retreat', a resolute commander withdraws northwards. Harried by Austrian cavalry, his forces plod through snow, sleet and mud, their determination not to be defeated increasing with each weary step.

# Seymour Hamilton

## River of Stones

More from the world of The Astreya Trilogy

Only three stones of power remain, and only the eight descendants of Zubin can wield them. A ruthless and power-hungry man is intent on stealing the stones, murdering the three leaders of the fleet, and torturing the secrets of navigation from their children. Grand master Astreya gives his daughter Mairi command of a ship with instructions to keep the younger members of his family far from danger. However, safety is elusive. Mairi must face political turmoil ashore, resolve conflicts with her twin brother Trogen, and lead her young crew through storms, dangerous passages, and battles at sea before she can discover the secret that will lead to the river of stones.

# V E Ulett

## Blackwell's Homecoming

In a multigenerational saga of love, war and betrayal, Captain Blackwell and Mercedes continue their voyage in Volume III of Blackwell's Adventures. The Blackwell family's eventful journey from England to Hawaii, by way of the new and tempestuous nations of Brazil and Chile, provides an intimate portrait of family conflicts and loyalties in the late Georgian Age. Blackwell's Homecoming is an evocation of the dangers and rewards of desire.

# Alaric Bond

## Seeds of War

1811 and the war with France continues although conflict of another kind is raging on America's Eastern Seaboard. For many years oppressive trade sanctions have soured Britain's relations with the newly formed United States; tensions rise further as seamen are illegally pressed and what had been a purely economic dispute soon turns into something far more deadly. Amid the conflict and confusion of fierce political debate, those aboard the frigate HMS *Tenacious* must also do battle with illegal slavery, powerful privateers, violent tropical storms and enemies that had once been the best of friends. *The Seeds of War* is a tale of loyalty, ambition and true camaraderie.

www.ingramcontent.com/pod-product-compliance
Lightning Source LLC
Chambersburg PA
CBHW070500200726
48293CB00007B/2314